LOSS

LOSS

JACKIE MORSE KESSLER

G RAPHIA

Houghton Mifflin Harcourt
Boston New York 2012

For information about permission to reproduce selections from this book,
write to Permissions, Houghton Mifflin Harcourt Publishing Company,
215 Park Avenue South, New York, New York 10003.

Graphia and the Graphia logo are registered trademarks of
Houghton Mifflin Harcourt Publishing Company.

www.hmhbooks.com

Text set in Adobe Garamond.

Library of Congress Cataloging-in-Publication Data
Kessler, Jackie Morse.
Rage / Jackie Morse Kessler.
p. cm.
ISBN 978-0-547-71215-4
[1. Bullies—Fiction. 2. Self-esteem—Fiction. 3. Diseases—Fiction. 4. Time travel—Fiction.
5. High schools—Fiction. 6. Schools—Fiction. 7. Four Horsemen of the Apocalypse—
Fiction.] I. Title.
PZ7.K4835Los 2012
[Fic]—dc23
2011031490

Manufactured in the United States of America
DOC 10 9 8 7 6 5 4 3 2 1

4500343569

*If you've ever been pushed around
and no one seemed to care,
then this one is for you.*

ACKNOWLEDGMENTS

First, a huge thank-you to Julie Tibbott, my extremely patient editor, and to the entire Houghton Mifflin Harcourt team, including Karen Walsh and Lisa DiSarro—you guys rock out loud.

Next, an enormous thank-you to Sammy Yuen, the brilliant cover god of *Hunger*, *Rage*, and *Loss*. Worship him. He deserves much worship.

To my tireless agent, Miriam Kriss: Thank you so much for asking, "So, which Horseman are you writing about next?"

To the Deadline Dames: You ladies have been my constant support. Thank you, thank you, thank you!

To the Mopey Teenage Bears: *Loss* began during the 2010 World Tour. Rah!!! Ty, thank you for "Ballard." Brian, you believed from the start. Amy and Heather—ladies, from punching bags to the TBF and beyond. You all are amazing. Rock on!

To Heather Brewer, who would have kicked my ass if Billy wasn't believable.

To Renee Barr, who continues to read every single thing that I write. Poor woman!

To my mom and dad: my biggest fans!

To my Precious Little Tax Deductions, Ryan and Mason, who understand the power of stories.

And to my Loving Husband, Brett. Always, forever.

LOSS

PART ONE

BILLY BALLARD AND THE ICE CREAM MAN

CHAPTER 1

THE DAY BEFORE DEATH CAME
FOR BILLY BALLARD . . .

. . . Billy was on the ground, getting the snot pounded out
of him. Again. No special reason this time; maybe it was because it was Tuesday, or because Eddie Glass didn't like Billy's
hair. Maybe, if you listened to Billy's mother all those years ago
when he'd first started getting pushed around by his classmates,
Eddie "secretly liked Billy" and this was how he showed it.

For whatever reason, Eddie was kicking the hell out of him,
and Billy was taking it. He knew it would be over soon, real
soon, and if he just protected his head and stayed curled into
a ball, Eddie would get bored and stomp away, and then Billy
could go on with his life.

The next kick didn't fall, so Billy made the mistake of glancing up through his laced fingers. The sun backlit Eddie for a
brilliant moment, and time stretched as Billy saw not a high
school bully but a man in white, fists by his sides, his face hidden in shadow . . .

. . . and then time snapped back into place as Eddie landed
one more kick, a brutal one that nearly cracked a rib. Billy
couldn't help it: He cried out.

Maybe that's what Eddie was waiting for, because he
stepped back, assessed Billy, and let out a satisfied grunt, like a
pig snorting after particularly fine swill. Eddie got the expected

high-fives from his fellow thugs as they moved on in search of other targets.

Billy lay on the filthy alley floor, alone and hurting, breathing in the stench of old pizza and spoiled cheese, thankful that Eddie hadn't done anything to his face. It was becoming harder for Billy to hide his injuries from his mom now that the weather had gotten better. No way he could have disguised a broken nose or black eye; the one time he'd tried to cover a bruise with his mom's makeup had resulted in a rash. Hell of a way to discover he had sensitive skin.

He let out a teakettle hiss through his teeth. He was grateful the beating was done, yes, but a small part of him seethed over the sheer indignity of getting beaten, again, of how dealing with the likes of Eddie Glass was just a piece of the daily routine. That part of Billy was disgusted by how he had to map out his routes to and from and inside school, how his mantra was Keep Your Head Down. Deeper than the disgust was the desperation to unleash his fury and fight back. But Billy's anger was overcome, as always, by the gnawing dread that defending himself wouldn't do anything but make the Eddies of the world return in packs.

"That's true sometimes," a woman said.

Billy jerked his head up to see not a woman but a girl in a red leather coat, pants, and boots, the color licking at her as if she'd caught fire. The girl loomed over him somehow, even though she was neither tall nor big, and though she wasn't that pretty, something about the way she looked, the way she stood, was altogether sexy.

"Other times," she said, "it's just an excuse."

"What are you talking about?" Billy's voice was scratchy,

breathy, betraying both his fascination and his fear—there was something terrifying about this girl who'd appeared from nowhere, something dark and wet and hot coating the air between them and making Billy think of freshly spilled blood.

"Why you don't fight back." She held her hand out to him.

He stared at the offered hand, surprised that her leather glove was a dull brown instead of red. *It should be red*, he thought as he took her hand; everything about the girl should be red.

Then all thoughts disintegrated as a rush of power charged through him, shooting up his hand to his head and down to his toes, instantly transforming his blood into lava. Just as he was about to scream, the girl released his hand. Billy, still on the ground, tried to catch his breath and failed. Gasping, he watched as waves of heat streamed from his fingers.

"You're good at caging it," the girl said. "But soon enough, it will claw its way free."

He wanted to say, "What?" but he was still in pain from Eddie's attack and the girl's whatever-the-hell-that-was, and now he was more than a little freaked, so the question came out as "Whuh?"

"Your rage." She said the word lovingly. "You're so angry. But you've talked yourself out of being allowed to feel that way. You've convinced yourself that if you fight back, that will make it worse. It might," she said. "Then again, it might not."

He stared up at her. It felt like his eyeballs were jittering in their sockets.

"You're angry," she said. "But you're also afraid."

His heartbeat confirmed her statement in triple time. Flustered, he shouted, "You don't know me!"

She smiled brightly, and Billy found himself momentarily

dazzled by the sheer delight on her face. "Of course I do," said the girl in red. "But you don't know yourself. Yet." And then she was gone, vanished like specters at daybreak.

He closed his eyes and took a deep, shuddering breath. When he opened his eyes again, the memory of the girl in red was nothing but a tickle in the back of his mind, a nudge telling him to get up.

Billy slowly hauled himself to his feet. His body was hurting—after a session with Eddie's boots, how could it not be? —but nothing seemed to be broken. His clothing wasn't even ripped. He probably had bruises, though. The same bruises he'd had for years.

There was a moment of bitterness, a sour churning in his stomach as Billy grabbed his fallen backpack by its single, dangling strap and hefted it over his right shoulder.

Get over it, he told himself. *Just grin and it'll be okay. Marianne's waiting.*

That was enough to get him moving. So what that he'd rather crawl under a rock and hide? Marianne was waiting for him.

He pasted a false smile on his face and walked—not limped, no, not today—out of the alley and around the corner to the front of Dawson's Pizza. Outside the store, he paused to look through the large front window. Teens filled the pizzeria, packing the tables and lined in rows three deep by the counter and in back by the video games. Over in the corner, right by the window, Marianne Bixby had snagged a table just big enough for two.

Billy's fake smile melted into the real thing as he drank in the sight of her. Marianne was in black, as usual, but the clothing paled compared to the raven black of her hair. Oblivious to the cacophony around her in the busy store, she texted on her cell phone as her bookbag stood guard on the other chair at the table.

In Billy's pocket, his phone buzzed.

He glanced at the message—it was from Marianne, who was wondering if he was weaseling out of his turn to buy the pizza—and then he put the phone back in his pocket and took a deep breath. This was always the hardest part: walking in. No matter how many times he did it, it never got easier. If not for Marianne, he'd never go to Dawson's Pizza; why choose to be adrift in a sea of sharks? Walking into the pizzeria meant that he was welcoming anything that happened, from being mocked to getting pinched to being shoved from behind. It terrified him. But knowing that Marianne was right there waiting for him was enough to make him forget his fear, just a little. Just enough.

He took two steps toward the door . . . and that's when he saw Eddie Glass near the front of the store, hulking over a packed table. Billy stood transfixed as he watched Eddie glower and the teens scatter. He flinched as Eddie and his cronies laughed and sat at the newly vacated table. He felt the echoes of pain in his side where Eddie's foot had slammed brutally home.

Billy shook off the memory of the beating, but the damage was done: He couldn't go inside. Marianne knew him far too well—one look, and she'd know that Eddie had jumped him, again, that Billy had been a punching bag, again. And she'd tell him, again, that he should talk to someone, try to get someone to help him make it stop, and he'd nod and say yes and would change the subject because he'd long since learned that adults don't always have the answers they claim to have, and the rest of the afternoon he'd see pity in Marianne's dark eyes.

No. He'd sooner stick needles under his fingernails than deal with that.

He turned away and trudged home, careful to take the longer, more populated route instead of cutting down side streets. Always Be Careful; that was right up there with Keep Your Head Down. Billy's life was about caution—at home, dealing with Gramps; at school, wondering when the Eddies there would lunge from the shadows.

Billy Ballard was sick of being careful.

Five blocks away from home, Billy fished for his house key, both to get him inside quicker and to give the appearance of a weapon, just in case he'd been followed. Not like he'd really fight, but still, appearances mattered. Everyone knew that. One look at Billy, and people saw right away that something was different. What was it about him that infuriated people like Eddie Glass? Was it his face? His hair? He had no idea. As far as he could tell, he was completely average. But there had to be something there, something he couldn't see, couldn't change with hair color or piercings or clothing. Something intangible and yet permanent, branding him forever as a target.

Billy was sick of being different, too. Maybe others wanted to stand out, to define themselves with proud, loud colors that screamed their independence. He wanted only to blend in with the crowd, because then he'd finally, *finally* not be the guy that anyone and everyone would push around.

By the time he walked up the front steps to his house, he was ready to shut himself away from the real world, ready to deal briefly with Mom and Gramps and then escape to his bedroom — except something pale green caught his eye.

Hugging the screen door was a sticky note, the sort used by deliverymen when no one was home to sign for a package.

Curious, Billy pulled off the note. He couldn't read most of the text on the paper; the ink was barely visible, like it had faded. The company name was all but nonexistent. Actually, the only things he could clearly make out were his own name and the checked message.

WILLIAM BALLARD
☑ SORRY I MISSED YOU — WILL TRY AGAIN LATER!

For no good reason, a shudder tripped up his spine. He had no idea what someone would have mailed him — he wouldn't be sixteen for another two months, and the winter holidays were long gone. Maybe he'd won a contest.

A whisper in the back of his mind — a memory, a dream, something tangled between fact and fiction — and he pictured a man in white, filthy and yet pristine. Billy couldn't see his face, and a part of him (the same part that so desperately wanted to stand up to Eddie Glass) was grateful. It was too soon to see that face, to know why the man's brow gleamed silver.

Billy distinctly thought: *The Ice Cream Man wants me to wear the Crown.* And then it was gone, snuffed out like a spent match.

He shivered again, and then he frowned at the slip of paper in his hand. It probably wasn't even real. Just some joke waiting to be told, a prank not yet pulled. And if it *was* a real message about a real package, then the deliveryman would return. He crumpled the note and shoved it into his front pocket, and then he unlocked the front door. Stepping inside, he called out a hello.

No answer. His mom and grandfather must have been out on an errand. Or maybe they were at the doctor's again. Fine by Billy. He relished the silence of an empty house.

He shut and locked the door, then stepped back to make sure the full-length poster was still in place, that it wasn't ripped anywhere and the black tape covering the doorknob didn't need to be changed. He stared at the poster critically and decided it was fine—where there had been a door was now a two-dimensional overstuffed bookshelf. The handle to the world outside was nothing but dead black.

Satisfied, he shuffled down the hallway, barely noticing the reflective tape on the carpet that led to the bathroom, or the barren walls that once had teemed with family photos. Outside his bedroom, he took out a second key to unlock the door. A memory teased him: Marianne a couple of years ago, marveling over the locked bedroom door and telling Billy how cool it was that he had so much privacy.

If the lock had been for privacy, Billy would have agreed.

He entered his room and shut the door, not bothering to lock it because Gramps was out of the house. The bedroom was standard fare: the bed, of course; the desk that had once been his dad's, complete with a computer that Billy had bought with birthday money; the closet with a hamper that only partially succeeded in housing clothes, whether dirty or clean. Bookshelves, overstuffed with paperbacks. Television seated on top of the bureau. And posters decorating the walls: various sports stars and bikini babes and rock legends all competed for attention in eye-straining colors and contrasts. Maybe his room was nothing out of the ordinary, but to him it was a sacred place. Here, he didn't have to worry about what lurked around corners, waiting to pounce. Here in his room, Billy was free. It was a gilded cage, perhaps, but he was grateful for the bars.

He dumped his backpack by his desk and pulled out his cell phone. His fingers glided over the keys and summoned Marianne's number, and he texted her an apology for not meeting her. He gave her a tried-and-true excuse: his mom needed him home because his grandfather was giving her fits. Not a lie; it just hadn't happened yet. Billy was used to making sacrifices to help out with Gramps.

Marianne texted back right away. No worries, she wrote; the pizza was lousy today anyway. But tomorrow, he was buying.

Reading her answer made him smile. For a moment, he imagined Marianne not as his best friend but as his girlfriend, imagined telling her how he felt . . .

That would be a mistake.

No, mistakes could be fixed. Telling Marianne Bixby he wanted to kiss her would be bad. Horrifically bad. The sort of bad from which there was no return.

He sighed as he pocketed his phone. Feeling more battered than he did when Eddie Glass was kicking him, Billy grabbed his iPod and flopped down on his bed. He didn't plan on falling asleep, but five minutes later, he was out cold.

Thirty minutes after that, he woke to his mother's screams.

CHAPTER 2

BILLY LURCHED OUT OF BED . . .

. . . and ripped the buds from his ears as he staggered to the bedroom door. He was on autopilot, his body reacting to his mother hollering "Dad!" again and again while his brain tried to process that he wasn't still sleeping. He'd been dreaming the sort of dream that felt like it was really happening. The images were already fading—the threads had begun unraveling as soon as his mom had started screaming—but one memory remained: the man in white.

The Ice Cream Man, Billy thought muddily as he opened his door, *the Ice Cream Man's going to let me ride the white horse . . .*

His mother raced down the hallway, screaming for her father. "Dad! Dad, where are you? Martin! Come out!"

Billy had to shout to get her attention. "Did Gramps get out again?"

"I don't know," she said too fast. "He might have, or he could be here in the house somewhere, there's so many places he could be if he jimmied the locks and . . . oh God, the kitchen cabinet!" She bolted down the hallway, banking the corner and heading for the kitchen.

Billy's heartbeat thundered in his throat, his ears, behind his eyes. *Here we go again*, he thought bleakly, even as he patted down his pockets to make sure he still had his keys and phone.

The last time Gramps had been alone, he'd almost set the house on fire. When Billy had gotten the matches away from him, his grandfather had slugged him in the eye. The rest of the night, Gramps had screeched at Billy, calling him horrible names and threatening to kill him.

"It's not him," his mom had told Billy all that night, the next morning, the next week. *"It's the Alzheimer's talking, not him."* As if that magically made everything better.

Billy locked his bedroom door and joined his mom in the kitchen. She was tugging on the cabinet under the sink, testing the child-safety lock. It was still on, so his grandfather couldn't have gotten into the drain cleaner. Billy asked, "Any doors open?"

His mom didn't answer. She was still pulling at the cabinet door, fixated on it, as if breaking the lock would somehow produce Gramps.

Billy tried the back door, but it was locked tight. Same with the door to the garage. But the front door, the one masked by the wall poster of a bookcase, was slightly ajar — the same poster that usually hid the door also camouflaged how the door hadn't been completely closed.

Gritting his teeth, Billy called out, "Front door!" And then he raced outside, looking around for any sign of his grandfather. "Gramps!" he yelled, then switched to cries of "Martin! Martin Walker! Can you hear me?" His voice echoed back at him like music.

That was when he realized the block was oddly quiet. Usually, midafternoon on a weekday, cars streamed up and down the street; on a warm afternoon like today, kids should be hanging out, riding bikes or skateboards. But today, the street was barren. Dead.

No, not quite. Down at the end of the block, a guy was playing a guitar.

Thank God, Billy thought, racing down the sidewalk. When Gramps escaped the house, he tended to walk a straight line, so there was a good chance he'd gone right by the street musician. The guitarist was blond and lean, doing the grunge thing like he'd sprung out of a Seattle 1990s brochure. Not bad at the guitar, either. The musician started singing as Billy approached—a familiar tune, but Billy couldn't quite place it. He stumbled to a halt in front of the guitarist's open case, which was lying open on the pavement and sparkled with coins reflecting the sunlight.

Pennies. All of the coins were pennies. Billy thought that was both odd and, for some reason, strangely appropriate.

"Years and years I've roamed," the blond guitarist sang.

That had to be a good omen. "Hey," Billy said, huffing from his sprint. "Did you see an old man walk this way?"

The guitarist stopped singing, but his fingers kept strumming, keeping the tune alive. He smiled lazily. "What, walking hunched over and gasping for breath? Nope. But I did see a man wander past not even five minutes ago."

Billy blinked, absorbed both the joke and the information, then asked, "Did he keep going straight?" He pointed farther down the street.

"Yep."

"Thanks," said Billy, then reached in his pocket for some change, just a small tip to thank the guy. But before he could toss the money into the guitar case, the musician grabbed his arm. Billy was stunned by the contact, and even more by the strength and chill of the guitarist's fingers. It felt like frozen branches had wrapped around his wrist.

"No need for that," said the musician.

Billy stammered, "Wanted to thank you."

The guitarist kept his smile, but now there was an edge to it. "Then give thanks instead of coin, William Ballard. Otherwise, you'll get what you pay for, and there's no time."

Shocked speechless, Billy couldn't ask how the musician knew his name.

"You have only three minutes before your grandfather causes a rather messy accident," said the guitarist. His blue eyes glinted wickedly in the sunlight. "He's walking in the street, and the driver's about to text his girlfriend."

Billy's mouth worked silently, gaping like a fish suffocating in air.

"Go," commanded the guitarist, releasing Billy's wrist. "Less than three minutes now. You'd better run."

Billy ran.

|||||||

The pale horse shook its head, as if shaking away a fly.

"What?" said Death. "It was just a little friendly advice."

The horse snorted.

Death smiled at his steed. "You're just annoyed that he didn't see you."

If the horse had a comment, the steed kept it to itself.

Still smiling, Death began to play the guitar once more.

|||||||

Rushing forward, Billy's thoughts were a mad jumble as he wondered how the street musician knew his name. *Not a musician. A Rider. He's the Pale Rider and he says Gramps is going to be in an accident, have to hurry, hurry, find Gramps . . .*

Lost in his mind's free flow, Billy sprinted down the street. He was thinking now about his grandfather, of the man who'd read him bedtime stories and chased away any monsters crouching in the closet. Martin Walker had been a bear of a man when Billy was young, a towering presence that had filled the house and made Billy feel safe—

(*even after the Ice Cream Man,* a voice whispered in the back of Billy's mind)

—even after his dad had gone away. Without Gramps, he never would have learned to ride a bike, or catch a fish, or so many other things. He vividly remembered the feeling of his grandfather's calloused fingers over his smaller, softer ones as Gramps taught him how to swing a baseball bat; he heard pride in the memory of his grandfather's voice, pride and love as Gramps encouraged him and congratulated him every time the bat connected and sent the ball sailing across the sky. *Just believe you can do it,* Gramps would say. *Believe, and stand tall.*

He had to find his grandfather. *Had* to.

You have only three minutes before your grandfather causes a rather messy accident.

How long had Billy been running? A minute? Two? Surely not three. Only three minutes, the guitarist had said, and never mind how the blond man knew that his grandfather would be in an accident; the street musician had declared it, and Billy believed him.

Of course Billy believed him; he was the Pale Rider, and he knew when people were scheduled to die.

Oh my God, Billy thought, wind-tears stinging his eyes, *I'm going crazy.*

No, he had no time for that. Muscles screaming, chest burning, Billy raced across the neighborhood, his feet slapping the ground in a backbeat to his labored breathing. No air to waste calling his grandfather's name. No air, no time, no . . .

Yes!

Up ahead, his grandfather was threading himself between parked cars. Each time he looped around, he wandered into the middle of the street and paused, then continued on, moving to another car and circling it before heading back to the center lane once more. His open jacket flapped around his body like a cape.

His gaze locked on his grandfather's coat, Billy snarled as rage flooded him, tinting his world red. *Didn't even take off his jacket,* he thought, *wasn't home long enough to take off his jacket. Mom was in a hurry and forgot to lock the door and she didn't even help him out of his jacket and this is* her *fault!*

Fueled with righteous anger, Billy rocketed forward, shouting, "Martin! Martin Walker, please stop!"

The old man froze, then slowly turned his head until he saw Billy. Even halfway down the block, he sensed the tension crackling along his grandfather's limbs.

Gramps was going to bolt.

Billy forced himself to stop, stumbling his way to a graceless halt. Hands out, imploring, Billy called out, "Mr. Walker, we've been worried about you."

His grandfather didn't move. There was a gleam in his eyes, something caged and frantic.

Billy took a step forward, and then another, keeping his arms out, palms up, showing Gramps that he meant him no harm. "Mom—Jane's been looking for you."

The name penetrated. The old man cocked his head and asked, "Janey?"

"Yes, Janey." So hard to project his voice and yet keep it soft, nonthreatening. Another step, and then another. Walking slowly now, he said, "She needs you, Mr. Walker. Janey needs you. Will you please come with me?"

His grandfather frowned, but he didn't run. Progress.

Billy took another step, and that's when he saw the car. It barreled forward, nowhere even close to going thirty—it was doing at least fifty, sixty, a hundred miles an hour, a moss green car gunning for his grandfather.

He launched himself at the old man, whose eyes widened in either fear or fury. Gramps didn't turn around, didn't see the pale streak of death careening straight toward him.

With a defiant cry, Billy tackled his grandfather. The two of them flew in a tangle of limbs, the old man screeching and Billy howling, wrapping himself around Gramps to cushion him from the impact. They landed hard against a parked car, a dirty white sedan. The pale green car drove past, veering slightly to the left. Billy caught sight of the driver suddenly looking up. The car straightened and continued going past, going, going . . . gone.

Billy let out a shaky, relieved breath. And that's when his grandfather punched him in the jaw. "Ow! What—"

"Off!" Gramps punched him again.

"Quit it!" Billy held on to his grandfather with one hand and tried to protect his face with the other. "Gramps, stop!"

The old man snarled, "Off me! Off!"

"Janey," Billy said, trying to be patient even with his heart thundering in his chest. "Janey needs you, Mr. Walker."

The name worked its magic once more: His grandfather's face softened. "Janey?"

"She's waiting for you. At home."

"Huh." The old man lowered his fists and stopped pulling away from Billy.

"I'll take you there, sir. Okay?"

"Hmm."

Billy nudged Gramps gently, and together they shuffle-walked the path back to Billy's house. They paused only twice: The first time was so Billy could maneuver his cell phone out of his back pocket and call his mom to tell her they were headed home, and the second was when they passed a particular corner where a street musician had been playing the guitar and singing about a man who'd sold the world.

Where the guitarist had been, two old pennies shone cheerfully in the afternoon sun.

CHAPTER 3

DINNER SUCKED WORSE THAN USUAL • • •

. . . because Gramps kept glaring at Billy like he wanted to kill his only grandchild, and his mom overcompensated by being the perfect mom and daughter; she was all "Here you go, Dad," and "Want some more mac and cheese, Dad?" and "Are there too many peas, Dad?" along with the usual "Can't believe how much you're eating, Billy," and "You're getting so tall, Billy," and "Isn't it nice having the three of us together for dinner?" —as if that last one didn't happen every night for the past who-knew-how-many years. She'd already done the Florence Nightingale routine and dabbed antiseptic on Billy's scrapes. At least saving Gramps had given him an excuse for the afternoon's bruises. See that? No scrambling to cover up the mementos left by Eddie's boots. Wasn't life grand?

"What's *he* doing here?" Gramps jabbed his spoon at Billy.

Billy's mother smiled. Through everything, she smiled. The world could be ending, and she'd still manage to smile. "Dad, Billy lives here." Her tone was soft, patient. It made Billy's skin itch.

Gramps stared daggers at Billy. "Malarkey!"

"I live here, Gramps. With you and Mom," Billy said for the thousandth time.

"Malarkey! He'll hit me! Knock me down!"

"Why do you think he'll hit you, Dad?"

"Steal my wallet," cried his grandfather.

"Do you have your wallet, Dad?"

Gramps paused, then felt in his back pocket. "Here," he said, voice filled with triumph. "See?"

"Do you have any pictures in your wallet?"

"I got pictures!" Arthritic fingers unfolded the wallet. A photo flap winked. "Here: my bride." A pause, and then Gramps's voice filled with tenderness. "My Bernice. My beautiful Bernice."

"And this one?"

"My baby girl. My Janey." Another pause. "That's you."

Billy's mom practically beamed sunshine. "Yes, that's me."

Three cheers for the redirect. Billy took a swig of milk. Conversations with Gramps were always like this: circular paths with no points other than to encourage the old man to cling on to memories of better times. And they had to be old memories; the more recent ones — which could be anywhere from now to twenty-some-odd years ago — had the potential to turn Gramps violent. At least at school, Billy knew where he stood. At home, it was a constant exercise in tiptoeing around landmines. It was exhausting. Billy had no idea how his mom did it.

"Would you like more macaroni and cheese, Dad?"

"Where's Jack?"

Billy's mother stiffened. She kept smiling, but it seemed brittle around the edges. Billy felt bad for her, but really, by now she should be taking that particular question in stride. Jack Ballard had walked out the door many years ago and hadn't looked back.

"Jack doesn't live here anymore, Dad. More mac and cheese?"

"What happened to Jack?"

"We divorced, Dad."

Gramps slammed his fist on the table, making all the plates rattle and the plastic cups jump. "I know that! What's *he* doing here?" He jabbed his spoon in Billy's direction.

Lather, rinse, repeat.

Billy shoveled food into his mouth without tasting it. Yeah, no doubt about it, Gramps was off his meds tonight. Or, to be more accurate, his grandfather's new meds were "underperforming." That was the doctor's favorite word, and Billy's mother had confiscated it, throwing it around in casual conversation as if a fifty-cent word would suddenly make Alzheimer's something manageable.

Stupid doctors with their stupid words. *Nothing* made it manageable. Didn't people understand that the old man ranting at the table wasn't Billy's grandfather? The real Gramps had checked out without paying the bill. Call it Alzheimer's. Call it dementia. Call it anything at all, but the thing sitting next to Billy's mom was nothing but a doppelganger. Gramps—his Gramps—was gone.

Billy's eyes stung. No, he wasn't going to cry. He mimicked his mother and smiled hugely, smiled until his cheeks screamed. His tears froze in his eyes, just like the smile froze on his face. Yes, his grandfather was long gone. All Billy could do was call the old man "Gramps" and pretend that it mattered.

Billy Ballard desperately hoped he'd get better at pretending, because this pantomime of normalcy was sucking him dry.

||||||

After dinner, Billy's mother kissed Gramps and told him to behave, kissed Billy and told him that she loved him, and then she escaped to work the late shift at the convenience store. When she had first taken on the second job—the money she made from her freelance projects just wasn't enough to pay Gramps's rising medical bills—Billy had suggested that he, too, start working. But his mom had smiled and shook her head. He had to stay home, she insisted, because he had two important jobs: take care of Gramps, and keep up his grades. "Full scholarship," his mom would say proudly whenever Billy brought home another A on a report or a hundred on a test. That was the plan: Billy was to get into college, any college, with a full four-year scholarship.

And then he could be just like his dad—he'd go away and never look back. Until then, it was bullies and bruises and babysitting Gramps.

Billy parked his grandfather in front of the television and checked all the locks on the doors and windows and made sure the hallways were empty so that the old man could wander without hurting himself. Checkpoints all clear, Billy told Gramps where he'd be and to just call out if he needed anything. His grandfather muttered something that was lost in Bob Barker's chatter about how the price was right. Once again, Billy blessed whoever had come up with the Game Show Network, and then he retreated to his bedroom to do his homework.

He was just getting into why the Battle of Vicksburg divided the Confederacy when the doorbell rang. Cursing, Billy tore out of his room and raced down the hall. His grandfather was actually having a decent night, but any disruption in the routine could ruin everything. Last week, some religious nut had come by, trying to simultaneously save them and drain their bank account. Gramps had capital-F Freaked. He'd thrown a glass at the visitor and howled like the devil. The nut took off screaming and Gramps crapped his pants. Right now, Billy's goal was to get to the door and shoo away whoever was hovering on the stoop before Gramps noticed.

He threw open the door, and there stood Marianne Bixby, her backpack hanging by her side. She smiled at him, a tentative thing that flicked at the corners of her mouth. "Hey."

"Hey." His own smile was surprised and pleased. Whenever he was with Marianne, the tension bled out of his shoulders and he remembered how to laugh—even when she showed up unannounced. Billy glanced over his shoulder to see if Gramps had noticed they had a visitor. So far, so good: His grandfather was hypnotized by the television. Turning back to Marianne, he grinned. "What's up?"

"The war zone's getting loud," she said, shrugging. "Can I finish my homework here?"

"Sure," he said, stepping aside to let her in. The Bixby War had been ongoing since Billy and Marianne were in middle school. Once, he'd asked her if her parents were going to get divorced since they fought so much. She'd said no, they were just the type of people who were only happy when they were angry. He thought that was messed up, but then again, he had a mom who smiled instead of shouted, so who was he to judge?

As Billy shut the door behind her, Marianne glanced at the family room. Televised sounds of some lucky winner filled the air with joyous screeches. She asked Billy, "Should I say hi?"

On good days, Gramps smiled at Marianne and called her "Debbie," whoever that was. Billy shook his head. "Don't want to push my luck. It was a bad afternoon."

The two of them slunk down the hallway and into Billy's room. He kept the door open so that he could hear if Gramps needed him. "Take the desk," he said, grabbing his laptop.

"Chivalry!" She unpacked her things and got settled. "Shouldn't be too long. Just have to finish up that history paper."

"Ditto." He sat on his bed, using his pillow to cushion his back. "Figure thirty minutes, then I'm done."

"Shame you weren't at Dawson's," she said as she opened up her report. "You missed all the fun. Amy and Michael hooked up, then Amy and Gary broke up."

He grinned. "You'd think Gary would've seen that coming."

"Shocker, right? He called Michael some interesting names. I'd tell you what they were, but you'd blush."

"My virgin ears," he said piously.

"So Gary stormed out, looking ready to grab a baseball bat and smash things. There's some colorful language on Michael's Facebook page tonight."

Billy took her word for it; he avoided social networking sites as a rule. The last time he'd done a search on his own name, he'd found an upsetting number of pages and comments calling him gay, and retarded, and stupid — and those were the nicer names. He'd been ten years old. Billy had learned his lesson: ego-surfing was bad, and social media sites were worse.

After they finished their homework and had a conversation discussing the merits of superhero comic books (better stories, according to Billy) versus superhero movies (better eye candy, according to Marianne), she asked what had happened that afternoon that had been so bad. So Billy launched into an abbreviated version of events, completely skipping over how he'd been jumped by Eddie and the Bruisers. Instead, he started with his mother telling him that Gramps had wandered off, so he'd had to go searching for him. And oh yeah, the old man had nearly gotten hit by a car.

Marianne shrieked, *"What?"*

Billy frantically shhhhhed her, then ducked out to do a quick check on the old man. All was well—his grandfather was snoozing in front of the television—so Billy quietly came back to his room and half closed the door. Then he told Marianne how he'd run for blocks, calling for Gramps. He sounded steady enough as he recalled what had happened, but his heartbeat throbbed in his ears and his throat constricted as he remembered the sheer panic of not knowing where his grandfather was.

"You must've been terrified," Marianne said breathlessly.

Shame flooded him as, for one brief moment, he wished that he hadn't found Gramps. "Yeah."

He skipped over his encounter with the street musician—he was having trouble remembering that part properly, sort of like chasing a dream—and instead he explained that he'd spotted his grandfather walking in the middle of the street. And then came the part about the oncoming car. He matter-of-factly described how he'd tackled Gramps to get him out of the way. Marianne oohed and ahhed at all the right points, and Billy felt his cheeks heat up when she commented how brave he'd been.

"Brave?" He let out a laugh. "Yeah, that's me. Brave. Right now, I'm in my mild-mannered disguise."

She glared at him. No one could glare like Marianne Bixby. It was a thing of lasers and fury. "Shut *up*," she said. "You were *too* brave!"

Billy shut up.

"Most people wouldn't throw themselves in front of a car to save anyone, family or not," she said. "If it was my family, I'd let them get run over."

"Yeah, well," he mumbled, embarrassed. "Your family has issues."

She rolled her eyes. "Billy, don't you get it? You *saved* your grandpa! You could've *died!*"

For some reason, that made Billy think fleetingly of the street musician. *Not a musician,* he told himself. *A Rider.*

Whatever that meant.

"Look," he said, "it's not a big deal. No one died. Gramps is fine. I'm fine. He was so mad at me for slamming into him, he punched me in the jaw." He pointed to the spot where his grandfather had slugged him.

She shook her head. "Billy Ballard, you were a hero today. You hear me?" Softer, she repeated, "You were a *hero*."

Now Billy's whole face was on fire, and his heart was beating too fast, and he couldn't think of a damn thing to say.

Marianne laughed quietly, a simple, musical laugh that went straight to Billy's heart. She said, "I made you blush."

"You're evil like that," he said, thinking seriously about taking a chance and kissing her. But in the end, he decided to play it safe. Heroes got the girls, but despite what Marianne said, Billy Ballard was no hero.

Later, after he'd checked on Gramps a half-dozen times but well before his mom came home, Billy walked Marianne to the front door. They kept their voices low so that the old man wouldn't be bothered.

"Want me to walk you home?" he offered. "We'd have to wait for my mom, because I can't leave Gramps alone, but once she's here I could take you back."

"Chivalry!" she chirped. "That's sweet, but I think I can make it the five blocks without getting mugged or raped or whatever."

Of course she'd say that. Marianne didn't believe in monsters. When she saw shadows, she assumed that's all they were: shadows. Not Billy. He knew enough to be afraid of what crouched in the dark. They said their goodbyes, and Billy watched from the doorway as Marianne walked down the block and aimed for home.

When she was out of sight, he started to close the front door — and then he swung it open wide. Frowning, he scanned the front yard, trying to find whatever it was that had made his internal radar ping. Despite Marianne's insistence of Billy's heroism, he was a coward through and through, and after years of getting jumped by bullies, he'd come to rely on his instincts. Right now, they were insisting that there was someone standing by the far end of the yard. He reached inside to flip on the floodlights, and for a moment he thought he'd seen a shadow retreat. He blinked and looked again.

Nothing.

His brow creased, but he couldn't deny what his eyes were telling him. There was no one on the lawn. *Just jumpy*, he told himself as he shut and locked the door. *Some hero.* With a sigh, he went into the family room to check on his grandfather.

||||||

Outside, a woman in black stood beside a black horse. When the boy had paused to stare right at her, she had been sorely tempted to approach him. But it wouldn't have changed a thing.

The White Rider was beyond her reach.

She clucked her tongue. "I'm getting as impatient as War," she said, shaking her head.

Next to her, the black horse snorted.

"Well, I am." She patted her steed's neck. "You've known him longer than I. Will he make things right?"

The horse cocked its head, considering the question. Finally, it lowered one ear, as if to say, "Maybe."

She fished out a sugar cube from her pocket. "I suppose I have to trust him," she said, tossing the treat over the horse's head. The black steed snapped its teeth and crunched sugar.

Turning once more to face the boy's house, Famine sighed. "I just hope he knows what he's doing."

The black horse, still chewing, declined to comment.

With a last look at the Ballard house, the Black Rider climbed atop her steed. Together, they disappeared into the night.

CHAPTER 4

BILLY'S IN THE SANDBOX . . .

. . . building castles and getting filthy and loving every second of it. It's a gorgeous spring day, complete with blue skies and singing birds. Other kids are in the playground, too, but Billy doesn't notice them.

A cloud passes over him, and he sneezes, once.

Five-year-old Billy scoops out more sand. He's sniffling now, his nose leaking and his eyes watering. He barely notices; he just uses his shirt as a tissue and keeps on playing in the sandbox.

The cloud doesn't move.

Something's not right, he decides as he frowns at the hollow tower, but he can't decide what it is.

A shadow falls over him.

"It won't last," says a man's voice—

||||||

—and Billy's eyes snapped open. His skin too cold, his breathing too fast, Billy stared at the alarm clock on his nightstand, stared at it until he finally understood that he wasn't in a sandbox but in bed. He'd had a dream, that was all.

Thank you, God. I don't want to remember the Ice Cream Man.

The dream was already blowing away, dandelion fluff in the

wind. He blinked until the numbers on his alarm clock registered, and then he let out a groan. 6:16 a.m. He could have
stayed asleep for fourteen more minutes. Ever since he'd hit pu-
berty, he'd come to appreciate the fine art of sleeping in — or, at
least, of staying in bed. Especially on school days, like this one,
Billy liked to stay hidden until the last possible second.

The thought of going to school made it rain fire in his
stomach.

He burrowed under his blanket and stayed submerged in
the muffled darkness, listening to the sound of his own breath.
Today was what, Thursday? That meant two classes with Eddie Glass's bruiser buddies, Kurt and Joe. Kurt had a laugh like
a donkey's bray. Billy knew the sound well; every time Kurt
pushed Billy or shoved him, the boy would let out that obnoxious laugh. Joe wasn't like Kurt. He was quiet. And mean. If
Kurt tripped Billy, Joe would kick him when he was down.

Billy's gut twisted, making him curl up like a shrimp.

He tried to focus on other things, like the biology class he
shared with Marianne. But he kept coming back to Kurt in his
English lit class and Joe in PE. What would today bring? Extended legs, tripping him in the aisle? Food spat into his hair?
A fist in his face? Something worse?

Billy's stomach lurched, signaled one pitiful warning.

He stumbled out of bed and ran toward the bathroom,
barely making it over the toilet before dry heaves ravaged his
body. His arms trembled as acid burned its way up his esopha-
gus and out his mouth. When his stomach finally settled, he sat
back on his haunches and blew out a shaky breath. He didn't
know if the dampness on his face was from sweat or tears.

Just another school morning.

A joyful sound yanked him out of his bleak thoughts, and Billy rushed back to his bedroom, where his alarm clock was chirping brightly. He shut it off and just stood for a moment, his head down and his back bent, breathing through clenched teeth. Maybe he should stay home sick today. All he had to do was knock on his mom's bedroom door and sound even more pathetic than he really was and say he was sick. No lie; didn't he just puke?

If he stayed home, he'd have to watch Gramps all day. Not fun, but certainly manageable, as long as he kept the house locked tight. He'd miss his test in English lit, but he could take a makeup exam. The teacher was laid back about that sort of thing, maybe because the subject matter was written by people long dead.

He wondered what Marianne would think if he didn't go to school today.

Billy closed his eyes and imagined he could hear the hum of her voice, the unique music of her laughter. Snapshots in his mind: Marianne Bixby at seven, gap-toothed and freckled; Marianne at fifteen, her grin infectious, her face perfect. He couldn't remember when she'd transformed from his best friend into the girl he wanted to kiss. One week, she'd been the buddy who liked to play hide-and-seek with him; the next week, she was pretty and curvy and suddenly much more than just a buddy. Time was funny like that.

Marianne would be at school, in his bio class.

Eddie and the Bruisers would be at school, anywhere and everywhere.

Stay home? Or go to school?

Billy counted to three and made his choice. He should have

felt confident or even brave—his mind kept replaying Marianne calling him a hero, ha, what a joke *that* was—but his
stomach was a mess and his head was hurting and his palms
turned clammy as he remembered the feeling of Eddie's foot
slamming into him.

Only two-plus more years of high school to go. His mom
insisted that a year went by quickly. Billy thought she was insane. A year was almost forever, and two years was an eternity.
How was he supposed to make it to college?

Billy forced himself to go back to the bathroom before he
could rethink his decision. He flushed away the vomit and
scrubbed his teeth to get rid of the taste in his mouth. Puking
always made him think of bugs for some reason, and now his
skin tickled as it felt like a colony of ants was working its way
along his body—imaginary, but still real enough to make him
want to scratch his arms and neck and chest until his flesh was
nothing more than bloody strips. *Stress*, the family doctor had
declared to Billy and his mom back when Billy first started
showing psychosomatic symptoms, and that announcement
had come only after a barrage of tests for allergies and maladies
and neuroses.

Yeah, being the local punching bag tended to stress him out.

Feeling itchy and angry and stupid, he took a hot shower
until any imaginary bugs left on his skin had been steam fried.

Back in his room, he outlined the day's battle plan. The
morning would be the worst part: trigonometry, biology and
American history, all of which bored him into a coma, immediately followed by PE, which meant somehow avoiding Joe in
the locker room. So he'd wear his gym clothes under his regular
clothing—in and out of the locker room in ninety seconds.

After, he'd throw his stuff on and run to the library instead of the lunchroom. Then lit, followed by creative writing, which was three doors down. Finally Latin, which sucked but at least was near the front door of the school; as long as he was first out of the classroom, he'd get a head start out of the building.

It was possible that he'd make it through the day without encountering Eddie at all. And if he was careful in gym, all that might happen was dealing with insults. He could handle that; he'd been called the worst of things ever since he was a kid.

Insults were just words. And words could be ignored.

Billy took a deep breath and started to get dressed, telling himself that nothing too bad would happen today.

Liar, whispered a small voice in his head.

That was okay; Billy was used to being called names, even when he was the one doing it to himself.

||||||

"Keep it up!"

Billy loathed the PE instructor almost as much as he de-spised Eddie Glass. The instructor was like a brick wall with overly large hands and a bullhorn voice, and he had a nasty habit of cracking his knuckles to punctuate his sentences. Like now: a resounding crack filled the gymnasium, the sound of spines breaking. Billy flinched; near him, Joe snorted. Of *course* he'd seen Billy's involuntary cringe. Of course. Joe made sure that Billy was utterly miserable in PE, and not just because the instructor preached the gospel of sweat.

The students were in a loose circle with one in the mid-dle, all of them tasked with keeping the volleyball in the air

—the middleman launched it, and the guys in the circle hit it back. Fingertips stretched high; forearms reached out. Sets and bumps all around as the ball hopped lightly from middle to circle to middle again. Calls of "mine" and "got it" echoed in the large gymnasium.

The instructor bellowed, "If the ball touches the floor, it's twenty pushups!"

Now groans joined the possessive declarations. Billy, though, kept silent. Complaining about things didn't make them go away. Eddie had taught him that a long time ago. More determined to keep the ball in play, he watched, his knees bent, his fingers twitching with nervous energy. He didn't want to be the one who screwed it up. Let someone else be the target of derision for a change.

Across from him, gangly Sean popped the ball up in a wide arc—overshooting Joe in the middle and heading toward Billy, but not close enough to reach. Billy jumped into the middle, fingers interlaced and his forearms out for a bump, his voice breaking as he shouted, "Got it!" The ball bounced solidly off Billy's arms.

He had a moment of sheer joy—he'd done it, he'd kept the ball in play—and then Joe shoved his elbow into Billy's stomach.

Blinding pain.

Billy couldn't stand. Couldn't breathe. He dropped to the ground and wheezed for air, body bent double. Tried to crawl and couldn't move.

Around him, a flurry of movement. The ball was still in play.

An eternity later, someone squatted next to him. Billy forced himself to look up into the instructor's small eyes.

"Get up," he barked. "Don't be such a girl."

Billy got up.

||||||

Eventually, PE ended and Billy was released into the wild of the boys' locker room. The agony in his gut had faded to a dull ache, just enough to slow him down to a shuffling walk. So much for zipping out of there before people realized he was gone. He clamped one hand to his side, which did nothing to stop his discomfort. Nasty bruise for sure. Maybe he was bleeding internally. Dead by sundown. That would be the end of Billy Ballard: done in by a sharp elbow and cruel coach. Rest in peace.

He suddenly remembered the street musician from yesterday, remembered the way the pennies in the guitar case had shone, beckoning. Remembered how he was going to toss in some change.

Remembered the cold bite of the musician's fingers on his wrist.

Billy shuddered, and he walked a little faster.

When he finally reached his locker, he blinked at the messenger slip stuck jauntily on the metal door. Frowning, he removed the slip from his locker door. Just like the one from yesterday, this message was mostly faded to the point of obscurity; once again, only his name and a checked message were legible.

WILLIAM BALLARD

☑ SECOND ATTEMPT—THIRD TIME WILL BE THE CHARM!

A joke. Just some stupid joke. No way was a legitimate messenger delivering something to a fifteen-year-old in his high school locker room. For a moment, he thought it wasn't merely a joke but the promise of something cruel, a horrific prank that promised pain and humiliation. Then again, his daily tormentors never bothered with anything so elaborate; they were more of the punch-and-point variety. This had to be nothing more than someone looking to get his hopes up, only to tear them down when there was no package. That, he could handle. He crumpled the slip and opened his combination lock.

Around him, the other guys were talking about this and that—girls, mostly, with some gaming chatter. Billy mechanically pulled up his jeans, only half-listening as one of the guys bragged about not needing cheat codes anymore. He was feeling like roadkill, but almost worse than that, he was feeling disappointed. Part of him had been hopeful that someone really had a package for him, something valuable enough that it had to be delivered and signed for. It didn't matter that he knew better; he still had hoped.

You'll get what you pay for.

He pushed his hoodie over his head, remembering the way the musician's words had chilled him, remembering how he had been completely certain the musician was right when he'd said his grandfather was going to be hit by a car in three minutes' time.

Remembering the face of the Pale Rider.

He had no idea what that even meant, other than it was completely true: He'd seen the Pale Rider yesterday and had survived to tell the tale. Score one for the coward.

It took him a moment to realize that the locker room had fallen silent.

Billy felt it before he saw the shadow on the locker door next to him: some guy, probably Joe, larger than life—or at least larger than Billy—looming behind him.

He stiffened. Should he just keep getting dressed? Should he just take it and be done with it?

Hadn't he already taken enough crap for today?

Anger flared, blotting out the ache in his stomach.

A voice whispered to him, like some guardian angel from on high: *You've convinced yourself that if you fight back, that will make it worse.*

His fists clenched. He should turn around and confront Joe. Yes, just turn around and look Joe in the eye and tell him to back off. He should . . .

Hands behind his head, fingers tangling in his hair. Pulling back hard enough to make his scalp scream, then pushing forward until his head slammed against a locker door, back again and forward with a slam, and back, and another slam, *boom boom boom*, and then the hands released him and Billy slid to the ground.

"Watch your head," said Joe.

Billy's limbs were rubber; his head was spinning, or maybe that was the world around him. It hurt, yes, but Joe clearly hadn't used his full strength. Billy felt absurdly grateful, and then immediately was flooded with rage—not at Joe, no, but at himself.

He should fight back. Except he could barely move.

With a satisfied grunt, Joe moved on. Soon conversation picked up, but none of it was about what had just happened.

Why bother? No one saw anything. No one ever saw anything. It was an unwritten law, the rule of the high school jungle: Mind your own business and maybe you won't get eaten today. Keep Your Head Down.

Joe's mocking voice: *Watch your head.*

Billy forced one hand onto the bench, then the other. Shaking, he pulled himself up. Half the guys had already cleared out, probably before Joe had shoved Billy's head into the locker. He looked around, bleary-eyed, at the remaining group of teens. All of them were busy getting dressed or getting out of there—all except Sean, whose older brother was captain of the football team. It didn't matter that Sean was a shy beanpole with zits like pepperoni; no one messed with him. He'd earned his immunity, at least until his brother graduated. Maybe next year Billy would have competition as the Most Picked-on Guy in School. But that didn't matter now; nothing mattered now, other than somehow making it through the day, every day.

Billy swallowed thickly as Sean stared at him. Sean seemed . . . what, unhappy? *Try being the one getting hit,* Billy wanted to shout at him. *Then you can be unhappy.*

Sean nodded at him before leaving, but Billy didn't know if the nod meant "Glad you're okay" or "You're on your own." Probably the latter. Billy couldn't depend on anyone to fight his battles for him. Not even himself.

His stomach hurt, but not from Joe's elbow.

Hating his life, Billy shoved his sneakers onto his feet and spotted the crumpled delivery slip next to his backpack. He stared at it, then picked it up, smoothing out the paper until he clearly saw his name again, and the text below it.

It was just a joke.

Even so, Billy carefully placed the slip of paper into his pocket before he picked up his bookbag, wishing that there really was some fantastic package just waiting to be delivered to him.

||||||

The package in question was no package at all, but a long piece of wood, black and polished to a brilliant sheen. It leaned in the corner of a small room filled with sickness. All sicknesses, really. The Bow gleamed, resplendent and sullen. It had been far too long since it was given the respect it deserved. And it loathed being ignored.

"Such drama," Death said. "I'm standing right here, you know."

The Bow said nothing. It couldn't; it was a piece of wood.

"Patience," said Death. "You'll meet your new wielder soon. Tonight, I should think. Yes," he murmured, far-eyed and all-seeing. "Tonight."

If the Bow could nod, it would have. Instead, it stood tall, propped against the wall of a room overflowing with illness. And it waited.

Chapter 5

MARIANNE TOOK ONE LOOK AT HIM . . .

. . . and knew something was wrong; Billy could see it in her face, in the way she squared her shoulders. In two seconds she transformed from Best Friend to Avenging Angel; her eyes flashed fury and her mouth twisted, ready to spit poison. She demanded, "What happened?"

Rather than tell her about what happened during and after PE, Billy pasted a smile on his face as he dumped his backpack under the table. "Lunch sucked," he said, sliding into the booth. "Think I got food poisoning."

She clearly wasn't buying it. Her voice flat, she asked, "Eddie find you?"

Damn it.

"No," he said truthfully. Not like he was about to admit it had been Joe. He borrowed a page from his mom's playbook and went with the redirect. "My turn to buy. You in a pepperoni place today?"

She frowned as she considered him, and Billy wondered if she was going to push. *Please let it go,* he thought. He'd barely had the guts to show up at Dawson's today as it was. If Marianne got on his case about how he needed to stand up to Eddie and his wrecking crew, he'd leave. Bad enough Joe had gotten him twice in one day; he couldn't take Marianne browbeating him. *Not today,* he thought desperately. *Please, not today. One thing more and I'll break.*

Maybe she'd seen the truth written on his face, because she sighed, then tried a smile on for size. "Broccoli," she said.

He made a face. "Why ruin a perfectly good slice of pizza with vegetables?"

"Feeling healthy today."

"Pizza as health food," he said. "Who knew?"

"It's got protein and carbs. And veggies," she added. "Specifically, broccoli. And green pepper."

"Gah." He escaped before she could add something nauseating like anchovies to the list. He'd do anything for Marianne, but watching her eat pizza with fish on it tested the limits of their friendship.

If only they weren't just friends . . .

In line to get their food, Billy daydreamed about going on a date with Marianne. Maybe it wouldn't start that way; they'd pick a movie to go to, as friends. A superhero movie, so Billy could roll his eyes at how it was different from the comic books and Marianne could appreciate the eye candy. They'd share a tub of popcorn, because that's what friends did: They shared. They'd reach for a handful at the same time, and their fingers would brush together, and Marianne wouldn't pull away as he slowly wrapped his hand around hers . . .

A jostle from behind—nothing too cruel, just a "Move it, buddy" sort of shove. Billy moved it.

Soon he was juggling pizza and Cokes—diet for Marianne, since she seemed to be health conscious today—walking slowly so he wouldn't drop anything.

Later, Billy would tell himself that it was his own fault.

He should have been looking. He'd known that Joe's sidekick, Kurt, was in Dawson's, seated at the Loud Table—the one that projected every taunt and jibe so that you felt each verbal barb, no matter where you sat in the pizzeria. Billy should have taken the long way around, circumventing the Loud Table and sticking to the crowded periphery. He should have known better.

But no, he'd been lost in his own world, thinking about Marianne and that superhero movie, their fingers interlocking in the popcorn tub, slick with butter. So he all but floated past the Loud Table.

Just not high enough to pass over Kurt's extended foot.

He had one second between walking and wipeout, just one second in which Billy stood suspended, perfectly balanced on one toe, his arms outstretched and hands clutching the overstuffed tray of food, and in that one second he gripped Marianne's hand tight, tight, squishing popcorn and refusing to let her go . . .

And then the daydream was wrenched away as gravity took over. His chin slammed into the floor.

He barely heard the raucous laughter, the jeers, the hoots and clapping. His jaw aching, he stared at the pizza, which had fallen cheese-side down, stared at the spilled cups of soda, stared and wondered *Why?* and *Why?* and *Why always me?* He stared as the soda pooled under the mess of cheese and broccoli and oil, and as he stared at the ruins of his meal, *his and Marianne's meal*, he felt Joe's elbow in his gut once more, felt his head bang into the locker door again, felt it all, and he had to get out of there, out of there now, *right now*, get out and get gone and not look back.

Billy scrambled to his feet and ran out of Dawson's, ran as fast as he could, ran so that the wind howled in his ears and muffled the sound of his furious screams. He hated them all — Kurt and Joe and Eddie and everyone who laughed at him, who picked on him, who looked the other way. He hated the teachers who saw what happened in school and ignored it, hated his dad for abandoning him, hated his mom and the old man that wore his grandfather's face. He even hated Marianne, perfect Marianne, for no reason he could name. He hated them all, but mostly, he hated himself.

When he finally arrived home, hoarse and trembling, he realized he'd left his backpack at Dawson's. He closed his eyes as he rang the doorbell, wishing to God that he could be someone else, that he could just run away and start over, that the world would end, something, *anything* to make it all just stop. When his mother opened the door, he muscled past her and locked himself in his bedroom and shoved buds in his ears and blasted music loud enough to liquefy his brain.

His life sucked. And that would never change because at his core, he was a coward.

A flash of red behind his eyes; a girl's velvet voice, saying: *You don't know yourself. Yet.*

Bullshit. He was a coward through and through. *So suck it up, cupcake,* he told himself as he tried to lose himself in the music and failed. *Suck it up.*

He pretended his eyes stung from the dust in the room. When the tears fell, he ignored them.

||||||

Billy's mother gave up trying to talk to him halfway through dinner. She was clearly annoyed; he could tell by the way her eyes glinted like diamonds, overly bright and sharp enough to slice with a glare. But she kept smiling. Billy wondered what it meant when people smiled through their pain. Did they scream when they were happy? Probably. No wonder the world was so messed up. People shouldn't have to lie through their emotions.

Even Gramps seemed to pick up on his black mood, because the most the old man did was mutter to himself and answer Billy's mother in monosyllabic grunts. Billy murdered peas with the flat of his spoon, killing vegetables along with time until dinner was finally over.

When his mother left for work, she cast him a troubled look before heading out the door. Billy let it wash over him, then parked his grandfather by the television and retreated to his bedroom. He couldn't do his homework because he didn't have his backpack, and he wasn't in the mood for music. Television was a waste. Reading? No. He was too messed up to talk to Marianne, so he wouldn't text her. Therefore . . . time for video games. Animated violence with a killer soundtrack: maybe not a cure-all, but it sure worked as a temporary fix.

He got six rounds in before the doorbell rang.

As he ran to the door, Billy had a sudden, consuming hope that it was Marianne standing on his stoop, offering his backpack and a sympathetic smile. On the heels of that was the fervent wish that it *not* be Marianne at his door, not after the scene at Dawson's. How could he ever face her again? His mouth twisted into something caught between a smile and a grimace. Steeling himself for the worst, he opened the door.

He didn't see Marianne Bixby.

"Oh good, you're home." The guitarist that Billy had spoken with yesterday smiled warmly as he held out a slip of paper. "I was starting to think I'd have to make a formal appointment."

Billy absently took the paper as he stared at the figure standing before him. Even though the street musician still wore a man's form, Billy now saw through the easy smile and mischievous blue eyes, down to the skull beneath the flesh.

Death had come for Billy Ballard, wearing a ragged brown sweater and a mop of blond hair. Strangely, Billy wasn't frightened. If he had to put a name to the emotion settling in his bones, it would have been resignation.

"You," said Billy.

"Me," Death agreed.

The Pale Rider, that's the Pale Rider, he's come to take me to see the Ice Cream Man.

He squashed that thought until it bled to nothingness, and he forced himself to consider the slip of paper in his hand. Anything to keep him from thinking about the Ice Cream Man. As before, the words on the message slip had faded to the point of illegibility—this time, even Billy's name was nonexistent. As he looked at the vague impressions on the paper, he wondered why he hadn't recognized Death yesterday.

"You were rather preoccupied," Death said cheerfully. "All you cared about was finding your grandfather. To see me for what I am, you need an open mind. Among other things. Oh, here's your backpack. Thought you'd want it back."

Billy, nonplussed by the casual display of mind reading, took the knapsack and mumbled his thanks.

"May I come in?"

"Um. Sure."

Death entered the house, whistling as he walked. Did he actually need an invitation, or was he merely being polite? Billy decided it didn't really matter. He closed the door and shoved the slip of paper into his pocket, wondering if he was going to die.

"Of course you are," said Death, glancing at the bookshelf poster on the back of the door. "Thou art flesh and blood. All such things die and decay and feed the worms. But not today, dude. Not for you."

Well then, there was only one other reason why someone— no, some*thing*—like this would be paying a visit, wasn't there? It couldn't be just to return his bookbag. Billy thought of his grandfather, of the man his grandfather used to be, and he told himself that it was for the best. It was long past his grandfather's time.

"Time is relative, of course," Death said idly. "Great poster, by the way. 'Outside of a dog, a book is man's best friend.'"

Billy struggled for a proper reply. "If you say so."

"I didn't. Groucho Marx did. And he added that 'Inside of a dog, it's too dark to read.'" Death chuckled. "Got to love the classics."

Nothing like a death god with a sense of humor. Billy glanced at Gramps, sequestered in the den but within easy eyeshot. The old man's gaze was studiously fixed on the TV screen. Billy wondered if his grandfather was ignoring the guest in the house, or if he really was just that into the television show. Maybe Gramps knew exactly what was about to happen, and he was pretending to be lost in a game show more than two decades old.

Maybe Gramps was scared.

"For the record," said Death, who was now ambling down the hallway, "I'm not a god. Those come and go. I'm more like a permanent fixture."

"Oh." Billy peeked at his grandfather again. Poor Gramps. Well, everyone had a time to go, and this was his grandfather's. Billy was okay with that. Actually, Billy felt . . . relieved.

He had to be the worst grandson in the world. He clamped a hand over his stomach, but that did nothing to stop the sudden churning in his belly.

Death, now standing in front of where a large family photo used to hang, turned his head to gaze at Billy. The wall behind Death was empty, with only the ghosts of snapshots to lend any color, but those eyes, Death's eyes, were even emptier.

Vacant, Billy thought, feeling the first stirrings of fear as his heart slammed in his throat, *the word is vacant, unoccupied. Unoccu-eyed. He's got no eyes in his eyes. How does he see?*

"I see quite clearly," said Death. "And I'm not here for your grandfather."

Billy went cold. It didn't come over him slowly, like blood draining from his face; this was a sudden frost, like he'd stepped into a meat locker and someone had shut the door behind him. Numb, he stammered, "Not my mom . . . ?"

A smile flickered across Death's mouth. "I'm here for you, William."

Now Billy wasn't numb at all. Sheer terror—far colder than the meager fear he'd felt just a moment ago—yanked at his spine and contorted it into a frantic knot. He squeaked, "*Me?* But you said I wasn't going to die today!"

"Who said anything about dying?"

Billy's mouth opened, but he couldn't think of a single thing to say.

"Get out!"

Billy spun to face his grandfather, who had pulled himself up and was shaking a fist in Death's direction.

"Gramps," Billy wheezed, "stop—"

"You got no business here," the old man shouted. "Ride somewhere else!"

"But I *do* have business here," said Death, not unkindly. "Just not with you, Martin Walker. This is between me and your grandson."

"Malarkey! He's just a boy! Can't speak for himself. Can't sign no deals."

"I'm not one to barter for souls or wager on people's natures." Death's voice was the subtle rot of fallen leaves, filled with both menace and promise. "And even if I were, it would not be for you to tell me otherwise. Leave us."

Gramps lifted his chin. "Get lost."

Billy wanted to run behind his grandfather and cower there until Death retreated. And Billy wanted to scoop his grandfather up and hurl him out of harm's way, like he did yesterday afternoon. In the end, Billy did neither of those things. Frozen, he watched the old man confront Death, and he silently cheered for his grandfather, *his* Gramps, returned at long last.

For a long moment, the room was painfully still. Billy didn't dare to breathe.

Finally, Death sighed. "Fine," he said, "let's do it the old-fashioned way." He grabbed his chin and yanked up, revealing the skull beneath the bloody flesh. "Boo!"

Gramps shrieked and bolted for his bedroom, the telltale

stench of urine wafting behind him. A door's slam echoed through the house.

Billy—far too furious to remember to be afraid of Death —whirled around and jabbed a finger at Death's chest. "You just terrified an old man!"

"Heh. Yeah." The skull's teeth gleamed. "Man, that was fun."

"That's my *grandfather!* You probably gave him a heart attack!"

"Not today," said Death, rearranging his face. "Not on the agenda. Oh, he'll probably have some bad dreams. But really, now, it's the least he deserved. I'm a patient sort of entity, but even I have my limits."

Enraged, overwhelmed, Billy shouted, "What do you *want* from me?"

Death paused. The humor winking in his eyes faded until they were empty once more. Finally, he met Billy's gaze. "I want your help."

B I L L Y   W A I T E D . . .

. . . for the rest of the joke. Because surely, Death had to be joking. No one wanted Billy's help, unless it was for him to act as a living target. When Death didn't elaborate, Billy said, "Help with what?"

"Moving a body."

Billy's eyes felt like they'd pop right out of his skull. *"What?"*

Death grinned. "Kidding. Well, sort of. Come on, I'll show you."

"Wait," Billy said as Death headed toward the front door. "I can't just go with you."

"Oh?" Death glanced over his shoulder. "And why is that?"

A thousand reasons screamed inside Billy's head, most of which boiled down to "Because you're Death, duh." But what he said was, "I can't leave my grandfather alone."

The man who was not a man looked at Billy, looked *through* Billy, before he replied, "Usually, it's the adults who whine about not leaving the children alone."

"He's got Alzheimer's," Billy said.

" 'It's got him' would be more accurate, but who am I to quibble about the nature of disease? That's not my forte." Death flashed a grin. "No worries. He'll still be in the throes of his particular ailment come morning."

"I *know* that." God, did he know that. "My point is, he can't be left alone."

"Can't he? Here in this fine house, with all its locked windows and obfuscated doors and rounded corners? You've all but swaddled him in safety." Death's eyes shone darkly, hinting at amusement. "As I said, no worries. No harm will come to him tonight."

"How do you know?"

That scored him an arched eyebrow. Translation: *Because I'm Death, duh.*

Billy felt his cheeks heat. "My mom will kill me if she comes home and I'm not here."

"She won't even know you've been gone. Neither will your grandfather. Time works differently for Horsemen."

A pause as Billy absorbed the words. He repeated, "Horsemen?"

"The Four Horsemen of the Apocalypse." Death's voice deepened as he proclaimed, "'They were given power over a fourth of the earth to kill by sword, famine, and plague, and by the wild beasts of the earth.' And all that jazz." He winked. "You have to admit," he said, his voice no longer booming, "it's terrific PR, even if it's overblown."

Apocalypse. As in the end of everything.

The world tilted to the left. Billy squeezed his eyes shut and commanded himself not to pass out. He'd understood that this creature dressed like a man was Death, and that was bad enough. But now this was Death as part of the Apocalypse, and that was infinitely more frightening. Throat dry, he whispered, "Is the world going to end?"

"Of course it will," Death said cheerfully. "But not today.

Really, you people get so hung up on the smallest things. *Apocalypse* is just a word, William. If everything were coming to a crashing halt, you'd know. There'd be signs. Wars on an unprecedented scale. Natural disasters. Human sacrifice, dogs and cats living together—mass hysteria. Okay, maybe not that last part." He chuckled, and the sound was like wind blowing through withered leaves. "Love that movie. Bill Murray rocks."

Death with a sense of humor . . . and who watched *Ghostbusters*. Somehow, Death loving one of Billy's favorite movies made the situation both more surreal and less terrifying. Billy opened his eyes. "So it's not the end of the world?"

"Nope."

"But you're a . . . Horseman."

"Indeed. The Pale Rider," he said with a showman's flourish. "But you already knew that."

Billy had. He'd known it since yesterday, just like he'd known that it was almost time to wear the Crown . . . whatever that meant.

No, he wasn't going to think about that, wasn't going to remember the dream about the Ice Cream Man or hastily made promises in the noonday sun. Feeling lightheaded, he asked, "So the Horsemen of the Apocalypse go riding even when it's not the Apocalypse?" Before he could stop himself, he added, "Isn't that false advertising?"

Death chuckled again. "Admittedly, 'Horsemen of the Daily Grind' doesn't sound as awe-inspiring. But end of the world or not, the Horsemen have a job to do."

"Which is?"

"Why, preventing the end of the world, of course. And

that's why I need your help." Death motioned to the door. "Coming?"

Billy blew out a shaky breath, nodded, and walked stiffly to the front door. It wasn't so much that he wanted to leave with Death but that he *had* to. Part of that was Billy was used to being bowled over, whether by fists or by words. Part of it was that Death wasn't one to be easily denied; there was a presence around him, an aura of power that Billy couldn't see but felt like pimples breaking the surface of his skin. Death wanted him to follow, and so he would follow.

But part of it — a small, hesitant part of it — was that Billy had to know why Death had chosen him. He was the one who no one picked, not for teams or friends —

(other than Marianne, amazing Marianne, who'd been there since pre-K and had stuck with him even when everyone else turned away)

— and adults either ignored him or dealt with him matter-of-factly, like he was a statistic instead of a person. Even his mom tended to treat him like a babysitter instead of a son. So why, out of all the billions of people in the world, had Death sought out Billy Ballard?

It's a joke, he told himself as he opened the door wide. *It's a joke and I'm the punch line.*

But it wasn't. In his heart, he knew this. He'd been chosen. And that small, hesitant part of him was grateful.

He stepped aside, and Death sauntered out, hands in pockets, humming a tune that Billy couldn't quite place. As the Pale Rider went by, Billy felt a chill on his face, like a breath of frost.

From the back of his mind, a man's voice whispered: *It won't last.*

Restraining a shudder, Billy cast a glance at the living room
—not nervously, exactly, and not anxiously. It was like he
wanted to memorize exactly how every stitch of furniture was
positioned, to remember the way each throw pillow was an-
gled on the overstuffed sofa. As spooky and weird as it was for
Death to come calling, Billy felt in his gut that once he walked
out the front door, life as he'd known it would be forever over.
That wouldn't necessarily be a bad thing. But it would be a
permanent thing. That's what was making his insides itch: the
finality.

It won't last.

A memory sliced through him: Billy, age seven, putting his
beloved stuffed Cookie Monster into a carton, to be tucked
away in the attic along with other toys and games he'd out-
grown. He was old enough to know his dad was never coming back; therefore, he was old enough not to need Cookie
Monster on his pillow at night. Billy remembered placing the
weathered blue plush figure into the box, remembered feeling
like someone was squeezing him too tightly because he'd found
it difficult to take a breath. The box was sealed, and Cookie was
gone.

Feeling hollow, Billy followed Death out of the house, pausing only to shut and lock the front door.

And then he turned and balked immediately when he saw
the horse.

||||||

The pale horse had no need to breathe, so it reserved that action for when it was near the other steeds. Over the years, it

had found that horses get nervous if one of their kind doesn't breathe, especially when snorts and blows were so essential to communication.

Living creatures, the horse had long ago discovered, were easily spooked.

As it watched its Rider and the boy exit the house, the steed took a dusty breath. Always best to relate to humans as if they were horses. Simpler that way, even though horses were far more noble than humans.

The boy slowly turned away from the door and saw the steed. His eyes widened, and as the boy stared mutely, the horse caught a whiff of moonlight and bedbugs: the scent of the White Rider.

Interesting.

The steed considered the boy's aura, a pulse of colors that indicated how much life had been already spent and how much was left in reserve. Through the colors was a thread of white, flickering from pristine to filthy. The horse squinted, and now it saw that the white was deeply tangled around the boy's core.

Very interesting. The boy had been marked — not by Death, who chose all Riders, but by the Conqueror.

Well now. That was something new. The horse's ears quivered. In its long, long years, the steed rarely came across anything new.

The boy was still staring at it. A fine sheen of sweat coated his forehead, and his mouth worked silently, opening and closing, opening and closing. Keeping background time to the breath of the world, the boy's frantic heartbeat drummed in his chest. The human was clearly terrified . . .

. . . of the horse.

Not of Death, who could end all existence with a simple word, but of the Pale Rider's steed.

The horse smiled, in the way that horses did. This, too, was new—and the pale steed was extremely amused.

▌▌▌▌▌▌

. . . At the edge of the park, he sees a white horse. Not a merry-go-round horse, either, but a real live horse, about a million feet tall and so white that it's like staring at the sun . . .

Billy blinked and the memory vanished, but the horse remained. Not his horse, no—that horse, the nightmare horse, the one that came with the Ice Cream Man, was a blinding white, and the one dappled in moonlight outside his house was, if anything, leached of color. It made Billy think of the plant hanging in the kitchen: amid the lush emerald leaves were scattered bits of pale green, the color leaning toward off-white. The horse was the color of those dying leaves.

"Come on," Death said, approaching the monstrous horse.

Billy's feet refused to work. He opened his mouth to shout, but his voice died somewhere along the way. He watched Death pull himself atop the horse in an easy motion, watched him adjust the saddle bag that absolutely hadn't been there a moment ago—for that matter, the *saddle* hadn't been there a moment ago—but all Billy could do was stare, horrified, at the pale horse.

"Plenty of room," Death said cheerfully.

Billy's voice had betrayed him, but he could still turn his head. He did so, slowly, emphatically if silently saying, *No, nuh-uh, absolutely not.*

The horse grinned at him. He knew that was crazy, because horses don't grin, but he would have sworn on his life that the thing was actually grinning at him.

"Is there a problem?" asked Death.

Oh yeah. There was a gigantic horse with glowing red eyes and looking like it had maybe drowned standing right there in front of his house. There was a problem, all right.

"It's my steed," Death said fondly, giving the creature a pat on its thick neck. "It won't harm you."

Billy shook his head once more, and managed to take a step back. The door was flush against his back.

Now Death was gazing at him like he had the word LOSER written on his forehead. In a soft, cold voice, Death said, "What frightens thee, William Ballard?"

Billy thought once more of the Ice Cream Man's giant horse, screamingly white and yet somehow dirty, just like the Ice Cream Man himself, and he heard the Ice Cream Man tell him that he's got something to show Billy . . .

No!

Shuddering, he looked away. No, he wasn't thinking about the man in white. He wasn't. That was a nightmare and nothing more.

"Even nightmares have elements of truth," Death murmured.

Billy shivered again, and this time his voice didn't fail him as he faced the Pale Rider. "I'm not riding a horse."

It was a pivotal moment: Billy Ballard, the most bullied kid in school, had chosen to stand his ground. It wasn't because he thought he could win. He'd reached his breaking point. Death could kill him, and that didn't matter. There was no way that Billy was getting on that horse. Period.

Silence echoed as Death stared at him, considered him. Judged him. At last, the Pale Rider grinned. "No worries," he said. "We'll go the pop culture route instead."

The horse snorted.

"Don't be grumpy," Death chided.

The pale steed snorted again, and then it wasn't a horse at all but a yellow car, its engine already running. It looked like the love child of a Volkswagen Beetle and a Delorean. Death, in the driver's seat, leaned his blond head out the window and said, "Well?"

Billy, stunned, said, "Your horse is a Transformer."

"Technically, a transmogrifier. But hey, whatever floats your boat. Get in."

Billy got in, pausing only to take in the name on the vanity plate. As he fastened his seat belt—which was purely habitual, because really, was he going to die when Death was driving? —he asked, "Um. What's 'Mortis Prime'?"

Death smiled, sighed, and said, "Dude, you've *got* to read the classics." And with that, he hit the gas.

|||||

One thing Billy could say definitively about Death: the personification had a lead foot.

Billy realized immediately that the horse/car wasn't limited to things like speed limits or physics: Death shifted gears, and suddenly they were in the air. Up they went, traveling across the sky fast enough to turn the images outside the window into watercolor blurs. One look was enough for Billy; he squeezed his eyes shut and recited Linkin Park lyrics in his head to keep from losing his mind. Bad enough they were inside a horse somehow, but inside a *flying* horse? Going at ridiculous speed? No. Just no. Mentally singing songs about pain and loss made it bearable. Sort of.

After a small slice of eternity (or, in real time, four songs), they came to a sudden, jarring halt.

He didn't open his eyes until Death said, "Here we are." That was when Billy realized that A) Death had gotten out of the horse/car and B) Death had opened the passenger door for Billy.

Well, at least he hadn't screamed during the trip. That had to count for something, right?

"Absolutely," Death said with a wink.

Right. Death could read his mind. He'd probably been bopping his head as Billy had channeled his inner vocalist. *Remember to think nice things about the grunger Grim Reaper*, Billy thought as he threw himself out of the car/horse/thing.

"Sage advice," agreed Death, shutting the door.

They were parked outside of a hospital; that was clear from the large red cross on the white building, even though Billy couldn't read the sign over the entrance. What language was that—Greek?

"*Né*," said Death.

"No?" Billy repeated.

"Not 'no.' *Né*." Death smiled and tapped his nose. "You got it in one, William: That's Greek. Appropriate, considering that we're in Greece. Follow me." And off he went, striding toward the entrance like he was about to take center stage.

They were in *Greece*? Billy stared at the hospital sign, then looked back at the yellow car that, another continent ago, had been a horse. Then he looked back at the sign.

Right. They were in Greece. This night couldn't possibly get any stranger. He hurried to catch up to the Pale Rider.

They walked briskly through the entrance, the automatic doors swooshing importantly. Inside, Billy was struck by the smell: a combination of antiseptic and ammonia, strong enough to sting his eyes. But beyond that initial stench was something subtler, deeper: a metallic tang, both sharp and yet soothing. It was a comfortable smell, one that made Billy feel at home even though they were in a foreign hospital.

Blood, he realized as he and Death turned a corner and strode down the hall. Beneath the hospital stench of Spartan cleanliness, he was smelling blood. And it smelled . . . good.

Great. Now he was turning into a vampire.

Next to him, Death laughed. It was a rich sound, so completely at odds with the sterility around them. "You're many things," said the Pale Rider, chuckling. "But a vampire isn't one of them."

Just as well, Billy decided. If he were a vampire, he'd be the one that got staked first. "So why does it smell so good in here?"

"Blood is life," Death replied, as if that answered the question.

As they walked, Billy noted that the people around them didn't look at them at all—not the doctors or nurses in their scrubs, not the patients in their seats or lying on the cots lining the hallway, not the people in the waiting areas, staring listlessly at television screens. A cluster of doctors grouped in the middle of the hall, chatting in an animated way in a language Billy couldn't understand — Greek, he assumed — but rather than steer around them, Death marched straight into them . . . and the doctors sidestepped at the last instant, not pausing in their conversation. Billy stared at the group as he walked past, wondering how they could react to Death's presence even if they didn't see him. He decided he really didn't want to know.

Soon they were entering a small room. Billy took in the lone hospital bed, the assortment of machines surrounding it, the staleness of the air, and his first thought was, *There's no one here.* And then, on the heels of that: *There's a man in the bed.*

He stared at the empty bed, frowning at its clean white sheets. And as he stared, he saw the impression of a man lying in the bed. Billy blinked, and the image vanished.

"Focus," Death murmured.

Billy squinted, and once again he saw the vague image of a man in the narrow hospital bed. As Billy peered, the man's shape solidified, and now Billy was looking at a man with a ruined face, lying in bed like it was a coffin.

Recognition slammed into Billy, tightening his gut and locking his knees. He choked out one word, one desperate plea: *"No."*

There, unconscious in the hospital bed, lay the Ice Cream Man.

CHAPTER 7

BILLY STAGGERED BACK . . .

. . . as he shook his head, saying, "No" and "no" and "no" again. The man in the bed *couldn't* be there. He was nothing more than a lingering terror from childhood. A bogeyman.

And yet there he was, shrouded from chin to toe in a dingy white blanket.

Horrified, Billy stared at the Ice Cream Man's waxy face. The skin, riddled with cold sores and pox, sagged as if overcome by gravity, pooling by the ears and jaw. His lipless white mouth hung open enough for Billy to spy rotted teeth. The eyes, thankfully, were closed, but Billy knew they would be rheumy with pus. Greasy black tendrils of hair fanned along the pillow like an oil-covered starfish.

"You know him," said Death. It wasn't a question.

Billy swallowed thickly. Oh, he knew the Ice Cream Man, all right. He'd been the central figure in Billy's recurring nightmare for years. Not trusting his voice, he nodded.

Death stood at the side of the bed, exactly halfway between the headboard and foot rail. His too-long blond hair curtained over his face, casting his eyes and nose in shadow. His mouth, though, was set in a wide grin, showing too many teeth for Billy's comfort. "Oh, he'd like that," Death said with a chuckle. "Ice cream and emperors go well together."

The words surprised Billy into speaking. "He's an emperor?"

"He was, long ago." Death glanced over his shoulder at the unconscious man in the hospital bed. "A ruler more than an emperor. And a ruler more than once. But more than anything else, he is a Rider."

"Like you," said Billy.

A pause, like winter frost gathering on a windowpane. And then Death said quietly, "None is like me."

Wind slapped Billy's face, bringing sudden tears to his eyes. In that moment, he thought he saw wings unfurling behind Death's back, spreading wide enough to fill the room and beyond—but then he blinked and the image was gone, leaving Billy with a vague sense of terror and awesome beauty.

The moment passed, and Death, no longer terrifying or awe-inspiring, grinned once more. "But you're close. He's a colleague of mine. Say hello to Pestilence, Conqueror of Health, Bringer of Disease, White Rider of the Apocalypse. Also, not a bad bridge player."

Thoughts whipped through Billy's head, some questioning what he'd just witnessed, others pouncing on Death's declaration about the man in the bed. Pestilence? The Ice Cream Man, the nightmare man, wasn't just real—he was a Horseman of the Apocalypse?

He shook his head. It was too much. Too crazy. He grasped on to that thought like a lifeline. Yes, he was going crazy. He could handle crazy. He'd enjoy crazy. The notion of being locked up someplace safe, far away from responsibilities and consequences, was extremely inviting. More likely, he wasn't crazy at all. He'd hit his head in the locker room—repeatedly, thanks to Joe—so maybe now he had a concussion. A head injury. Yes, that had to be it—he was hallucinating from pain. Or maybe he was dreaming. He'd gone home after being humiliated in front of Marianne, and he'd probably thrown himself on his bed, his iPod buds snug in his ears, and he'd fallen asleep to a soundtrack of angst.

That made Billy laugh, a strangled sound that bordered on a scream. Death and Pestilence and the flying horse/car, those were all just symbols of his stress. He wondered what it meant if you knew you were dreaming when you were in the middle of a dream, and he decided he didn't care. This wasn't real, so he didn't need to care.

This wasn't real.

Suddenly Death was right in front of him, peering at him with those empty blue eyes, and he said, "This is more real than you have allowed yourself to know, William Ballard." A cold finger touched Billy's forehead, and it seared him down to his soul.

Death's voice, penetrating, insistent: *Remember.*

And Billy remembered.

||||||

. . . *Billy's in the sandbox, building castles and getting filthy and loving every second of it. The castle's going to be the setting for the ultimate battle of Good versus Evil—in other words, the battle of every single toy, creature, and superhero he's ever owned, created, or seen on television. Billy's got a tremendous imagination. His mom tells him so every day. She's there somewhere on the periphery of the playground, sitting on a bench and reading a book. Billy doesn't need to look around to know she's watching. His mom al-*

ways watches. It makes him feel safe. He smiles as he adds more sand to reinforce the towers.

It's a gorgeous spring day, complete with blue skies and singing birds. Trees talk to each other in the breeze as the sun smiles down on everyone. Other kids are in the playground, too, but Billy doesn't notice them. He's lost in his sandcastle architecture, already planning on building an extension for the mega-round of the tournament. He's got to be thorough; he doesn't want anyone left out of the superhuge battle.

A cloud passes over him, and Billy sneezes, once.

Wait—maybe he should make this part of the castle open to the sky. That way, the flying aliens and superheroes don't have to worry about bumping into the ceiling. He scoops out more sand.

The cloud hasn't moved.

Billy's sniffling now, his nose leaking and his eyes watering. He barely notices; he just uses his shirt as a tissue and keeps on playing in the sandbox. Something's not right, he decides as he frowns at the hollow tower, but he can't decide what it is. Maybe he'll make another castle right next to this one.

A shadow falls over Billy.

No, not a castle, he decides. A fortress. With wings, so that it can fly. He grins, inspired, and he reaches for more sand.

"It won't last," says a man's voice.

Billy jumps, and he whips his head around to see a huge man dressed in white looming over him. There's something wrong with the man's face—it looks like it's melting. Billy is about to shout for his mom, but then he feels three things, one right after the other. First, he's horribly thirsty. Second, he has a sudden urge for potato chips. And third, he's calm, extremely calm. There's no reason for Billy to panic; if the man in white does anything scary,

Billy will run to his mom. Billy is proud of himself for being so grown up.

"Addison's disease," says the man in white. His voice sounds like it's being pulled out of his mouth and dragged along gravel. "The adrenal glands don't produce enough cortisol, which helps the body respond to stress. A feel-good disease. Just for you, Billy."

Billy cocks his head to the side as he looks up at the man. He's positive he hadn't told the man his name, and he's not wearing a shirt with his name printed on it. Instead of feeling uneasy or scared, Billy just accepts it. "I'm thirsty," he announces.

"Of course you are. Dehydration is one of the symptoms of Addison's. You should be thankful that I'm repressing most of the other symptoms, like vomiting and diarrhea."

Billy isn't sure what diarrhea is—it sounds like a girl's name—but he's familiar with vomiting. The last time he'd puked, it was because he had what his mom called a "tummy bug." Billy hates vomiting. By extension, he hates bugs. "I'm getting some water," he says. When he stands up, there's a moment of dizziness. The man in white catches him before he can fall. His gloved hand is cold on Billy's back.

"Sudden low blood pressure," the man with the runny face says. "Another symptom. Nothing to worry about. This is all temporary."

"I'm not worried," says Billy. And it's true: He's not. He walks over to where his mom is, going slower than usual because his legs feel a little rubbery, and he frowns when he sees her sleeping on the bench. The lady next to her is also sleeping.

Actually, everyone in the playground is sleeping. Everyone except for him and the man in white.

"Narcolepsy," says the man, who's watching Billy. "Extreme daytime fatigue, resulting in falling asleep at inappropriate times.

Again, temporary. Get your drink. Then I have something to show you."

Billy rummages through his mom's large shoulder bag and produces a juice box. Straw in place, he sips his apple juice as he walks back to the man. "*Are you an ice cream man?*" he asks, staring at the man's pristine white clothing.

The man in white smiles slowly. It's rather horrible to look at. "*I am many things. Why not an ice cream man as well?*"

Billy ponders this as he drinks his juice.

"*Come with me,*" says the Ice Cream Man, who turns his back on Billy and starts to walk off the playground. "*And throw out the empty box. Littering is a disease of the world, and I don't abide by it.*"

Billy follows, tossing his juice box in a garbage can. He knows he's not supposed to talk to strangers or go with them anywhere. But this man knows his name. And besides, Billy is feeling so calm that he feels good, really good, like he just ate something tasty and is feeling it settle comfortably in his belly.

The Ice Cream Man walks, a cloud of dust in his wake, and Billy Ballard follows as if in a dream.

At the edge of the park, Billy sees a white horse. Not a merry-go-round horse, either, but a real live horse, about a million feet tall and so white that it's like staring at the sun. Billy grins in delight.

"*Tell me,*" says the Ice Cream Man, "*would you like to ride the white horse?*"

Stunned by his good fortune, Billy nods.

"*All you have to do is agree to wear the Crown when the time comes.*"

Billy scrunches up his face as he tries to understand the Ice Cream Man's words.

"Will you wear the Crown, Billy Ballard?"

Billy says, *"A crown. Like a king?"*

"This Crown," says the Ice Cream Man, motioning to his forehead.

Billy squints, and now sees there's a thin silver band nestled over the man's eyebrows. Even looking hard, Billy can barely see it, thanks to the man's long greasy hair and his misshapen forehead. It's like the crown is being eaten by the man's terrible face.

"Why?" asks Billy.

"Because I've picked you."

"Why?" Billy asks again.

The man in white smiles. *"Because it makes more sense to pick my predecessor now than to have the Pale Rider do so post mortem."*

Billy knows with crystal-clear certainty that even though the man is telling the truth, he's also lying.

"Omission isn't the same thing as lying," the Ice Cream Man says with a sniff. *"But it's your choice. Either agree to wear the Crown when the time comes and get a ride on my fine white steed, or say no and run back to your meager little life."*

Billy looks at the horse. The huge animal seems to be smiling at him, like it's trying to tell him that riding on its back would be the best thing in the whole world.

"What do you say, Billy?" The man's voice is smooth now, not at all like the rough voice he'd used back in the playground. Hearing the man speak makes Billy think of a glass of cold milk. Or maybe vanilla ice cream, the soft kind that swirls into a point. *"Do you want a ride on the horse?"*

Biting his lip, Billy nods.

"Do you agree to wear the Crown when the time comes?"

Again, Billy nods.

"You have to say the words, Billy. Say that you agree to wear the Crown."

Staring at the white horse, Billy says, "I'll wear the Crown."

The Ice Cream Man grins, and Billy feels the calmness inside of him begin to erode. There's a pit in Billy's stomach, and it's white and filled with bugs.

"Excellent," hisses the Ice Cream Man. "Come here, Billy, and I'll get you saddled up . . ."

The man in white reaches out to Billy, and Billy sees that the man's gloved hand is twisted into a monster's claw. The last shreds of calm are torn away as Billy opens his mouth to scream . . .

|||||||

"No!" Billy cried, throwing himself back to avoid the Ice Cream Man's touch. The cold spot on his forehead vanished, and warmth flooded through him. He stood, shaking, panting for breath.

A dream, he told himself as he shivered. *Just a dream!*

"It was no dream, William."

Billy looked up to see the Pale Rider leaning against the bed rail, hands stuffed in the pockets of his faded blue jeans. His hair hung almost artfully in front of his eyes, casting them in shadow. "It's amazing to see just how far you people go to lie to yourselves," Death said idly. A smile teased his lips — just a hint by the corners, almost too subtle to be seen. "Imagine how much you could accomplish if you stopped insisting on denial as the norm."

It was Death's bemused smile that nudged Billy over the edge. He'd been elbowed, slammed, and tripped, that last in front of the girl he still dared to dream about, not to mention countless others in the pizzeria. He'd changed his grandfather's adult diaper and put up with monosyllabic insults from the man who'd stepped in when his father had stepped out. He'd gotten through all of that because that was his life and that's what he did: He got through it. He hated it, but he understood it.

But then Death had shown up, and everything Billy thought he'd understood got flushed down the toilet. And now Death had the gall to mock him?

In his mind, the PE coach sneered, *Don't be such a girl.*

Voice tight, Billy demanded, "Why am I here?"

Half-hidden by golden hair, Death's eyes sparkled like caged sunlight. "Depends if your worldview is Maileresque or more along the lines of Vonnegut. Are you a 'huge purpose' fan, or more of a 'fart around' sort of guy?"

"You said you needed my help," Billy said flatly. "And then you brought me here. Tell me why."

"Ah, the direct approach. Groovy." No question about it now: Death was smiling fit to burst. "I brought you here because of your connection to the man lying unconscious in this bed. The Conqueror cannot ride. And so the mantle of the White Rider falls to you."

A heartbeat, then Billy said, "I have no idea what you're talking about."

"You, William Ballard, are now Pestilence. Well," added Death, somewhat sheepishly, "sort of."

Billy's stomach roiled. He couldn't tell if he was angry or afraid or something else completely. He wanted to run until his legs turned to rubber; he wanted to throw his head back and scream until the sound was etched in his throat.

A lick of fire burned behind his eyes, and as the fire crackled it said: *You've convinced yourself that if you fight back, that will make it worse. It might. Then again, it might not.*

Billy didn't know about fighting back. But he did know that what Death had just said was ludicrous. The Ice Cream Man was real, and now Billy was . . . what, the Ice Cream Boy? No. Absolutely not.

"'Fraid so," said Death. "You agreed to wear the Crown when it was time. And it's time."

"I *agreed?* I didn't agree to anything!"

"For the price of a ride on the pretty white horse, you agreed to wear the Crown."

The words sank in. "You're talking about my dream."

Death said nothing as he watched Billy, but the smile on his face stretched wider.

"You're telling me that because of something I said in a dream from when I was a kid, that makes it a done deal?"

"It wasn't a dream. You made an agreement with the White Rider when you were five." Death paused, then said, "Sorry, William. That's lousy, but it's binding."

"It's *bullshit!* You can't hold me to something I said when I was a kid!"

"Actually, I have to," Death said gently. "Rules, you know. They suck, but they're still rules. And these aren't the kind you can break, or that I can overlook. Thou art Pestilence, William Ballard. Of a sort." Shadows passed behind Death's eyes. "I can't give you the White Rider's Crown because he wears it still. It would have made you the conqueror of health and sickness alike. That title remains with him. He is the Conqueror."

Billy glared at the figure lying in the hospital bed. Indeed, on the man's pox-ridden brow lay a thin band of silver, barely visible between the greasy strands of black hair. Billy thought the silver band was called a circlet. He also thought it looked completely nasty, resting there on the man's lumpy face. There was no way he would ever let that band of silver touch his flesh.

"I can, however, give you his Bow," said Death. "A consolation prize, perhaps, but still a good one."

Eyes locked on the Crown, Billy shook his head. "I don't want anything of his." He wasn't going to take over for the Ice Cream Man, or the Conqueror, or whatever he was called.

"He has many names, and even more titles. Before you prattle on about what you want and what you don't want, look at the Bow."

Something about Death's voice made Billy turn to face the Pale Rider, who was motioning to the back corner of the room.

"You have to admit," said Death, "you've never seen anything like it."

Despite himself, Billy gazed at the object tucked in the corner of the room. At first glance, it seemed far too short and thin to be a bow—more accurate, he thought, to call it a walking stick. It was black and polished to an opulent sheen, its ends tapered to narrow points. It was beautiful to look at, almost hypnotic, like fire. It couldn't have been carved from an ordinary tree, not something that marvelous, that radiant.

"The tree it hails from, the Wattieza, is long extinct," said Death. "But even when its siblings filled the land, this particular wood was already ancient."

"No string," Billy murmured. "No arrows."

"It requires neither of those trappings," said Death. "As you already know."

And he did. Billy didn't know how he knew it, but he understood it to be true—just as he understood that it belonged in his hand. He found himself walking over to it, reaching out to touch it before he could tell himself otherwise. His fingers stroked the polished wood once, lightly.

A shock of power jolted him, searing every nerve. With the pain came a burning clarity: The Bow was an extension of the White Rider, a tool that would bring disease to the world.

Among other things, Death murmured in his mind. *But as with the other Riders, you will learn as you go.*

With a yelp, Billy jerked his hand back, knocking the Bow to the ground. It landed on the linoleum floor with an unceremonious thump.

"That's no way to treat such a relic," Death commented.

Billy slowly backed away from the fallen staff. Death, and flying horse/cars, and the Ice Cream Man, and the Conqueror, and an unstrung bow that would let him spread sickness through the world. He shut his eyes and wrapped his hands over his head. Enough. He was done. He could barely handle his own life, such as it was; he couldn't also cope with the supernatural.

"I thought you wanted to escape your life, William."

He did, but not like this. He whispered, "Take me home."

A touch of frost on his shoulder, and then a popping sensation in his ears.

"Jiggety-jig," Death said, sounding terribly chipper.

Billy opened his eyes to find himself standing on the steps outside his front door. Thank God they hadn't had to get back into the horse/car.

"Usually," said Death from behind him, "Riders prefer to ride."

Billy's hands squeezed into fists. "I'm no Rider."

"Thou art the White Rider, William Ballard. Thou art Pestilence, Bringer of Disease. Go thee out unto the world."

"I don't want to be Pestilence!"

"It matters little what you want. The Conqueror tricked you into agreeing to wear the Crown when the time came. That time is now."

No, Billy thought desperately. *No. No. No.* In his mind, he saw the Ice Cream Man with his waxy brow, saw the silver circlet winking around the folds of skin and lanky hair. Desperate, he said, "But he's still wearing the Crown."

"True," Death agreed cheerfully. "But as you have seen, he's fallen down on the job. It's up to you to pick up the slack. Or, if you'd rather, you can convince him to get out of bed." A chuckle, like the sound of soil eroding. "Either way works for me."

"No," Billy said through gritted teeth. After having denied Death once—no way would he ever ride a horse, especially Death's horse—doing so again was slightly easier. Perhaps facing his mortality (or, more accurately, *everyone's* mortality) helped him put things in perspective. "I don't care what you say," Billy insisted. "I'm not doing it."

With that, he dug out his house key and jammed it into the lock. The knob turned, and he stormed inside.

"Don't forget your Bow," Death called after him.

Billy slammed the door and jerked the locks in place, then tore down the hall to his room. Buds secure in his ears, music blasting on the iPod, he buried himself in his blankets, his clothes and shoes still on, and he hid himself from the world.

‖‖‖‖

Famine stepped out from the shadows, black separating from black. The echo of the front door slamming still rode the air. Turing to face the Pale Rider, she huffed, "That didn't go well at all."

Death winked at her. "Trust me."

CHAPTER 8

THE ONLY REASON BILLY
HEARD THE ALARM GO OFF . . .

. . . was because one of his ear buds had popped out over-night. His iPod was still blaring his five-star playlist, but over the sounds of My Chemical Romance was the insistent beeping of his clock, telling him that it was 6:30 in the morning and therefore time to start the school day.

Autopilot kicked in. He shut off the alarm. He shut off his iPod. He pulled the remaining bud from his ear. He staggered out of bed and made his way to the bathroom, where he peed like a racehorse. He was vaguely aware that he was still in yes-terday's clothes, sneakers and all. Whatever. He stumbled back to his room. And standing in the doorway, he stared at the long black bow lying atop his unmade bed.

He blinked, and blinked again.

The bow was still lying on his bed.

As he stared at the polished limb, two things hit him like Eddie's fists: One, everything that had happened last night, from Death appearing at his door to seeing the Ice Cream Man in a hospital bed in Greece, was real; and two, the Ice Cream Man—the Conqueror, the decrepit White Rider of the Apoca-lypse—was not only real but had tricked him when he was a kid.

And because of that, he now had a bow that magically ap-peared on his bed.

A consolation prize, perhaps, but still a good one.

The Bow waited on his bed, daring him to pick it up.

Death had told him that he was to use the weapon to bring disease to the world. He snorted. Yeah, he was supposed to use his magic bow with its pretend bowstring and imaginary arrows to shoot people. That was insane. Clearly, he'd gone crazy somewhere along the way, and now he was having some weird revenge fantasy.

Thou art the White Rider.

He shook his head at the thought. He couldn't even bear the idea of riding a horse, let alone shooting people with arrows brimming with sickness.

It's amazing to see just how far you people go to lie to yourselves.

Billy stood in the doorway to his bedroom, Death's taunt echoing in his mind, and he stared at the unstrung bow on his bed. And he allowed himself to consider the possibility that he wasn't insane and that the Bow was real.

One way to find out. He walked into his room and reached for the Bow.

Just before his fingers would have brushed against the polished wood, he felt a jolt of power spiking from the limb like a live wire. He jerked his hand away and scrambled backwards.

On his bed, the Bow waited.

It was real. And more than that: It was dangerous.

Breathing hard, Billy scrubbed his fingers through his hair and stared at the black wood. Inanimate objects couldn't smirk, he told himself, and yet that's exactly what it looked like the Bow was doing.

"Go away," he whispered. It had appeared by magic; it could leave by magic as well. "Get out of here. Abracadabra. Shazam."

The Bow didn't move.

Thou art Pestilence.

No.

Billy ran out of his bedroom and yanked the door shut. Panting, he called himself three kinds of stupid for running away from an unstrung bow, but that didn't change the fact that he wasn't going back in his room. Not now. Not yet, at any rate.

Down the hallway, his grandfather's door opened. As the old man wandered out, Billy was hit immediately by the toxic stench of urine and sweat. Scrunching his face against the smell, he saw that Gramps was plastered in yesterday's clothes, and the pants were darker by the crotch.

Billy bit back a curse as he remembered Gramps screeching and running into his bedroom last night. Instead of getting his grandfather ready for bed, he'd left with Death and paid a call to the Ice Cream Man. Of course Gramps had peed himself; Billy hadn't even bothered to get him into an adult diaper.

This was his fault.

Billy, already tense to the point of snapping, clenched his fists and ground his teeth and counted to five before he pasted a tight smile on his face. It didn't matter that he was in the middle of freaking out over a magic Bow and being charged by Death; he had to take care of his grandfather. "Come on, Gramps. Let's get you clean."

The old man let Billy walk him to his room and strip off his clothing. At least he wasn't fighting this morning; if anything, today he was like a life-sized doll, allowing Billy to dress him quickly, if mechanically. Billy then stripped the single bed and bundled all the soiled laundry into a tidy pile by the corner. He'd leave a note for his mom, telling her to grab the dirty things from Gramps's room and to make sure he got a bath.

Done with his chores, he said, "All set, Gramps."

His grandfather stared at him, or at a spot just over Billy's eyes. And then he said, "Mark."

"No, Gramps," Billy said, trying to be patient. "Not Mark. Billy. I'm Billy."

"Marked," his grandfather wheezed.

"Yes, Gramps." Uneasily, Billy wondered if the old man was trying to say "Malarkey" and couldn't remember the word.

"Marked so's you won't get lost."

"Yes, Gramps."

"You find your way," said his grandfather, shaking a finger at him. "You find your way, and you come back home."

Maybe the old man was talking to himself, telling himself not to go wandering out of the house. Or maybe he was just rambling because he had Alzheimer's and that's part of what people like him did. Billy forced himself to smile placidly. "I hear you, Gramps. Want some breakfast?"

With those words, Billy slipped into the comfort of routine. He led his grandfather into the kitchen and helped him into a chair at the small table. He served Gramps orange juice in a plastic cup, fed him overly buttered toast, and cleared the plate when only crumbs remained. He walked the old man into the family room and got him settled in his favorite chair, then he turned on the television to a *Wheel of Fortune* rerun.

"I have to get ready for school now, Gramps."

"Hmmm."

"Mom will be up soon. If you need anything, she'll be here."

"Hmmm."

Billy took that as both agreement and approval, so he retreated to the bathroom. He'd almost forgotten about the Bow and the White Rider and Death, almost slipped quietly back into his life—but then he splashed water on his face and looked at his reflection in the mirror over the sink. And he froze.

There was a blotch of white in his hair.

He leaned closer to the mirror, his gaze locked on the splat of white staining the lock of hair dangling over his forehead. It wasn't the pristine brilliance of new snow but more like the paleness of dandruff flakes: The color had been dried out, leached away, leaving the strands empty.

Dead.

Hair is dead, he thought wildly, *it can't just turn white overnight no matter what happens in movies, it can't it can't it can't—*

And yet, it had.

His fingers shaking, he reached a hand up and touched the white lock. The hair felt like . . . well, hair. He finger-combed it back, but when he removed his hand the lock slumped back over the center of his forehead.

It hung directly over the spot where Death had touched him the night before, commanding him to remember the Ice Cream Man.

Marked, his grandfather had said. And he'd been right.

Billy ripped off his clothing and jumped in the shower. He tried to scald away the white hair, then scrubbed it with a ton of shampoo and rinsed until the water ran cold. He toweldried his hair hard enough to make his scalp scream. But when he wiped away the steam in the mirror, the stark-white patch winked at him.

For a long moment, he did nothing but stare at his reflection and get caught in the undertow of physical stress: the headache throbbing behind his eyes; the acid churning in his belly; the muscles of his shoulders and neck and back tensing to the point of rigid pain. It hit him in waves, bruising him and leaving him breathless.

Brush your teeth.

The thought was simple and direct, and he grabbed on to it to keep from drowning. *Yes, brush your teeth and get dressed. It's a school day. Get ready for school.*

And so he managed to brush his teeth without giving into panic. Maybe his breathing was a whisker shy of hyperventilation, but at least he wasn't curled in a ball under his blanket and wishing the world would just go away.

Besides, Billy couldn't hide in bed; the Bow was still resting on his cover when he returned to his bedroom.

Get ready for school, he told himself again. And so he did. He grabbed clothing and got dressed in baggy jeans and a hoodie. He went back to the bathroom and stared at the white patch in his hair, and then he slowly pulled up the hood of his sweatshirt until his hair was completely hidden and his face was obscured with shadow.

||||||

Keep Your Head Down.

Billy's mantra had never been more appropriate. Hood pulled down to his nose, he slunk from class to class and did his best to be invisible. Even so, his morning was peppered with the usual taunts that ranged from "asswipe" to "zitface," punctuated with the occasional shove. Normal stuff, at least. He breathed; he pretended he was numb to the physical pushes and the verbal punches. He survived. (And the pop quiz in second-period bio was surprisingly easy.)

After bio, Marianne walked with him to the lockers. She frowned at his raised hood and asked if he was okay. He really didn't know how to answer that, but he smiled and shrugged and said that it could be worse. He supposed that was even true.

During English, as his teacher went on and on about the Shakespeare, Billy thought about a man with a melted face and rotten teeth.

"Tell me," said the Ice Cream Man, "would you like to ride the white horse?"

Billy never did get that ride. He remembered that now, sitting at his desk and staring at the poorly spelled insult about him that had been etched into the plastic tabletop: That fateful day in the playground, after he'd agreed to wear the Crown, he'd been so terrified that he'd run screaming to his mother. He'd found her blinking sleepily on the park bench, and she'd held him as he'd wailed. He'd been too scared to say why he was upset, so instead he told her that his belly hurt and he wanted to go home. No horse ride for him.

The teacher droned on, and Billy pretended to take notes. The Ice Cream Man hadn't pursued Billy when he'd run away all those years ago. There'd been no need: The White Rider had gotten his promise. That thought made him grip his pen tight enough to whiten his knuckles. The Ice Cream Man had tricked him, and now he had a white patch in his hair and a Bow lying on his bed.

"You have to admit," said Death, "you've never seen anything like it."

As the end-of-period bell sounded, Billy stuffed his books into his backpack and thought about the Bow. He remembered the polished sheen of the black wood, how it gleamed like it had been carved from obsidian. And he remembered the jolt of power he'd felt as his fingers brushed its surface.

Power.

What could he do if he wielded such power? Not that he wanted to bring disease to the world—no, not that, not at all —but wouldn't it be sweet to be the one that people respected? The one that they feared?

What would it be like to be powerful?

He pictured himself standing with his back against the school lockers as Eddie Glass got in his face. This time, Billy wasn't paralyzed by fear. He saw himself blocking blows instead of taking them, saw himself landing a solid punch in Eddie's gut. Billy's mouth twitched, and as he imagined Eddie doubled over and wheezing, Billy pressed his lips together in a grim smile. Yes. That was what he wanted—to be strong, to be unafraid. To be confident.

To be powerful.

He thought now not just of Eddie but also of Joe and Kurt and all the others who'd hurt him, everyone who'd ever beaten him until his body was awash in a rainbow of colors—the bruised purples, festering greens, sickly yellows, wounded reds. He thought of laughter, of jeers, of faceless mockery and brutal hands.

"You're good at caging it," said the girl in red. "But soon enough, it will claw its way free."

Rage surged through him, and he thought of how good it would feel to finally put them all in their place. He had a Bow. Why not use it?

"Look at the birdshit in your hair!"

Startled out of his dark thoughts, he looked up to see Kurt grinning down at him, surrounded by three cheerleader types giggling like rabid hyenas. Kurt pointed at Billy's white-streaked hair and started guffawing.

"Birdshit," Kurt said gleefully around his chortles. "Birdshit!"

Billy bolted out of his chair, throwing his backpack over his shoulder as he rushed out the classroom. *Stupid hair!* he thought as he stormed down the hall. He should have just cut the offending white hairs off. Too late now; the damage had been done.

He shoved the top of the hood down to his nose, but it wasn't enough. Like a communicable disease, knowledge of his white hair stripe spread everywhere—he could see it in people's wicked grins and pointing fingers. Kurt or one of the hyena cheerleaders must have texted it. Or maybe the rest of the school was linked telepathically. However it had happened, everyone suddenly knew that Billy Ballard's hair had been skunked. Halfway to PE, the hallway morphed into a sea of hands, all reaching out to yank on the white lock to see if it would tear away from his scalp. Fingers and arms and elbows sprang from everywhere, swarmed over him like ants on a honeypot. He slapped them away, but that did nothing to stanch the flow or to muffle the jeers and taunts. Bombarded by flesh, he watched, helpless, as a teacher walked right past him.

See that? he thought wildly. *They don't care. They never care.*

They promise to protect you but then they leave you they ignore you they look the other way—

A beefy hand yanked his hood back so quickly that the seam popped. And then he was face to face with Eddie Glass.

"Nice stripe," said Eddie, leering. "Does it come out?" He grabbed a chunk of Billy's hair and pulled. Hard.

Something in Billy's head quietly snapped. It was an audible sound, a soft click that flipped off everything that paralyzed him at the thought of fighting back. It was the sound of Billy hitting his breaking point. He looked at Eddie's face and didn't see the bully who'd been tormenting him for years.

He saw a target.

Billy lifted his hand, knowing the Bow would already be in his grip. And it was: It felt *right*, as if the wood had been carved for his hand alone. He didn't worry about the way the Bow had simply appeared, or about the way the hall was now warping and stretching, pulling Eddie back until the larger boy was twenty feet away from him. The Bow was in his hand and his prey was before him; the time for worry was long past.

The world around him grew silent as he took aim. His fingers hooked on the bowstring and drew it back smoothly, easily. He couldn't say if the pull was five pounds or five hundred; he pulled, and the string drew back, as naturally as him taking his next breath. It didn't matter that he couldn't see or feel the bowstring. He *believed* it was there—oh yes, Billy believed. The bow was his religion and the drawstring, his faith. And the arrow fletching that kissed his cheek was proof of God. His vision tunneled, giving him a clear view of the surprise flickering in Eddie's piggy eyes.

Billy Ballard let fly his poisoned arrow.

In front of him, Eddie staggered. He blinked, then blinked again, and his wide face suddenly flushed. One hand covering his mouth, he drunkenly turned and stumbled down the hall. He didn't make it ten feet before he doubled over, vomiting. Around him, other students screeched and leaped out of the way.

Billy lowered the Bow and watched Eddie succumb to another bout of nausea. And then, as the other boy fell to his knees and cradled his stomach, Billy began to smile. He barely noticed how all of the students who'd been accosting him just moments ago were now scuttling away, and when the next-period bell rang the sound seemed muffled, distant. Billy's gaze was locked on to Eddie's form, and he watched as the large boy huddled next to a pool of vomit. Sweat gleamed on Eddie's pimpled brow, and he shook uncontrollably.

Billy knew that Eddie had just spiked a dangerously high fever. He didn't know how he knew. And he didn't care.

Soon a teacher — the same one who'd ignored Billy's plight a few minutes earlier — ran over to help the fallen boy. He didn't look up at Billy, didn't seem to realize he was even standing there.

Billy watched as he gripped the Bow tightly. His smile took on a hard edge.

He was done with keeping his head down.

He was done with being afraid.

Billy spun on his heel. Bow in hand, he marched down the hallway, the sounds of Eddie's feverish whimpers a sweet harmony to his ears.

CHAPTER 9

BILLY HAD NEVER . . .

. . . felt so confident, not even those times as a kid when he'd hit the baseball that Gramps so patiently threw. Seeing the great and powerful Eddie Glass reduced to a vomiting mass of flesh had been a wakeup call.

And Billy intended never to go back to sleep, not as long as he had the Bow.

Head high, white forelock dangling over his eye, he walked past the locker room and headed for the main gym doors. He was late for PE, but that didn't matter. The handful of stray students rushing to class ignored him, as did the vice princi-pal, who usually had a gimlet eye for anyone not tucked inside a classroom after the bell rang. A small part of Billy's mind noticed this and thought it odd—the vice principal lived for assigning detention—but the rest of Billy, the newly confident part of him that wielded the Bow, merely shrugged this aside. Of *course* he wasn't noticed. Only the Horsemen could see the White Rider.

He thought fleetingly of a girl in red, a girl who spoke lov-ingly of rage and told him that soon enough, his anger would claw its way free. Was she a Horseman too? Billy felt the answer was yes. He didn't know the girl, and yet part of him did—he saw her standing over him in the alley behind Dawson's Pizza, offering him a hand, and just beyond that, like an afterimage, he saw her on a red horse, one hand hefting a sword high as they galloped through the sky, leaving bloody trails in their wake.

But blood wasn't the province of the Red Rider alone. He knew this, just as he knew the girl in red was War. The White Rider, too, knew of blood. Bronchitis. Pneumonia. Tuberculosis. And so much more. So much to learn. And to teach, oh yes, to show everyone who'd ever hurt him just what he could do now.

Picturing Joe and everyone else doubled over with coughs that left their throats raw, Billy approached the gymnasium. They wouldn't see him, not even when his arrows pierced their skins. Finally, after years of being tormented by them for no reason he could name, it would be *their* turn to play the victim, their turn to have their stomachs clench and insides twist from nausea. Their turn to be sick with fear. Or, barring that, their turn to be sick, period.

He grinned. The Bow wouldn't fail him. However many arrows he needed, he'd have. He knew this, just as he'd known how to strike down Eddie. He would storm inside, a soundtrack of righteous fury blaring in his mind as he'd let arrow after arrow fly. He'd take down Joe first and the PE coach right after, and then anyone else who'd ever picked on him or who'd looked the other way instead of extending a hand. Everyone. Billy laughed softly as he reached for the door handle. He would rain sickness down upon them all and watch their diseases blossom. They'd whimper and groan as they lost themselves to fever and chills, and he'd rejoice in their pain.

That thought stopped him cold.

It wasn't that he wanted to hurt those who'd hurt him for so long—that was nothing more than justice. What froze him in place was the realization that he would *enjoy* hurting them.

He'd be no better than Eddie Glass.

Standing outside of the closed gym doors, he pictured Eddie writhing on the floor next to a pool of his own vomit . . . and then the fallen boy looked up at him, a perverse grin twisting his face. Billy felt the ghost of a booted foot slam into his side, and the breath whooshed out of him as he stumbled backwards. Over the sounds of muffled shouts from behind the doors, he heard Eddie's soft laughter—laughter that sounded frighteningly like his own from just a moment ago.

No. He loathed Eddie Glass. No way in hell would he become him.

With a cry of disgust, he flung the Bow away. It skittered across the linoleum floor and came to an unceremonious halt by the janitor's closet.

Thou art the White Rider, William Ballard. Thou art Pestilence, Bringer of Disease.

He clenched his fists. It didn't matter what Death told him, or showed him, or even what he'd done to him. Billy couldn't wield the Bow. He *wouldn't*.

On the floor, the black wood seemed to chide him, telling him to finish his tantrum already because there was work to do. Infections to spread. Diseases to riddle healthy minds and bodies. All he had to do was pick up the Bow and throw open the gym doors, and then Pestilence would do the rest.

Billy tore his gaze away.

Had he really thought he was done with being afraid? At least before, all he'd had to fear was the inevitable daily beating, whether physical or verbal or both. He'd never imagined that he'd be afraid of himself.

Nauseated, he made his way to the bathroom and hid in a stall as fourth period ticked by.

When the bell rang, he went to the lunchroom, his hood pulled down low over his face. Once he got his lunch he sat near the door, alone, numbly eating a PB&J. At the far end of the table, other kids clustered—losers like Billy, wimps who Kept Their Heads Down and took pains to be one another's shadow. Billy could have told them that numbers don't stop bullies if they've got you in their sights. He'd learned that lesson back in elementary school, when he'd still had a smattering of people he called friends. Then came the day that Eddie transformed from Just Mean to Mean and Pushy, and Billy wound up eating dirt. He did what he'd been taught and told a teacher, who did nothing about it because she hadn't seen Eddie shove Billy. Eddie promptly labeled him a tattler. When it became clear that Billy would be the local punching bag for the near future, his friends peeled away like dead skin until only Marianne remained.

Billy Ballard, you were a hero today.

His shoulders sagged. A hero. Yeah, right. What would Marianne say about what he'd done to Eddie? About what he'd been about to do to his entire PE class? He wasn't a hero. Heroes didn't fire a weapon at unarmed teens. And if they did, heroes certainly didn't enjoy it.

Oh, how he'd enjoyed watching Eddie puke all over the floor and then whine like a kicked puppy.

With a sigh, he lifted his carton of milk and drank. He wondered if anyone would see the Bow lying on the hallway floor. Maybe their eyes would slide over it as if it were invisible. Or maybe someone would pick it up, and then Billy would be off the hook—the mantle of the White Rider would fall to that new person, someone better suited for the role. But as he took another bite of a sandwich he couldn't taste, he understood that no one would be able to wield the Bow but him.

Him, and the Ice Cream Man.

"He's fallen down on the job," Death said. *"It's up to you to pick up the slack. Or, if you'd rather, you can convince him to get out of bed. Either way works for me."*

Billy had to talk to Death. He needed help, needed information. *Pestilence for Dummies,* maybe. Something. Anything. He couldn't do this alone.

From behind him, a maliciously gleeful voice said, "Hey, look! It's Birdy! How you doing, Birdy?"

Billy stiffened. His heartbeat slammed into overdrive as Kurt brayed laughter.

Another voice said, "Missed you in PE." That was Joe, leaning down now so that Billy could smell the mint gum of his breath. "Hear you got you a new look."

Go away, Billy wanted to shout, but his mouth had locked around his bite of sandwich. His head suddenly ached where Joe had slammed it into the locker door yesterday, or maybe it was the spot that Death had touched, hidden beneath his white patch. His stomach cramped in anticipation of pain yet to come. He screamed silently, the words muted by peanut butter and fear: *Leave me alone!*

"I want to see." A hand snaked out and grabbed Billy's hood, then yanked it back, exposing his stained hair. "You were right," Joe said to Kurt, sounding pleased. "It *does* look like a bird took a shit on his head."

"Looks stupid," said Kurt.

"So does his face."

"You don't want stupid hair, do you?" Kurt clamped one hand on Billy's shoulder.

Billy flinched, and hated himself for doing so.

"See that? He wants us to help him."

Joe got right in his face. Billy swallowed tightly and counted the blackheads on Joe's nose. "You want our help?"

Hoping that the cafeteria monitor would step in, knowing that would never happen, Billy clenched his jaw and said nothing.

"Say it," Joe commanded.

"You have to say the words, Billy," the Ice Cream Man insisted. "Say that you agree to wear the Crown."

No.

He didn't realize he'd said the word aloud until Joe's eyes widened.

"Listen to him," sneered Kurt, giving Billy's shoulder a squeeze, "thinking he's too good for our help."

"Know what I think?" said Joe, his eyes gleaming. "I think he needs more white in it." He grabbed the milk carton and poured the contents over Billy's head.

Cold liquid pooled over Billy's hair, streaming down his face and ears and chin, christening him in rivulets of white. Shock and horror gave way to outrage, and then embarrassment as Kurt and Joe and too many others to count laughed at him.

And then fury, white hot and blinding.

He reached out his hand, and his fingers closed around the

familiar width of the Bow. Power surged through him, and he smiled coldly. The part of his mind that would have questioned how the weapon could have just appeared in his hand simply shut down. Pestilence had summoned his Bow, and so the Bow appeared.

Billy stood as time thickened around him, trapping everyone in the cafeteria like fossils in amber. He stepped away from the table, turning slowly to face Joe and Kurt. The two boys stood frozen, one still holding the upturned carton of milk, the other nearly doubled over with laughter. As Billy looked at them, he felt the damp weight of his hair, smelled the sweetness of milk mingling with the oil and sweat of his skin.

He judged them and found them guilty.

Billy pulled back the bowstring he could neither see nor feel, an arrow of disease nocked and ready. Distance warped as he took aim at Joe, who stood now more than twenty feet away, and he let fly. In the same breath he drew, aimed, and released another arrow at Kurt. He didn't bother to see if his arrows would strike true; of course they would. Pestilence didn't miss. Instead, he turned to consider the living backdrop of students and the occasional adult scattered throughout the room, and his gaze locked on the cafeteria monitor. She sat, her face mostly hidden by a book, a food-laden fork halfway to her open mouth. A third arrow flew, and this time Billy watched as it buried itself deep into her flesh, then evaporated.

The arrow's disappearance made Billy blink—and time kicked into gear. The laughter in the cafeteria continued once more, but he ignored it as he saw Joe and Kurt clutch their stomachs, their fingers splayed wide. Kurt's face paled, and as his belly let out a liquid growl he lumbered to the door, one arm thrown out before him and shouting at anyone who dared to get in his way. Joe swayed and crashed onto the cafeteria bench, his face dripping with sweat, heat and sickness wafting from him like perfume gone to vinegar.

Billy's head swam as he stared at Joe, who stank of diarrhea and fever. Salmonella, Billy knew, without knowing how he knew. Even pasteurized milk wasn't always safe. Watch that first sip.

The cafeteria monitor barreled out of the room, her stomach a gurgling mess. The group of misfits at the far end of Billy's table erupted with laughter, joining the rest of the students in their schadenfreude. No one pointed to Billy or shouted at him or accused him of firing a weapon. No one seemed to see him at all.

And that made him want to shoot them all the more.

He stared at the Bow, horrified by what was happening to him. But along with the horror, there was a building fascination, a sense of wonder. Of possibility. He could finally fight back. With the Bow, he could put everyone in their place. They'd know he wasn't someone they could push around any longer. And if they didn't know it, he'd teach it to them, arrow by arrow, sickness by sickness. And finally, wallowing in bacteria and drowning in viruses, they'd respect him. More than that: They'd *fear* him, the way that he'd feared them for so very long.

It would be so very easy.

No. *No.* He wouldn't become what he detested. He *wouldn't!*

He lifted the Bow high and brought it down hard against the cafeteria table. And again. And again, smashing the weapon with all his strength. With every contact he screamed his frustration and his fear until his fury dwarfed all other sound. No one saw him. No one stopped him. He was the White Rider, invisible as a germ.

In his hands, the black wood gleamed, unscarred.

Bellowing his denial, he brought the Bow up one final time — and froze as a cold hand gripped his wrist.

"Dude," said Death. "There are easier ways to get my attention."

CHAPTER 10

"YOU'RE HERE," BILLY SAID . . .

. . . and nearly sagged with relief. Everything would be okay now; surely, Death could see that there had been a horrific mistake and would take the Bow away. Billy Ballard wasn't White Rider material.

As if to counter the argument, Joe chose that moment to double over and vomit loudly on the cafeteria floor. Cue the mass exodus: The lunchroom cleared out in a wave of screeching teenagers until the only figures remaining were Billy, Joe, and an all-too-bemused Death.

"Ah, school food," said the Pale Rider, smiling down at Joe, who was now curled up in a tight ball. "Who knew they had regurgiburger on the menu?"

"Please," Billy said, "you have to take it back."

"Fine, it's not a regurgiburger. We'll just stick with 'mystery meat' and call it a day."

"The Bow," Billy said, desperation pitching his voice high. "Please, you have to take back the Bow!"

The Pale Rider's smile turned sly. "I have to do many things, William, most of them centered around life and death. What I absolutely don't have to do is claim a tool that is not meant for me."

"But look what I did!" Billy flailed his free arm in Joe's direction. "I made him sick! Him, and Kurt, and Eddie!"

"Don't forget the cafeteria monitor."

"Yeah, and her! And you don't know what I was about to do!" Thinking of how close he'd come to attacking his classmates made his stomach drop to his toes. "You don't know," he whispered.

"Oh, I know." Death finally released Billy's wrist. "All that power can be overwhelming at first. Happens all the time. Well, almost. There was a Famine once who accepted the Scales and attempted to stop the Flood. Shortest tenure of the Black Rider, ever. But she proved her point."

With Death's words, Billy saw a woman in black holding her arms high as a mountain of water loomed over her. He blinked and the image was gone, leaving him lightheaded and gasping for breath. He stammered, "What point?"

"That you people are worth saving." Death was no longer smiling. "And yet here you are, demanding that I take back the Bow—which, by the way, does not appreciate being bludgeoned against the table."

Suddenly queasy, Billy repeated, "Appreciate?"

"Would you like it if someone tried to break you into splinters?"

Eddie's boot, slamming into his side and nearly cracking a rib.

Billy's throat went very, very dry. "No," he said hoarsely.

"Of course not. So treat the Bow with respect."

He held the weapon at arm's length, wanting to hurl it away but afraid to let it go. "You said yesterday you needed my help. If this is it, then I'm not helping you. Get someone else to be Pestilence, someone who's okay with making people sick."

"Usually, I'm rather open-minded about who stays a Horseman. If those chosen decide not to wield their symbols of office, I find someone else. But your case is different, William. You were chosen by the White Rider. Behind my back, which I don't appreciate, but I understand why he picked you." He wagged a finger in a no-no-no gesture. "Never antagonize kings. Their memory is long for grudges."

The words made no sense. The only kings Billy knew were names in his history textbook.

"As for your help, well, I already told you what I need you to do. Either be Pestilence, as you agreed to be when you were five, or get the White Rider out of bed and back on his steed."

"That's not me *helping* you," Billy shouted. "That's you *forcing* me to make a choice I don't want to make!"

"I suppose it's a matter of perspective." Death shrugged, the perfect image of slacker-may-care whatevertude. "I don't want to make the choice, either. I find the entire situation distasteful. The White Rider played us both, but you're far too caught up in your own drama to be mindful of that."

Billy felt his cheeks flush.

"I had this notion that you'd spare me from choosing your fate by doing it yourself. Foolish of me." Death grinned, showing far too many teeth. "No good deed, and all that. Let's be clear. If you don't help me by making the choice yourself, I will choose for you."

Of course he would.

"Decision time, William Ballard. You stand at a crossroads, and now must choose your path. Will you wield the Bow of the White Rider? Or will you call the Conqueror back to duty?"

It didn't matter; whichever path he chose was paved in White.

Billy squeezed his eyes shut and shook as emotions surged through him — anger, first, searing every nerve; on the heels of that, resentment, slathering over him like balm.

He took a deep breath, and with the air came a quiet focus, a sense of quietude, of clarity. He breathed, and he opened his eyes, and then he turned to face the Pale Rider. Locking his gaze on to Death's empty blue eyes, Billy Ballard made his choice.

||||||

The hospital room was no different from last night: small and stale, with machines scattered haphazardly and a single, narrow bed with crisp white sheets. At first glance, the bed was empty. But as Death closed the door behind them, Billy saw the unmistakable form of the Ice Cream Man, a white blanket covering him from chin to toe. His ruined face was all too visible in the harsh florescent light.

Staring hard at those waxy, pox-ridden features, Billy swallowed thickly. "What's wrong with him?"

"All manner of things," Death said idly. "The White Rider houses all diseases. There are any number of things wrong with him."

"So you don't know why he won't get up?"

"Oh, that. Easy peasy. He's not home."

Billy frowned at the Pale Rider, who was leaning casually against the door.

"He's not here," Death said, tapping his own head. "His body is well enough, all things considered. But his mind has gone wandering to a place where even I cannot seek him. He's lost somewhere in his past. It's up to you, William, to find him."

In a world where a horse can be a car and travel halfway across the globe in a matter of minutes, the notion of time travel was almost quaint. Billy was surprised to find himself rather blasé about the whole thing. Have Bow, will time travel.

"Return the White Rider to himself," said Death. "Find him and bring him home."

(*You find your way, and you come back home.*)

Thinking of his grandfather, Billy set his jaw. Ice Cream Man or no, the Conqueror was just another old man who'd gone wandering. And if there was one thing Billy had experience with, it was tracking down wandering old men and bringing them home again. "Okay," he said, determined. "How do I find him?"

"You are Pestilence; he is the Conqueror. White beckons White. You can't help but find him, wherever he is. The more difficult part," said Death, "will be convincing him to return."

"I'll do it," Billy insisted. No way was he going to be stuck being Pestilence. "I'll get him back."

"Then touch the Bow to the Crown on his brow. And think White thoughts," Death added, perhaps whimsically.

Billy looked hard at the Ice Cream Man, the nightmare man of his past, and he held out his hand, knowing the Bow would be there. As his fingers closed around the black wood, he thought, *I'm going to find you. Whatever it takes, I'm going to find you. And I'm going to make you take back the Bow.* His heartbeat quickened, but not from fear. A hum of power danced along his skin, but it didn't come from the Bow.

He could do this.

Chin high, Billy Ballard touched the tip of the Bow to the silver band half hidden on the Conqueror's forehead. And the world erupted in White.

PART TWO

INTO THE WHITE

CHAPTER 11

HE SEES THE END OF THE WORLD . . .

. . . and it arrives on a sheet of white/

/he drapes her in a white *chiton*, her favorite, even though he's always preferred her in green/

/he is surrounded by lush greens and earthy browns, here in the heart of the Greenwood, and peace settles over him as he smiles, content, for here he'll stay, away from the world with its never-ending diseases and hunger and battles/

/he's seen centuries of battles, of wars erupting over the face of the world like a pox/

/the pox has ravaged his kingdom, but now he wears the Crown and wields the Bow and he will make it right, he will set the balance in his people's favor/

/he holds her favor, this woman in black, with her whip-thin smile and set of balances in her hand/

/and she tells him the Four are out of balance and he must return, but he cannot, he will not, not even for her/

/not for the woman in red with her laughter of fire and blood, handmaiden of the one who shall lead them in the end/

/he sees the end of the world, and it arrives on a sheet of white/

||||||

—and with a gasp, Billy pulled himself out of the White.

He floated in a world of smoke the color of a winter sky heavy with snow; not white, not pale, but somewhere caught in between. Nearby—so near that all he had to do was close his eyes and leap—the White beckoned to him like a will-o'-the-wisp, urging him to return. Fainter, he sensed the Ice Cream Man lying desiccated and empty on his sickbed, and he felt the presence of Death, so cool and aloof beneath his mask of flesh, but they were little more than peripheral flickers, ghosts hovering at the edge of his vision. Here, in the space between present and past, they weren't real.

Here, Billy was completely alone.

A shiver worked its way through him. What he'd seen, what he'd felt, was a raw wound in his mind, echoing around him and through him in a free fall of sensation: loss and stolen solitude, despair and bitter determination, and, above all, a lingering terror that started and ended in an expanse of white. Still shivering, Billy rubbed his arms. He'd expected to go into the Conqueror's memory like a time traveler going back in history: There would be a proper beginning in which he found the Horseman; a satisfying resolution, once the Conqueror agreed to return with him to the real world; and an adventurous middle that neatly connected start to finish. What he'd gotten instead were flashes, like pieces of a movie spliced together out of order. Along with those flashes were thoughts and feelings, swirls of emotion that threatened to drown him. Somewhere within the jumble of images and sensations was the thread of an idea, of an experience, that linked everything together in a way that Billy didn't understand.

Good, he thought, shuddering. He didn't want to understand. Those flashes had been so overwhelming that he'd had to jump out of the White, to distance himself from the insistent *now* of those memories. He hadn't been merely witnessing what had happened to the Conqueror; they'd felt real, in the way that dreams sometimes felt real. And more than that: Deep in the White, it had been as if those memories, those events, had actually been happening to *him*.

Death's voice, patient and knowing: *White beckons White.*

But Billy hadn't merely been beckoned. It had felt like he'd been absorbed, eaten away by a cancer of the mind. For those brief moments, he'd lost his very identity. In the White, Billy Ballard had ceased to exist.

What would happen if he lost himself completely in the Conqueror's memories?

(*You find your way, and you come back home.*)

He thought of Gramps, manic and violent when he walked a world adrift in the past, torpid and monosyllabic when he was anchored in the present. Would that happen to Billy? If, in the embrace of the White, the Conqueror hooked Billy's mind and pulled him down, would he be no better off than his grandfather, forever battling with dementia?

Would he be worse, because he'd be reliving memories that weren't his own, and he wouldn't even realize it?

How was he supposed to go back into the White, knowing that everything he was could be erased?

(*You find your way.*)

Even if he succeeded and found the Conqueror without losing himself, what then? How was he supposed to pull a Horseman out of a memory and into the real world? How was he supposed to rescue someone else when he could barely hold on to himself?

I can't do it.

Billy hugged himself tightly and curled into a ball. His life was a series of *can'ts*—he can't fight back, he can't deal with his grandfather, he can't kiss the girl, one *can't* after another with no end in sight, building on one another until they paralyzed him. He can't go to school. He can't get out of bed. He can't face the day. He can't.

He was sick of his life being defined by can't.

A hint of frost as a cold breeze whispered along his neck. It almost sounded like laughter.

He was scared to move forward; he felt that fear claw its way through his stomach and squeeze his throat, felt it tighten his chest and shrivel his spine. But staying where he was did nothing other than suffocate him with that fear.

He could lose himself; that was true. He could try and still fail, and therefore be forced to travel the path of the White Rider. That, too, was true.

He could succeed, and be thrown back into his life. That was also true, even if deep in his heart he didn't think it likely.

If he didn't try, he would never know if he could have succeeded. And that was the truest thing of all.

Billy took a shaky breath, then unfolded his limbs. Slowly, he pulled himself up so that he stood tall, floating in the gray world of in between. He had another moment of *I can't*, one that stole his breath and threatened to release his bladder. And then, before he could talk himself out of it, he launched himself once more into the White.

|||||||

He sees the end of the world, and it arrives on a sheet of white/

/he drapes her in a white *chiton*, her favorite, even though he's always preferred her in green and violet. The cloth settles over her like a shroud, and he touches her face, once ivory perfection and now mottled with reds and yellows. Her skin is cool beneath his fingers, but he knows she had burned fiercely within, burned her enough to cook her very flesh and turn her fingertips a purple so bruised it looked black. He strokes her cheek once more, then pulls his hand away, and he gazes at her ruined form. He'll bury her in her beloved garden, will cover her in roses, thorns and all, so that her sickness will be hidden in a bed of blushing petals and lush green leaves/

/he is surrounded by lush greens and earthy browns, here in the heart of the Greenwood, where the very ground thrums with life. Peace settles over him and he smiles, content, as he leans against the broad trunk of an oak tree. Here he'll stay, away from the world with its never-ending diseases and hunger and battles at every corner/

/he's seen centuries of battles, of wars erupting over the face of the world like a pox until land and sea were awash in red, but nothing affects him as much as this one boy with his golden hair and honeyed voice convincing thirty thousand children to march to Jerusalem. Dumbstruck, he watches them advance, row by row, an army of them, a river of them, all enchanted with the possibility of succeeding where their elders have failed. Tears wind down his cheeks as the children's call to battle spreads like an epidemic of the most sinister pox/

/the pox has ravaged his kingdom, indiscriminate of poor or rich or old or young. The healthy had suddenly been taken by a violent heat that started in the head and slowly worked its way down, transforming their eyes to embers, inflaming their throats and causing them to spew blood and reek of sickness. He feels their agony even now, though he himself remains untouched by distress: the coughing, the sneezing, the endless vomiting and spasms, the compulsion to rip clothing away from his overheated body, the urge to throw himself into a rain tank or the river in the desperate need to slake a maddening, ceaseless thirst. But now he wears the Crown and wields the Bow, and he is rejuvenated. He will cleanse his land and heal his kingdom. He will make it right; he will set the balance in his people's favor/

/he holds her favor, even though he had not sought it. She's looking at him now, boldly, this woman in black, with her whip-thin smile and set of balances in her hand. The instrument of her office gleams in the sunlight, but it cannot compare with the hungry sheen of her eyes. They share a look, these two Riders, and around them, Romans fall victim to famine and plague. He hardly notices the bodies littering the streets; he's enamored by the swirl of the Black Rider's linen *peplos* around her shapely ankles. Something about this woman calls to him, stirs his blood and upsets the balance of his sanguine humor/

/and she tells him the Four are out of balance and he must return, but he will not listen to her. She may wear the mantle of the Black, but she is not his Famine. He turns his back, bristling when he feels the weight of her hand on his shoulder. She speaks of sickness and starvation and dares to tell him of his duty, and he whirls to face her, his mouth twisted in a snarl. Shadows play behind her eyes as she quietly asks that he do this for her, and he laughs in her face. He cannot. He will not, not even for her/

/not for the woman in red who laughs at him when he accuses her of whispering to the golden-haired boy, of dazzling him with images of glory and coaxing him from his home, encouraging him to stir the souls of thirty thousand children and lead them to slavery and death, all in the name of war. She mocks him with her laughter of fire and blood, and she declares herself as the handmaiden of the Pale Rider, the cold one warmed only by her passion, the one who will lead them all to the greatest battle of all time before the end of everything/

/he sees the end of the world, and it arrives on a sheet of white/

‖‖‖

—and Billy screamed as he threw himself out of the White. He dropped to his knees and retched, dry heaving in the gray of in between past and present. When his body stopped convulsing, he hugged his knees and rocked.

Too much. It had been too much. All the sickness, all the death, the overwhelming sense of despair and horror—how could the Conqueror stand it?

He shook violently as he rocked, alone in the gray. He remembered the looming presence of the Ice Cream Man, standing over him as he played in the sandbox all those years ago, remembered how his face had run like wax melting in the sun. Had his experiences done that to him? Had he literally fallen apart because of everything he had seen, had done?

How was Billy supposed to jump back into the White and not drown?

(*You find your way, and you come back home.*)

A memory winked: Gramps and Billy and Marianne at the community pool, back when his grandfather had been whole and Billy and Marianne were just kids. Gramps was pitching pennies all along the deep end of the pool and giving them thirty seconds to scoop up as many coins as they could. Marianne went first, using one huge breath and managing to grab thirteen pennies. When it was his turn, Billy took a breath and dove, grabbed the few pennies within reach, then swam back up for more air and back down again. And again. And again. By the time thirty seconds were up, he'd scored the entire twenty cents. He'd won, said Gramps, because Marianne had been so busy trying to do it all at once that she'd forgotten she needed to breathe. Billy had won because he'd paced himself.

Yes, he thought, pulling himself to his feet. *Yes.* He didn't have to jump into the White and nearly drown; he could take a breath and dive, then come up for air before going back in. One memory at a time; that was the key. One at a time, instead of all at once, and he'd get all the pennies.

The end of the world arrives on a sheet of white.

For a long moment, he stood at the edge of the White and wished he were brave.

Shut up, chided Marianne. *You were* too *brave!*

Fine. Time to prove it.

Billy Ballard took a deep breath and stepped once more into the White.

CHAPTER 12

HE SKIMMED THE SURFACE . . .

. . . of the White, treading the waters of memories not his own. Above him, the bleached sky glittered with stars; around and below him, the White flowed and churned, rolling softly and hinting of storms. He floated, mesmerized. Before, he had just plunged into the depths without acknowledging the power and presence of such a force as the White; if the gray of in between was a place of nothing and nowhere, the White was on the edge of everything, everywhere. Billy felt both insignificant and magnificent, as if he were a speck on the face of grandeur as well as the eyes on that face, the one who could appreciate such awesome splendor. It was a sublime moment in which Billy was both completely empowered and thoroughly humbled, and the combination stole his breath.

His arms and legs moved easily, and each motion brought forth ripples that sparkled like gemstones.

Billy sensed such amazing possibilities, all just waiting for him to dive down and lose himself in the throes of sensation, of experience, of thoughts not his own. The Conqueror was old, Biblical old, and there was so much for Billy to see. To *feel*. Skimming the surface was just a taste, a tease, a tantalizing hint of what else waited for him.

Around him, ripples of memory glinted.

So what if he lost himself? What was he really losing? The

identity of a bullied boy who didn't have the stomach or the
spine to defend himself? Who let his mother bulldoze him into
babysitting his demented grandfather? Why would he want to
go back to that?

In his mind, Death chuckled. *I thought you wanted to escape
your life, William.*

He did. He wanted out. He wanted to be free of Eddie Glass
and his thugs, free of the chains locking him to the man who'd
been his grandfather. He wanted to escape the hypocrisy of
school with its willfully blind teachers, to run away from the
specter of the Ice Cream Man, looming over him as he played
in a sandbox.

If he stayed here, in the White, he wouldn't have to go back.

A shadow passed close by, and for a moment Billy thought
he saw his favorite girl in black next to him in the pool, floating
in the water and daring him to go down to the deep end.

If he stayed here, he'd never see Marianne again. He'd never
know if he'd finally find the courage to kiss her.

Treading in the White, he looked down. He thought he saw
pennies scattered on a pool floor. *One at a time*, he told himself.
Remember to come back up for air.

Billy took a deep breath and dove down.

▌▌▌▌▌

/he drapes her in a white *chiton*, her favorite, even though he's
always preferred her in green and violet. The cloth billows in
the cool morning air, then settles over her like a shroud, covering her ravaged form.

Kings do not cry, he tells himself. And so Mita, king of Phrygia, does not cry as he tucks his daughter into her deathbed. He touches her face, once ivory perfection and now mottled with reds and yellows. Her eyes will remain forever sealed; her mouth will never again pull into a delighted grin. She will never smell her favorite roses in her garden, or feel the grass wiggle between her toes. Never laugh; never sing. Never grow up.

So many nevers, all for his daughter, who will never see her ninth birthday.

Kings do not cry.

Her skin is cool beneath his fingers, but he knows she had burned fiercely within, burned enough to cook her very flesh and turn her fingertips a purple so bruised it looked black.

"Plums," he says softly. The disease turned her fingers the color of plums.

"A sweet fruit," a cold voice says from behind him, "with a pit that can be poisonous."

(And Billy shivers.)

Mita stiffens, but he does not turn to face the speaker. He would be furious, if only he could summon the strength. Instead, he feels hollow. Perhaps at one point, fury will fill those empty places within him, but for now, all he manages is a bitter sigh.

"You have done a noble thing, you who were Mita."

"My daughter is dead."

"But your kingdom survives. What is the life of one, when you have saved thousands?"

Mita's lip twitches once, pulling into a snarl before his mouth presses into a thin line. He looks over his shoulder at the tall man wrapped in a plain woolen *chiton* from neck to knee, a simple *fibule* fastening the fabric at the left shoulder. His legs, as his arms, are bare, and no sandals adorn his feet. The inelegant clothing and unkempt yellow hair make the figure seem unimportant, perhaps even a slave, but Mita knows better. The thin limbs, the pale flesh — that is just as much a costume as the *chiton*. Only the man's eyes hint at the truth, but Mita cannot meet that cold gaze for long.

"She was my *daughter*," he growls. "She was everything to me."

The pale man's face is impossible to read; if he feels any emotion at all, it does not show in his eyes or his mouth. He is blank. Cold. "Everything to the mortal known as King Mita, perhaps. But you are no longer he. You are the White Rider."

The words are like punches to his chest. "I'm still a father!"

"Even when your child is dead?"

Mita turns back to his daughter. His left hand still rests on her cheek, but now there's a fine tremor in his fingers that he cannot quell. Beneath his shaking fingers, her skin flakes like ash. "One doesn't stop being a parent."

"Why do you still touch her?" asks the pale man. "That is nothing more than empty flesh. The spark that had been your daughter is gone."

Mita squeezes his eyes shut, as if that would take away the sting of the man's words. "You would not understand."

"Your people are calling you Mita with the golden touch," says the man that is not a man. "They are saying one touch from the king is all it takes to heal them from the great pestilence that walks the land. Is that why you are touching her? Are you trying to heal her from death?"

"One such as you can *never* understand," Mita says through

clenched teeth. "To you, people are as ants. Just ants. All alike, all so easily crushed underfoot."

"There are more than twenty thousand different types of ants. They live and die, as do all mortal things."

"But whether ants or humans, parents should not outlive their children." Mita's voice cracks, and he tells himself again that kings do not cry.

The pale figure does not reply.

In a hoarse whisper, Mita asks, "Can you bring her back?"

A long pause, and then the Pale Rider asks, "Why?"

Mita bows over his daughter's deathbed. "Because she's everything to me. My child, my life. My light. Everything that makes this world worth living is all because of her. Please," he begs, "please, bring her back."

"Her *psyche* is gone, you who were Mita. Mourn your daughter, in the way of your kind, and then forget her."

"*Forget* her?" Hollow no longer, Mita whirls to face the embodiment of Thanatos. Enraged, he lifts his chin high. " 'And there the children of dark Night have their dwellings, Sleep and Death, awful gods. The glowing Sun never looks upon them with his beams, neither as he goes up into heaven, nor as he comes down from heaven.' "

"Hesiod," says the pale man. " 'Theogony.' Trite creation stories. I prefer the works of Homer."

" 'And the former of them roams peacefully over the earth and the sea's broad back and is kindly to men. But the other,' " declares Mita, pointing at the Pale Rider, " 'has a heart of iron, and his spirit within him is pitiless as bronze! Whomsoever of men he has once seized he holds fast, and he is hateful even to the deathless gods!' "

Mita's last words echo in the cold, cold chamber.

"You speak out of grief," Thanatos says. "Because of that, I forgive your outburst." A flash of a smile. "You see, little king? One such as I can understand. Sometimes."

At his sides, Mita's hands open and clench, open and clench.

"Bury your child, you who were Mita. And then continue doing the job you agreed to do."

"No."

The pale man stills. He neither blinks nor breathes as he waits for Mita to speak again.

"No, I won't do it." Mita's lips peel back in a snarl. "I will not work for a creature that tells me to forget my daughter! Take back your Crown!" His fingers move to the circlet on his brow.

"It is not mine to take," says Thanatos. "You are the Horseman of Pestilence, not I."

"Then I will be a Horseman no more!"

The silence echoes in the small chamber. When the Pale Rider finally speaks, his voice is flat and dead.

"Would you undo all the benefits to your kingdom, you who were Mita? Would you undo your golden touch of health and plunge Phrygia back into the depths of plague? Because that is the choice you are making."

A tremor works its way up Mita's spine.

"Do you really think you have eradicated the sickness from your kingdom for all time?" A smile quirks Thanatos's lips, a flash of bemusement that does not touch his empty eyes. "It will return. It always does. Whether that is in five weeks' time or five centuries' time is completely up to you."

"No," Mita whispers.

"The choice is yours. Refuse the Conqueror's Crown, and watch thousands of your people sicken and die, or keep your Crown and do your duty. It makes no difference to me."

"It doesn't, does it?" Mita wraps the folds of his *himation* around himself, but it does nothing to stave off his sudden chill. "You are the lord of life and death, and you don't care which one we choose, do you? You walk like a man, but beneath the skin, you're inhuman."

"I never claimed to be human."

"You're a monster."

"I am nothing you have ever seen," says Thanatos. "But this is not about me. Tell me, you who were Mita. Are you a Horseman? Or are you a little king who will condemn his kingdom to death?"

Mita bows his head, defeated. "I am the Conqueror of Disease," he says bitterly.

"For what it is worth, you have chosen wisely."

He cannot bring himself to look upon the Horseman of Death. When he speaks, his voice is that of an old man, broken by loss. "Can you at least tell me that her *psyche* is content? That she rests in the Underworld? That her suffering is over?"

"Her physical suffering is past," says Thanatos, and for a moment, Mita feels a weight lift off his chest. Then Thanatos adds, "Her body is dead; it feels no pain." And with those words, the Pale Rider disappears.

Mita's eyes burn, and this time he allows the tears to fall.

Kneeling next to his daughter's deathbed, he strokes her cheek once more, then pulls his hand away. He knows he should summon his slaves and have them lay out his daughter's body properly, to begin the lamentation for the dead, but the thought exhausts him. Gazing at her ruined form, he decides that there has been too much of death on display for his taste; he'll not add his child to the spectacle of grief. Instead, he will bury her in her beloved garden. He'll give her a blanket of flowers and a pillow of blossoms.

Mita leans down and kisses his little girl goodnight one final time. His tears land on her cheeks, and there they shine like diamonds.

Yes, he will cover her in roses, thorns and all, so that her sickness will be hidden in a bed of blushing petals and lush green leaves/

/he drapes her in a white *chiton*, her favorite, even though he's always preferred her in green and violet—

|||||||

Billy pulled himself away as soon as the memory began to replay. Once again on the surface of the White, he caught his breath.

The Conqueror was King Midas.

He thought of the Greek myth about the man with the golden touch. According to the story, Midas had done something nice and scored a boon from one of the gods—he could have anything he wished. So the greedy king wished for everything he touched to be turned to gold. And the wish worked, but as in the way of such stories, it worked too well. Midas couldn't eat without the food turning to gold, which was a hell of a choking hazard. Even worse, when his young daughter ran up to hug Midas, she transformed into a golden statue.

He'd never heard the version where Midas's golden touch was one of healing.

He remembered Mita's crushing sorrow, his bone-numbing grief over the loss of his only child. The king had given up everything to save his kingdom, only to lose his daughter.

"You are the lord of life and death," said Mita, *"and you don't care which we choose, do you?"*

Floating in the White, Billy shuddered as he thought of Thanatos, the Pale Rider. Was that *his* Death, the grunger god who had a penchant for guitars and flying horses? They didn't look alike, and clearly, Horsemen could change over the years. Even so, Billy knew, just *knew*, that it was the same person.

No, not a person. A monster, as Mita had said.

"I am nothing you have ever seen," said the pale man.

And on the heels of that, Billy heard Death once more, and he imagined he saw wings unfurling as the Pale Rider declared: *None is like me.*

Billy was suddenly very, very glad that he'd met a more laid-back version of Death. He wouldn't have lasted two minutes with Thanatos.

A voice like liquid fire: *You don't know yourself. Yet.*

He blew out a breath, then looked down. At the bottom of the White, memories waited for him to scoop them up. Pestilence waited to be found.

All right, Billy thought. *Ready or not, here I come.*

He took a breath and dove down.

CHAPTER 13

THE WHITE GAVE WAY . . .

. . . to green as Billy dove deep.

||||||

/he is surrounded by lush greens and earthy browns, here in the heart of the Greenwood, where the very ground thrums with life. There is no whiff of sickness, no pulse of disease to distract him from the simple majesty of nature. A welcome change. The illness is still there, of course, if he were to look for it; trees and foliage sicken just as all living things do. But today he is willfully blind to all maladies. Let the insistence of decay come on the morrow; today he will relish the false appearance of good health of the world around him.

The White Rider breathes deeply, pretending he's still completely human, and the smells of dirt and resin sting his nostrils. It's a pleasant sting, a reminder that life brings its own sort of pain. Only lepers feel no pain.

Be a leper, he tells himself as he weaves around massive oaks and unobtrusive ashes. *Feel no pain. Feel no fear.*

But how could he not be afraid? He'd seen the end of the world. How does one return from that unscathed?

He blinks—

(and Billy stumbles)

—and the natural wonder of the forest gives way to white, a massive sheet of white, empty of color, barren of life, and it yawns forward—

No. *No.* Whether memory or harbinger of the future, it is not *now. Be in the now,* he tells himself, even though he's watching as the gaping white advances and he feels a scream building in his chest, *be in the now!*

A flash of white, and then it's back to soft greens and calming browns, and he sinks to his knees.

(And Billy catches his breath.)

Beneath him, the groundcover of dead leaves and fallen twigs crunch under his weight, reminding him that he's truly *here*, that he has substance. Above him, hidden somewhere in the leaf canopy, birds squawk and scold and gossip. His shoulders loosen, and he allows himself a relieved sigh. He's in the forest, not at the end of the world. He's here.

There's still time.

He has to think. If only he knew what to do. A lifetime ago, he had wise men at his side to advise him before he made any decisions that affected his kingdom. But now? Who understands the plight of a Horseman? He thinks of Famine, the dark lady wrapped in shadow, and he wishes he could turn to her. But no, he can't chance it—for though they are close, she stands by the Pale Rider completely. He certainly cannot approach War, not unless he wants to see her double over with laughter.

All that remained was Death.

He lets out a bitter laugh. No, he learned his lesson about Thanatos's understanding of humanity centuries ago. Sometimes, when he closes his eyes, he still sees his daughter's ruined face, imagines he's holding her violet-tinged hand.

"Plums," he whispers, the word like a sigh.

If not the other Horsemen, then who? He'd talk to his steed, but he can't trust it; for all that it's been faithful to him, the white horse answers to the pale, and he has no doubt about *that* particular creature's loyalty. When the end comes, Death will ride his pale horse; in his wake, the world will wither and die.

The world will end in a sheet of white—

No! Be in the now!

He hugs his knees. He knows he's been slipping, losing pieces of himself as he is flung from present to past and back. A disorder of the mind, surely; nothing can travel from one time to another. He knows this. But when he slips, it feels so very real. It's completely terrifying, especially because knowing what he does about how the world will end, the notion of fleeing to the past is so very inviting . . .

A shudder ripples through him. *It's not the end of the world.*

He tells himself once more to be a leper, but that doesn't stop him from feeling a sense of despair so deep that it scoops out his chest and leaves him hollow. Lost, he begins to rock.

If time passes, he does not notice.

The snapping of twigs; the crunching of leaves. And then a strangled sound, followed by a thud, like a sack of flour being tossed to the floor.

The sounds penetrate his despondency, and he finds that a man has fallen to the ground in front of him. He watches the stranger writhing on the forest floor, and he appreciates the way the man's clothing blends with the colors of the woodlands, all greens and browns, but the purplish tinge to his face ruins the camouflage. The White Rider cocks his head and wonders why the man seems to be struggling for breath. And then it occurs to him.

"Oh," says the Conqueror. "My apologies."

With his words he quiets the flare of disease that had attacked the man's lungs, and the stranger takes in a great heaving gasp of air. His face slowly returns to a more normal color as he continues to breathe deeply.

"And who are you," asks the Conqueror, "that you go crashing about my woods without permission?"

The man freezes, then looks around cautiously, even as he reaches for a bow and quiver that must have fallen to the ground during his fit. His gaze passes over the White Rider without seeing him.

The Conqueror sighs. It's been so long since he's tried to talk to mortals that he'd forgotten to make himself *real*. The man must have sensed something, based on his careful reaction, but that something is no more than a whisper of wind in the ear, or a flash of sunlight at the corner of the eye. The Conqueror shakes his head and scolds himself for his foolishness. With a bit of effort, he anchors his presence in the human world of the real, and then he repeats his question.

Now the man sees him and falls backward with a shout. He scrambles to his feet and grabs his bow, quickly nocking an arrow. The White Rider is amused by the way the man's face hardens, removing all signs of the terror that had been so clear a moment ago.

The archer takes quick aim at the White Rider's chest.

The Conqueror is so surprised he actually laughs. It's a rusty sound, and the motion makes his cheeks hurt, but it's a welcome sort of pain. Threatening a Horseman? And to threaten *him* in particular with an *arrow?* Oh, humanity! It never ceases to amaze him.

"Are you a madman," asks the archer, "who laughs in the face of death?"

"Oh, you're not Death," says the White Rider. "I'd never laugh in his face. That's not good for my health. And I know all about health."

The archer slowly turns his head, as if to get a better look at his potential victim. "You are delirious, sirrah."

"Sire," corrects the Conqueror, for he is still a king, even though his name escapes him.

"Sire," mocks the archer. "Are you King of the Greenwood, perhaps?"

"Perhaps." A smile unfurls on the White Rider's face. King of the Greenwood. Yes, he likes the sound of that. "I have a Bow as well. It's nothing like yours, though."

The man's gaze darts over the Conqueror. "I see no bow."

"No, you wouldn't."

"No bow, no sword, no staff. Knives, perhaps, hidden on your person."

The White Rider's brow creases. "Why would I need a knife?"

This seems to fluster the archer. Scowling, he says, "You snuck up on me! To attack me, eh? Steal my things and cut my throat?"

The Conqueror blinks with surprise. "How would I cut your throat if I have no knife? And I've been here all along. You didn't see me until now."

"Didn't *see* you?" The man lets out a choked laugh. "You're wearing bright white in the middle of the forest. I'd have to be blind not to see you!"

The Conqueror considers testing the man at his word—a sudden stroke, perhaps, or a clouding of his eyes—but then the man lets out a cough, then another. Soon he's doubled over with spasms as harsh, barking coughs wrack his body. He drops the bow and arrow to cover his mouth with one hand and clasp at his chest with the other. When the coughing fit finally passes, the archer collapses to his knees, wheezing.

The White Rider frowns. He's fairly certain that was his fault. He delves and discovers blackness within the man's lungs, a blackness that is eating away his insides.

Well then. Not his fault after all.

The blackness makes him think of the Black Rider, and he marvels over how he and Famine work so well together; she from without, he from within, both of them depleting sources of nourishment and sustenance and health. He imagines the two of them working in other, more private ways, and he smiles as he thinks of a feeling like shadows and velvet moving over his skin. Not a memory, that, but a wish, a desire. A hope.

A dream.

He feels himself begin to slip away, and he bites his gloved finger, hard. *Now*, he commands himself through the flare of pain. *Stay in the now!* It is enough; instead of flashing to the past with the one whose company he enjoys best, he remains in the Greenwood with the dying archer who would rob him. Releasing his finger, he lets out a phlegmy sigh. He must be as mad as the archer claimed.

"The coughing will worsen," he says idly, "as will the pain in your chest."

The archer doesn't look at him. When he replies, his voice is hoarse. "So says the physician in the woods. I thought you claimed to be a king."

The Conqueror smiles briefly. "The King of the Greenwood is passing familiar with the art of medicine."

"Of course you are." The archer wipes his mouth, and the back of his hand comes away bloody.

"And yet," says the Conqueror, "I still don't know the name of the man who is trespassing in my woods."

Staring at the blood on his hand, the archer says, "Robert Hode."

"What brings you here, into the heart of the Greenwood?"

Now the archer looks up and meets the White Rider's gaze. "I murdered a man."

"Ah, a cutthroat. Now I see why you were so concerned with knives."

"He had it coming," growls Hode. "He was trying to arrest me, all for hunting deer. How am I supposed to eat if I can't hunt?"

"I'm quite the cutthroat, myself," the Conqueror says, trying to make conversation. It's been so long since he's actually spoken to a human directly, and he's surprised to find that he's missed it. "Although I've never actually slit a person's throat, so perhaps the designation is misleading. But I am certainly a murderer, if indirectly."

Hode frowns at him. "You? Tell me, who has the mad King of the Greenwood killed?"

"I've sent numerous men to their deaths. Men who could have been saved, I allowed to die. Women too. And children," the Conqueror says, his voice soft and haunted. "Children are the worst. Their cries of pain and betrayal stay with you, long after their voices have been forever silenced."

"You . . ." Hode's voice breaks, as if he's horrified by what he's just heard. "You've killed children?"

"Oh, yes. Thousands, over the years. Well, everyone dies," the Conqueror says defensively. "And life span is so relative. Did you know the mayfly lives only for one day?"

"You *are* insane," says the wide-eyed archer.

"Sometimes," admits the Conqueror. "Now that you have run away to the Greenwood, what will you do?"

Hode stares at the White Rider for a long moment before he replies. "I'll hunt. I'll lay snares. I'll find a cave for shelter and weave together a blanket of leaves." He's warmed to the sound of his own words, and he declares with passion, "I'll survive here in the woods, outside the shire-reeve's law!"

Based on the blackness in his lungs, Hode is a human mayfly. But the Conqueror sees no reason to bring up the man's imminent death. "So you came to the woods to escape your fate."

The archer nods. "Here I am a free man, and I will live on my own terms."

"As long as you're not caught."

"I won't be caught," he says, scoffing. "I know enough to stay away from the well-trod places in the forest."

"Clever little outlaw," says the Conqueror, but he is no longer thinking of the archer.

"The Greenwood will shelter me," insists Robert Hode. And then his body is wracked with another coughing fit.

The Conqueror barely notices. He is too busy thinking of what it would mean to escape his fate. He has seen the end of the world. He hears the Red Rider's mocking laughter as she tells him of his final purpose, and he bats the memory aside, forces himself to stay in the now. An idea flits across his mind, and he reaches for it, desperate.

As long as he is here in the Greenwood, without his steed, he cannot ride.

If he cannot ride, he cannot achieve his final purpose.

Therefore, if he stays in the forest, he escapes his fate.

Yes.

He's nodding now as he plans, and his fingers twine together as if they are trying to keep others from peeking at his thoughts. Yes, he will take his leave of the Horsemen. Not a permanent leave; if he forsakes the Crown, Death will simply find another to wear it. As long as the Conqueror does not resign his position, the White seat will remain filled.

And as long as he chooses not to ride, he cannot achieve his final purpose. Even Death will not be able to stop him.

Simple, really.

He murmurs to himself as he thinks of what he must do next. He will have to hide the Crown and Bow. More than that: He will have to hide among humanity.

He slides a calculating look at Robert Hode, who is shaking as he coughs up blood. And the Conqueror thinks, *Why not?*

And so, a plan: Once the archer meets his maker, the Conqueror will hide the Crown and Bow, and take over the reins of Robert Hode's life. He will have to hide himself as well for a full three days after the man's life ends, to ensure that he does not come across his Pale colleague.

And then? Dressed as a mortal archer, he will stay in the

shire-wood and live as an outlaw. For in truth, he will be the greatest of outlaws—he will be the one who cheats Death.

Making the decision lifts a massive weight from his shoulders and chest, and for the first time since wearing the Crown, he feels lighter. He lifts his head and feels sunlight dapple his face, as if giving him a blessing. He hears the sounds of Robert Hode's sickness, and he is at ease. The man's death, unlike so many others, will serve a purpose. *His* purpose.

One that will keep the world from ending.

Peace settles over him and he smiles, content, as he leans against the broad trunk of the oak tree. Here he'll stay, away from the world with its never-ending diseases and hunger and battles at every corner/

/he is surrounded by lush greens and earthy browns, here in the heart of the Greenwood, where the very ground thrums with life—

‖‖‖‖

Billy broke through the surface of the White. He treaded, pondering what he had just witnessed. All this time, he'd lived in terror of the Ice Cream Man, the bogeyman in white. It was extremely disconcerting to see that same man absolutely terrified. Whatever the white thing was that the Conqueror claimed was the end of the world, it was enough to send the White Rider into hiding.

(The end of the world arrives on a sheet of white.)

Billy had no desire to see that particular memory. Which meant he had to find the Conqueror soon.

He looked down at the pool of White, and he wondered how he was supposed to find the modern-day Conqueror in memories of the White Rider's past. Would he see two identical Horsemen? Would the real Conqueror, concealed in the memory, appear not as a strong middle-aged man with solid features but instead as a living horror with a melted-wax face? There had to be some way to tell.

White beckons White.

This time, Billy swore to look not just at the memory playing for him but also for any hint of the Horseman's true presence. "Be in the now," he said aloud, but he had no idea if the Conqueror heard him. He took a breath and dove down.

CHAPTER 14

SOMEWHERE WITHIN THE WHITE . . .

. . . the Conqueror hid. Not some figment of the past mourning a dead daughter or deciding to run away from the Horsemen, but *Billy's* Conqueror, the Ice Cream Man who'd tricked him into making a choice he hadn't understood. Billy was going to find the White Rider, the man who had stolen his future.

And when he did, he was going to force the Conqueror to return to the real world and do his job. Somehow.

You can't hide from me. Down in the White, Billy reached for another memory. *I'm going to find you.*

And White touched White.

||||||

/he's seen centuries of battles, of wars erupting over the face of the world like a pox until land and sea were awash in red, but nothing affects him as much as this one boy with his golden hair and honeyed voice convincing thirty thousand children to march to Jerusalem.

The boy is sitting in a brightly painted cart, its canopy sheltering him from the brutal effects of the sun. Even though the Conqueror is half-blind with a cataract temporarily clouding his left eye, he can see that the boy's hair is poorly shorn and his clothing is barely rags. But even with his pauper's image, the boy smiles beatifically as he waves at the cheering crowds lining the streets: the adults who have come to witness the spectacle of France's children going off to war.

Seated atop his steed, unnoticed by the masses, the Conqueror watches. Disgust and outrage battle within his chest, and his stomach twists as if he'd eaten something rotten. Do these children truly believe they can take the so-called Holy Land with nothing but love in their hearts and faith in their God? And their parents—why are their parents allowing such folly?

The white horse sneezes a question.

The Conqueror absently rubs the bald spot behind one of the steed's ears as he replies, "It's a type of insanity, certainly. But that doesn't make them mine. I can't stop them."

His steed lets out a phlegmy snort.

The Conqueror sighs, and the sound rattles in his throat. The horse is right; he could stop them. He could unleash minor illnesses upon the lot of them and force them to retreat, to return to Tours and Lyons and Vendôme and forget this eloquent preacher boy with his talk of rescuing Christiandom. But no—he dares not. One of the Four may not stand against another, not without consequences.

And these children have already been claimed.

The boy is leading his army in song as they slowly wind their way toward the large port of Marseille; the sound of thousands of footfalls mixes with the swell of voices, forming a sonorous melody that is both hypnotic and horrifying. Over the sounds of their campaign, the Conqueror hears War's booming laughter. He can't bring himself to look overhead and watch the Red Rider soar over her army of children.

(Billy hears the laugh and he thinks of a girl in red.)

The next human waves rolls past him, and he spies one of the few girls who have been swept up in the madness of righteousness. She must be no more than eight years old, and when she grins she shows off a gap-toothed mouth. She's marching off to die along with thousands of her brothers, and still she grins.

He sees his long-dead daughter grinning at him, and he thinks of plums.

"Is it not glorious?"

War's voice is like thunder, and the words are the spatter of winter raindrops. He frowns up at the Red Rider as she and her steed spiral down toward him. Her armor catches the sunlight and slashes it back at him in blinding strokes. Around one gauntleted hand, the reins of her warhorse are wound tight. The other hand wields a long sword as immaculate as his own coat and pants. Like his uniform, the weapon's cleanliness is a lie—beneath the pure white of his clothing are the diseases and filth of the world, and buried in the metal of War's sword is the blood of humanity waiting to be shed. Her face is hidden, as always, by her helm, but within the shadows of her visor, her eyes glow like twin fires.

(And Billy finds her both a complete stranger and strangely familiar.)

"Red," the Conqueror says, inclining his head slightly as her steed lands. The warhorse snaps its teeth, but its Rider pulls back on the reins at the last second. The white steed blows out a sound that comes across as vaguely insulting. Picking up on his horse's tone, the Conqueror gives voice to his derision. "Admiring your work?"

"Of course. There is so much to admire!" She takes in the swarm of child soldiers with one sweep of her gauntleted hand. "Thirty thousand! Even in my wildest dreams, I did not imagine one half-mad shepherd could be so successful."

"Shepherd *boy*," says the White Rider. "They call him prophet and treat him as a saint, but the boy is barely twelve."

"And not even three months ago, that boy was tending sheep in Cloyes." War booms laughter. "There is much to be said about shepherds and leaders, White! They exchange one flock of followers for another."

He doesn't know if the knot of anger in his belly is due to War's presence; she has the unsettling habit of amplifying people's emotions, even those of the other Horsemen. What Death sees in her, he'll never know. He supposes she must be beautiful beneath her armor, but it would be the beauty of an inferno feasting on the air—all-consuming, deadly. But then, who better to be Death's handmaiden than one who gleefully encouraged slaughter?

"They are not a flock," he snarls. "They're *children*."

"They're strengthened by their innocence and thus certain of their victory." War laughs again. "As if innocence has anything to do with it. Might makes right. Anything else is just wishful thinking. Did you know that the boy is claiming that when they reach Marseille, the waters will part for them as the Red Sea did for Moses? Such lovely lies people tell themselves!"

Curious despite himself, he asks, "Did the waters actually part for Moses?"

"That was before my time, White. And that incarnation of Red was far more concerned with the war of the Egyptian firstborn than the escape of the Hebrews." Within her helm, the fire of her eyes brightens. "After plagues upon plagues, the slaves slaughtered lambs to smear blood upon their doorposts, claiming it would save their own firstborn from the final plague upon Egypt. The Egyptian firstborn adults had no wish to feel Death's cold touch, so they approached their pharaoh and demanded that the Hebrews be set free. It was the Egyptians who struck against their own pharaoh and his generals when he refused to grant his precious slaves freedom." She laughs, and the sound is like the clanging of swords. "Did the waters part? Does it matter? The Egyptians brought War and Death to their doors. Who cares whether the waters parted or swallowed the slaves whole?"

"It might make a difference to the thirty thousand children who think they won't drown." The Conqueror looks for the grinning girl among the throng of boys, but she is lost, adrift somewhere among the sea of her brothers.

"Their faith will buoy them." War kicks her steed, and it begins to trot in a circle around the Conqueror and his white horse. "Even though their own Pope doesn't bless their so-called Crusade, the children believe their God is on their side. I *love* people, White! They can convince themselves of anything, given the right motivation."

He slides her a look. "And the right push."

"Of course. Whether sheep for herding or lambs for slaughter, people are wonderfully responsive." Her sword gleams in the harsh sunlight. "And they are so easy to cut down."

His teeth grind together. "They are not *lambs.*"

"No? Tell me, White—where is their precious Pope? Why does he remain silent when the footfalls of thirty thousand children shake this country's very foundation? The Church could stop it," she says, one confidant to another. "But it doesn't. It doesn't stop a similar movement happening even now in the Rhineland, with another shepherd boy leading thousands more children to the seaside. Why is that, White? Could it be that their religious leaders hope these toy soldiers will shame their rulers into yet another, proper crusade?"

Fury sears him, and it takes all of his control not to summon his Bow and let disease strike War's bloody heart. "*Another?* There's been a hundred years of crusades! And for what purpose? To claim a city?"

"Not just any city. A holy city. So say these humans— therefore, it must be true." War jerks back on the reins, forcing her red steed to halt. Pausing to watch the children's ongoing march, she says, "So many truths, these humans have, but only one world to fit them in. How can they not always be at the brink of war?"

"You'd drown the world in an ocean of blood," he shouts, "and it still wouldn't be enough for you."

"Of course not. There will always be war."

"Phaugh!" The Conqueror leans over and spits; where his saliva lands, the ground sizzles. "You've whispered to the boy, dazzled him with images of glory—coaxed him from his home, encouraged him to stir the souls of thirty thousand children and lead them to nothing but pain and death. And for no purpose other than war!"

"You complain of a century of warfare," she says casually as she looks at thousands of children happily striding toward their doom, "and you forget that our domains cross. Warfare and disease are good bedfellows. Think of the sicknesses that embraced the Knights of the Cross: heat stroke, food poisoning, fevers, epidemics, spreading from soldier to soldier. Where I go, White, you follow."

"I follow no one!"

"Is that what you think? How charming."

"You twist things to make them fit your narrow worldview," he snarls. "And worse, you pervert your station. Instead of moderating war, you have kept the crusades in motion for more than a century. A century! Now you're leading these children to the battlefield. We are supposed to provide *balance*, not encourage their baser instincts!"

War turns to look at him from over her broad shoulder. Her face is hidden, but he can feel her glance stabbing through him. "*Balance*," she says, turning the word into a curse. "You sound like Famine. Does the Black Rider speak for you now? Are you nothing more than a puppet?"

His nostrils flare; he feels something on his face blister and crack. "I am not the only one who adheres to her philosophy. When Death offered me the Crown years gone, he told me the same thing. Balance, Red. We are to balance the ills of humanity, not tip the scales."

She laughs mockingly, and it's the sound of fire cauterizing a bloody stump. "And you say that *my* worldview is narrow. Didn't our Pale lord tell you our final purpose when he gave you your pretty crown?"

His good eye narrows, while his milky eye remains wide and shocked. "What purpose?"

He cannot see her mouth, but the smirk in her voice is all too clear. "Where is your philosophy now, White? Why aren't you quoting your sweet Black's words to me? Could it be that Death's handmaiden knows more than you?"

He snorts, and mucus flies from his nose. "You talk but say nothing."

"I say much," she purrs. "I say to you now what our cold Pale lord said to me one moonless night when I warmed him with my passion: This world is ours to do with as we will, until the time comes when we Four shall ride."

"We Four ride all the time," he says, trying to ignore his sudden chill. "You speak nonsense."

"We ride, certainly. But not together. Even when our paths cross, we never truly are together. That time will come, White. When this sorry world has reached its end—when our Pale lord has decided that the end is nigh—then we shall ride!" She hefts her sword high, and she shouts, "We Four together, War and Pestilence and Famine and Death, will split the world asunder! We will crush humanity and all manner of living things, slaughtering and infecting and starving them until this world is nothing more than a charnel house!"

His eyes have widened with her every word, and now he's breathless. "No."

War bellows her challenge to the heavens: "Our Pale lord will lead us in the greatest battle of all time! We are the Riders of the Apocalypse, and we herald the end of everything!"

His throat tight, he once again whispers his denial. *"No."*

"You complain of this small sacrifice of children," War says, lowering her sword. "Have you not considered that what we do now is a mercy, compared with what awaits them elsewise?"

The Conqueror slides off his steed and stumbles to the ground. His body shaking, his head spinning, he tries once more to insist that War is wrong, to say *no*, but his tongue is dead and his mouth is dead and the word sticks in his throat.

With a roar to crack the skies, War and her steed leap into the air, and they hover once more over her latest converts; beneath her, thousands upon thousands of children sing of triumphs to come.

The white steed bumps its muzzle against the White Rider's back, but its Rider does not respond; War's revelation has ripped away his ability to speak, to move, to do anything but watch, dumbstruck, as the children advance row by row—an army of them, a *river* of them, all enchanted with the possibility of succeeding where their elders have failed. Tears wind down his cheeks as the children's call to battle spreads like an epidemic of the most sinister pox/

||||||

Billy barely made it out of the White before he doubled over and vomited. His body shook with spasms as he retched, trying to void himself of the sickness he'd witnessed.

We herald the end of everything.

When the heaving finally stopped, he sat back on his heels and closed his eyes, feeling heat flush his face and neck. Sweat popped on his brow, but it did nothing for the fever of truth searing his soul.

The White Rider was supposed to help end the world.

Billy Ballard was the White Rider. Therefore . . .

No. Impossible. He couldn't.

War's lying, he told himself. *She has to be. No one actually* wants *the world to end. Not even War. Right?*

Perhaps in answer, he heard the Pale Rider's voice: Apocalypse *is just a word, William.*

But in his memory of the Greenwood and the archer Robert Hode, the Conqueror had been babbling about the end of the world.

Another memory, Billy's own memory, shining as brightly as War's sword gleaming in the sun:

Death told him, "End of the world or not, the Horsemen have a job to do."

Billy replied, "Which is?"

"Why, preventing the end of the world, of course. And that's why I need your help."

Floating in the gray of nothingness, Billy groaned. It made no *sense*. He was supposed to find the Conqueror and bring him back to the real world. The Conqueror was convinced that he, the White Rider, would help bring about the end of everything. But Death had told him, Billy, that he needed Billy's help finding the White Rider, who, like all Horsemen, had a job to do—namely, preventing the end of everything.

So had War been lying to the Conqueror all those years ago?

"So many truths, these humans have, but only one world to fit them in."

What to believe?

Maybe he should do what the Conqueror had done: Keep the Bow and refuse to ride. Not like he had a horse, anyway (certainly not the huge white beast he'd never had a chance to ride after the Conqueror tricked him). A Horseman without a horse couldn't ride. Keep the Bow, say all the right things to Death—*sure thing, I'll shoot infected arrows at people, you bet*—and then just go on with his life. Just because he had the Bow, that didn't mean he needed to use it.

An image flashed in his mind: Eddie Glass, puking all over

the floor. Another image, worse than seeing Eddie in regurgitation mode: Kurt, racing out of the cafeteria as his bowels threatened to let go, and then Joe, too overcome with illness to move from where he sat, staying in his seat and trying not to soil his pants as diarrhea and fever wrack his body.

With Eddie, Billy hadn't understood what he'd been doing; he'd just reacted. But with Kurt and Joe, Billy had known what could happen, and never mind how he'd thrown the Bow away before going into the cafeteria. He'd known that he could summon the Bow, and he'd known what the Bow could do, if only he'd use it.

And he'd used it, all right.

But maybe, if he was really careful, he could manage. He was good at not acting on his feelings — hell, he was an expert on getting the snot beaten out of him with barely an arm up to protect his face — so maybe he could have the Bow and not use it.

Maybe —

Before he could think any further on that, the White leaped up at him, wrapped itself around him and dragged him down.

CHAPTER 15

BILLY STRUGGLED . . .

. . . against the tendrils of White pinning him and pulling him into itself, but it was no good; the White had him, and memories not his own sucked him in.

||||||

/the pox has ravaged his kingdom, indiscriminate of poor or rich or old or young. The healthy had suddenly been taken by a violent heat that started in the head and slowly worked its way down, transforming their eyes to embers, inflaming their throats and causing them to spew blood and reek of sickness.

And yet Mita, king of Phrygia, remains untouched.

He presses a clean linen cloth to his daughter's lips to help quell her coughing. Lying on her sickbed, she's in the throes of the great pestilence that has captured his land; he watches, helpless, as she struggles to breathe. The group of royal physicians trained in the works of Hippocrates and Galen had warned him that the time would come when her throat would close, and then nothing would allow the passage of air. Mita had dismissed them all, first individually and then as a group, when they, too, began coughing. Even so, many stayed, determined to perform their duties to the end. The last doctor to walk the halls of his palace had collapsed in a heap not two days gone; the last priest had died yesterday, his appeals to Apollo unanswered, save by the cold embrace of Thanatos.

Mita touches his daughter's cheek, and he flinches from the heat he feels there. She's burning up. His child is dying before his eyes, and there's nothing he can do.

His kingdom is dying, and he's powerless.

(Billy struggles but he's powerless.)

On Mita's brow, his crown threatens to crush him beneath its weight.

He squeezes his eyes closed and prays to the gods—all of them, any of them, whichever one will show mercy and be moved by his words. "Please," he says, "tell me what to do."

The answer comes like a whisper of wind: one word, one action, one request. *Die.*

Perhaps his daughter listens to the wind, because she takes one last strangled breath, and then she breathes no more.

Mita throws himself over her small body, screaming his rage and grief and impotence to Olympus and Tartarus and all places in between. His wails eventually give way to harsh, shuddering sobs that wrack his body and rip his soul. Only when his voice is hoarse and his tears are spent does he bow his head and pray for the safe passage of his daughter's *psyche* to the Underworld, where she will drink from the river Lethe and forget her mortal life.

Forget the pain, he wishes for her, pressing her hand to his lips. *Forget everything that has ever hurt you.*

Forget me, the father who could not save you.

Mita places her hand gently across her chest, and he slowly rises. His heart is too heavy and his head is too thick, and barefoot he walks, stooped and broken, out of his daughter's bed chamber. He cannot think; his body moves and his mind follows, nothing more than a quiet passenger. His steps are unsteady and his mind is blank, but still he walks, compelled by some unknown presence to leave the palace grounds and enter the sprawling city below. The wind kicks up, strong enough to blow Mita's long black hair away from his face. He walks on, breathing in the perfume of sickness, all spoiled meat and feces and blood. Around him is the cacophony of panic: terrified citizens shuttering their windows and doors and hearts, turning away those already suffering with the plague, even as they beg the gods to forgive them, to show mercy, to spare their lives. Mita hears their words, but they are nothing more than noise, the buzzing of flies lighting on a carcass. If any of his subjects tries to stop him, he does not notice. He is blind; he is deaf. He is an impotent king of a diseased land.

He is lost.

When Mita comes to his senses, he is at the entrance of Apollo's temple, deep in the center of Phrygia. Inside the doorway is a stone table—the god's altar. On the slab is a metal dish, used for the sacred fire but now gone cold, and a curved dagger. Next to the table rests a jug. The priestess's body is sprawled on the ground, her face swollen and discolored from the sickness that killed her. Other corpses litter the temple: the bodies of the devoted, whose prayers did nothing to stop the great pestilence from annihilating the kingdom. The temple smells of stale incense and despair.

And death, of course. And death.

Mita stares at the dagger on the altar, and with the clarity of an epiphany, he knows what he must do.

He has no proper sacrifice to offer; the shepherds are dead

and dying, so none are tending their flocks. He himself is not proper, for instead of being freshly bathed and wearing the appropriate purple tunic, he is filthy and his *chiton* is stained. There are other missteps to the ritual of sacrifice as well: There had been no procession, led by a maiden carrying a basket filled with barley covering the sacrificial blade at the bottom. And the priestess is dead.

But he has a crown for the sacrifice, which is important, and there in the jug is holy water, which is necessary.

And he has flesh, as unworthy as it may be.

He strips off his dirty *chiton* and takes the jug in his hands. Naked save for his crown, he spills the contents of the jug over his head. The water hits him, and with it he is purified. So what that he has no barley to sprinkle? The gods will have to understand. He sets the jug back on the ground and takes up the dagger, and then he climbs atop the stone table.

Kneeling, Mita presses the tip of the blade to his bare chest. "Take me," he begs, "and spare what remains of my kingdom. Let my blood be enough to appease, and to make right whatever it is that we have done wrong." Closing his eyes, he hopes that his plea does not fall on empty ears. His fingers tighten around the handle, and he takes a deep breath, preparing himself for the end.

A cold grip catches his wrist.

"Hold, King Mita," says a man's voice. "I would have a word with you."

Mita's eyes snap open, and he sees a tall figure clothed in a coarse brown robe, his face hidden by a cowl. Mita is so stunned by the interruption that it doesn't occur to him to reprimand the man for daring to touch a king.

"Before you spill your blood," says the hooded man, "I have an offer for you." His voice is oddly hollow, as if coming from some great distance.

"What could you possibly offer me?" Mita asks bitterly. "My daughter is dead. My kingdom is dying. I wear a crown, but it is sickness that reigns in Phrygia."

"There is a different crown you could wear," says the stranger, "one that would allow you to banish the sickness from your land. For a price."

Something flutters in Mita's chest, a mixture of hope and caution. He stares at the figure in the dark brown robe, and he frowns at the shadows beneath the stranger's hood. "Let me see your face," he says.

The stranger stiffens. "I come with an offer, and yet you make demands?"

"I don't bargain with those who hide their face." Mita wonders why he gives any reason at all. He is king; that he commands it should be enough. Beneath the stranger's strong fingers, his wrist has gone numb.

Finally, the figure releases Mita's arm. "Then look," he says, and draws back his hood.

Mita looks, and his eyes widen and his mouth drops open and his breath catches in his throat. Before the horror truly sinks in, the stranger *ripples*, and now Mita is staring at a young man's face. A shock of yellow hair crowns him; his skin is pale yet not sickly, even though his cheeks are sunken and the angles of his face are sharp. Only his eyes touch upon the truth: They are blue and yet bottomless, and they swirl with the secrets of the stars.

With that one look, Mita knows him, recognizes him for

what he is: Thanatos. Not a god, but something older, something *other*. Something far more terrifying. It is the embodiment of death, masquerading as a human.

Mita quickly drops his gaze. His heartbeat thunders in his chest and ears and eyes, and a tremor settles in his hands, causing the sacrificial dagger to tremble. He'd been ready to die minutes ago, and yet now, with Death right in front of him, he suddenly very much wants to live.

"You know who I am."

"Yes, Lord Thanatos," Mita replies, his voice cracking.

A sound like the wind rustling dead leaves, and then: "I am no one's lord, but you may call me by that title if it sets you at ease. Tell me, King Mita: Do you want to save your kingdom?"

Mita swallows thickly. Bargaining with one such as Thanatos is folly at best, but what choice does he have? "Yes, Lord."

"Well then, we each have something the other wants. You want to save your land from pestilence, and I want a new Horseman."

"You . . . wish me to be a soldier?"

"I wish nothing," says Death, "and the role of War has long been cast. But I offer you a place as the White Rider of *Apokalyptein*."

A pause, as Mita struggles to make sense of Death's words, but he is at a loss. "The White Rider of Revelation? I don't understand, Lord. What would be revealed?"

"Pestilence."

With the word, Thanatos presents Mita with a long white box. Where it came from, Mita cannot say; it's as if the box has always been in Death's hands, and Mita has only now just noticed. Still keeping his head bowed, Mita asks, "What is inside, Lord?"

"Open it and find out. But know that once you open the box, you agree to be the White Rider."

The pronouncement rings in the air like doom.

Mita's head pounds in time with his heartbeat. He thinks of Pandora and how her curiosity doomed mankind to all manners of evil. Is that what waits for him inside the plain white box?

"Pandora's Box is nothing more than a story that lets people pretend they have nothing to do with the existence of evil." Again, the sound of dead leaves rustling, and Mita realizes that Thanatos is laughing. "Humanity's imagination is both its greatest achievement and its greatest disappointment."

Mita is still weak with fear, but he raises his head to meet Death's bottomless gaze. "Humanity did not create the plague that is killing my kingdom."

Thanatos nods his head slightly, acknowledging the point.

"What does it mean," Mita asks slowly, "to be this White Rider? How would pestilence be revealed?"

"I could spend years telling you the meaning of the White Rider," Thanatos says, "and it still would not be enough, for with every answer you would ask another question. Do you accept the box, and therefore accept the role of White Rider?"

The king lifts his chin. "You offer me the chance to save my kingdom, and I am grateful. But I am also blind as to your intention."

Death's eyes narrow.

Mita forces himself to remain still. The urge to beg forgiveness is nearly overwhelming. He wants to hide his face in his hands and cower before the terrible creature before him that makes even the gods tremble. But he is king, and so he must pretend to be brave.

"You presume much," Thanatos finally says. "I'm not certain I like that. But I do admire it. My intentions remain my own, and are no business of yours."

Mita holds out his hands, imploring. "Tell me one thing, at least, before you would have me make a decision that would leave me forever changed. What does a Horseman of *Apokalyptein* do?"

"Mediate the ills of the world."

Mita's heartbeat is galloping again, but this time it's not from fear. "If I become a Horseman, I can eradicate illness?"

The shadows on Thanatos's face darken until his eyes are blue stones in a sea of midnight. "There must be balance. There can be no health without sickness, no peace without war, no satiation without starvation." A lightning flash of a smile. "No life without death. These things must exist so that all living things exist. But the natural order is one of push and pull. There are times when the ills of the living become too great to bear. And that's when the Horsemen set it right."

"Set it right?" Mita repeats.

"To put things back in balance," says Death. "There can be no health without sickness, but as the White Rider, you would be the Conqueror of Disease. You would help ensure that no pestilence becomes so great as to wipe out humanity. Starting, perhaps, with your own land."

A sound escapes Mita's lips, a soft cry of relief. Tears sting his eyes, and muscles in his neck and shoulders and back that have been pulled taut with stress for too many days to count finally begin to loosen.

"What say you, ruler of Phrygia? Will you exchange one crown for another, and take up the mantle of the White? Will you be one of the Riders of *Apokalyptein* and help save the world from itself?"

How can he not?

And so Mita, king of Phrygia, naked and on his knees, puts down the dagger that was to spill his blood and instead takes the long white box offered by Death. Inside is an unstrung bow, cut from polished black wood, and a silver circlet. Both are intricate in their simplicity.

"For thee," says Thanatos.

With numb fingers, Mita removes the crown of Phrygia from his head and replaces it with Death's gift. The metal is cold upon his brow.

"Thou art the White Rider," says Thanatos. "Go thee out unto the world."

With those words, a door opens in Mita's mind, and he throws back his head as he feels the agony of his people suffering from the plague that has infected his land. The coughing, the sneezing, the endless vomiting and spasms, the compulsion to rip clothing away from his overheated body, the urge to throw himself into a rain tank or the river in the desperate need to slake a maddening, ceaseless thirst—he feels it all, and so much more. Because deeper than the sickness is the embodiment of health, part of the world itself, and that health reaches up and touches all living things. He senses it all, and he knows he can separate the pestilence that is causing such a destructive imbalance of the humors and, once separated, he can decimate it forever.

He can even heal his daughter. In his heart, he knows it. He believes it with all that he is.

He is rejuvenated; he is ecstatic. With the Crown he will cleanse his land and heal his kingdom. He will set it right, as Thanatos has promised, that and more: Mita will set the balance in his people's favor/

/the pox has ravaged his kingdom, indiscriminate of poor or rich or old or young—

▌▌▌▌▌▌

With a shout, Billy tore himself out of the White. *No more!* He didn't want to see any more, not when bearing witness meant feeling compassion for the man who'd stolen his future. He didn't want to understand the Ice Cream Man, to sympathize with him—to think he was a hero. No, not the terrifying monster that had hurt him, betrayed him, before he was old enough to know better.

"Let go!" he yelled, yanking against the stems of White wrapped around his arms and waist and legs.

But the tendrils held him fast, and they were already pulling him back down. After a lifetime of accepting the role of victim, Billy didn't know how to fight back. Even so, he tried. He howled and thrashed, but the White claimed him and dragged him under. His last thoughts, before his thoughts were no longer his own, were of Marianne, and how he wished he'd had the courage to kiss her.

And this time, the White gave way to Black.

CHAPTER 16

THE BLACKNESS WRAPPED
ITSELF AROUND BILLY . . .

. . . almost intimately. Embraced by shadow, he watched what
happened as the world shifted.

||||||

/he holds her favor, even though he has not sought it. She's
looking at him boldly, this woman in black with her whip-thin
smile and set of balances in her hand. The instrument of her
office shines in the dim light, but it cannot compare with the
hungry sheen of her eyes.

The Conqueror, as always, is struck by Famine's exotic
beauty. Her skin is darker than his and unflawed by any im-
perfection; it is the color of russet skies moments before sunset,
and it is magnificent. Her eyes are ringed with kohl — a testa-
ment to her former mortal life, as is her long braided wig. She
is swathed in a black pleated dress held in place by two broad
shoulder straps; beneath her belted waist, the long skirt splits
down the sides to allow for riding. As usual, she is barefoot.

And, as usual, she has shown up exactly where he needs to
be. Whether that is due to famine naturally leading to pestilence, or due to the Black Rider's whim, he can only guess. For
whatever reason she is here, out of duty or out of desire, he is
glad to see her.

She pats the black horse standing next to her, and then she turns her head away from the Conqueror, presenting him with her back. Had she been War, it would have been a sign of haughtiness, indicating that he was no threat. From Death, the gesture would have been dismissive. But from Famine, it's an invitation to come to her side.

As the Conqueror dismounts, the white steed lets out a coughlike nicker. The black horse answers with a thin whinny, and then the eager sound of clopping hooves fills the air. He watches the white and black horses gently intertwine their necks in an equine hug, and he thinks of the closeness between the two animals, an intimacy that is so much more than the cautious distance the white steed always gives War's horse or the respectful air it offers to Death's. Not for the first time, he wonders if the steeds pick up on their Riders' feelings or, perhaps, if it's the other way around. But in the end, it doesn't matter; whether Horsemen or horses, white and black work well together. They always have.

The Conqueror approaches Famine, who is standing near the docks of Alexandria, watching scores of men fill cargo ships with boxes. Between their work and the dense, dry fog that has overtaken the land, none of the humans notice the two Horsemen—although soon enough, all will feel the White Rider's presence. He already senses the fever at work on at least three of the sailors, and it will be only a matter of days before they experience the telltale swelling in the groin, the armpits, the ears. It's a particularly nasty disease, one that Pestilence feels a vague fondness for; it was his first plague, so it holds a special place in his heart.

Something about that thought nags at him, but the more he

tries to examine it, the more abstract it becomes until he's left with a faint discomfort, like a fading rash.

(*They died,* Billy thinks, quite horrified, *they all died, his daughter, his people, but he doesn't remember that.*)

As the Conqueror stands beside the Black Rider, she inclines her head, setting her beaded braids clacking. "King White," she says, her voice like honey.

"Lady Black," he replies with a nod. The titles are something of a joke between them, for he has not been king for more than five hundred years, and it has been two thousand years since she was the vizier of Upper Egypt and called the Lady. "It's good to see you."

"And you." A smile spreads across Famine's face. It's a subtle thing, that smile; it begins with a twitch of her lips, and then with every breath the corners of her mouth tug just a little farther until there is the barest sliver of teeth. She is not one given to excess, and even her mirth is measured. He treasures every hint of delight she reveals to him as the most precious gift.

They stand close enough to be holding hands as they watch the dockworkers laboring. The Conqueror knows there are odors twining through the air, smells that capture the essence of humanity slaving by the riverside, but his senses are dazzled by Famine's perfume of cinnamon and sweet wine.

"They wear cloaks," Famine says.

The Conqueror regards the men as they go back and forth between ship and dock, storing their cargo. "It is much colder than it should be," he replies. "They have to keep warm."

"It's so odd to see. Winter in the desert."

"It's not yet winter."

"It might as well be. Krakatoa erupts, and the world shivers from a volcanic winter. Ash falls, sunlight fades, and bread fails. That's what some call it: a failure of bread." The Black Rider smiles again, tightly. "Humans can be so poetic in their understanding of destruction. Have you noticed that?"

"It's a way to ease their pain." He thinks of the Furies of old, of how mortals appeased them with the name "Kindly Ones," and he adds, "Or maybe it's a way to soothe our Pale colleague. Lull him with poetry, and maybe he'll be too charmed to ride."

"Only humans would dare to think they could control one such as him."

"Not control," he says. "They beseech. People have discovered that he has an appreciation for the arts. It's his soft spot."

She arches a kohl-painted brow. "You call *him* soft?"

"We Four have our affinities," says the Conqueror. "We simply show them in different ways." He smiles wryly. "Say, for example, Egypt's crops being spared, while the rest of the world has 'a failure of bread.'"

The Black Rider laughs softly. "Am I that obvious?"

"Only to one who knows you."

Thin fingers brush against his arm, a touch and then gone. A sip of affection, but rather than slake his thirst he finds himself parched and desperate for more.

Time ripples—

(and Billy feels dizzy)

—and the Conqueror is in Athens and Famine is by his side. The two Riders share a look as around them Romans fall victim of famine and plague. He hardly notices the bodies littering the streets; he's enamored by the swirl of the Black Rider's pleated skirt around her shapely ankles. Something about this woman calls to him, stirs his blood and upsets the balance of his sanguine humor—

He blinks—

(and Billy stumbles)

—and the Conqueror is back in Egypt with Famine, who is looking at the doomed dockworkers. *Memory*, he thinks, restraining himself from placing a hand upon his brow. *Merely a powerful memory.* He knows he is lying to himself, but that doesn't matter. He won't think of diseases that affect the mind, not now. Standing next to the Black Rider, he imagines what it would be like to crush her to his chest and seal his mouth upon hers and steal her breath away.

(And Billy thinks of Marianne, of kissing Marianne, of finally being brave enough to kiss the girl.)

"I saved them," Famine says, her black gaze locked on the sailors and their cartons. "But it won't matter. I spare their harvests, yet here you are."

"Here I am," the Conqueror agrees, wanting to kiss her and knowing he will not. His chest aches. How could he feel loss for something he never had?

"Grain," she says with a sigh, and the Conqueror hears a wealth of meaning in the word. "The same grain I spare feeds the mice, and the mice bring disease."

It's true; the rodents are already boxed in with the cargo, feasting on wheat—and plague-carrying fleas bloat themselves on the rodents. "If starvation didn't lead to illness," he says, "it would lead to war."

"It already does. It always does." Her mouth twists as if she's bitten something sour. "Except when starvation follows in the wake of bloodshed."

While he doesn't care for War, what passes between the Red and Black Riders borders on hatred, and has ever since he first took the Crown. The Conqueror has never asked about the cause of their animosity, and Famine has never offered to tell him. "Black and white and red, intertwined. And it all leads to death," he says.

"War and plague and starvation, all centered around a box of grain." Another sigh. "What gives life also brings death."

"And now we're back to poetry."

That coaxes a small smile from her. "Indeed." A long moment passes before she speaks again. "You are so very different from your predecessor."

In all their time together, she has never spoken of Conquerors past. "Who was he?"

"Just a man, wearing a borrowed crown."

"As am I."

"Wearing a crown, no matter how potent, does not make one a king." She's gazing at him now, her eyes telling him things that her voice does not. "But you, White, are a king. Take the crown away, you still would be king."

The words squeeze his heart, and a lump forms in his throat —a different sort of sickness than he is used to. For a reason he cannot name, he thinks fleetingly of plums.

Perhaps she senses his distress, for she steps away from him and lifts her scales high. "I must go bear witness to the great failures of bread. Until next time, King White."

"Wait." He doesn't know what else to say, only that he

doesn't wish her to leave. And so, he scrambles for conversation. "How long do you think the sun will stay dark?"

"Months. Years." She shrugs, and her beaded braids clack musically. "If you really wish to know, ask our Pale colleague."

"He knows the future?"

"He knows *everything*."

It's not her words that chill him, but the easy way in which she delivers them. He thinks of Thanatos's bottomless eyes, how they hold the secrets of life and death, and he fights back a shiver. " 'He knew the things that were and the things that would be and the things that had been before.'"

"More poetry." Famine smiles again, broadly, as if she's forgotten the notion of restraint. "I did not realize you housed such an artistic soul."

"It's from Homer." His voice is heavy with phlegm, and the name comes out sounding strangled. "*He* once told me he prefers Homer to Hesiod."

She considers him, studying his face, reading each line and pockmark, searching his eyes for hidden meaning. "Maybe humans aren't the only ones who try to appease him."

He's so cold, it's a wonder his breath doesn't frost.

(He sees the end of the world, and it arrives on a sheet of white.)

"It's a careful balance we Four must keep," says the Black Rider/

— and the world shifts —

(and Billy lurches)

/and the Black Rider tells him the Four are out of balance and he must return, but he will not listen to her. She may wear the mantle of the Black, but she is not his Famine.

Instead, he takes aim at a distant ash tree. The weight of the drawstring feels good in his hand, and he enjoys the way the fletching tickles his cheek. Mortal bows need real strings and arrows. In his seventy years playing at being a human outlaw, this has been a constant joy: truly feeling things the way mortals do. He'd been too long a leper—numb inside, his heart withered and half-dead.

He releases the shaft. The arrow slices the wind and lands true.

"White," the woman in black says. "Are you listening to me?"

To tune her out, he opens himself up to the majesty of the Greenwood. His senses sharpen; sounds and smells and colors become dizzyingly crisp. He can make out each leaf fanning the trees, every thorn tangled in clusters of underbrush. The air is so fresh that it sears his nostrils when he inhales. A blue jay shouts from above, and the distinct *rat-a-tat* knocking in the distance announces the presence of a woodpecker questing for food hidden in a tree's bark. Beneath the leaf carpet under his feet, he feels bugs and earthworms as they scuttle and writhe and dig; farther away, he feels the moisture trapped on the strands of spider silk threading along thin branches, hears the angry buzz of an unfortunate insect fighting to break free from the web. He senses all this and more, so much more that he can't help but smile as the thrum of the forest works its way though his bones and plays along his skin. Here in the Greenwood, he is alive in a way he never has been before.

Here in the Greenwood, he is safe from the world. And the world is safe from him.

He takes another arrow from his quiver and nocks it.

"White," the woman in black says again.

His smile falls away. "I am Robert Hode," he says curtly, refusing to look at her. "No more. No less."

"You are the White Rider of the Apocalypse. And I have come to return you to your senses."

"I never took leave of them." He pulls back on the drawstring and takes aim.

The rustling of leaves in the wind doesn't quite cover her snort. "You abandoned your responsibility to parade in mortal form and forester's clothing. How is that not insane?"

"Insanity is a disease of the mind. I know disease. My actions sprang from clarity of thought." He lets fly, and once again, his aim is true: The second arrow splits the first, to land solidly in the ash's trunk.

"So you chose to run away and pretend to be human."

"Call it pretense if you must. My conscience is clear."

"Only because your ego is outpaced by your ignorance!"

A surge of fury swells in him, filling him with fire. He turns his back on her. He'd saved the world, and this was his thanks? Being insulted by a sorry excuse of a Rider? Gnashing his teeth, he draws another arrow.

"Do you not even care about what is happening outside of your precious forest?" Her voice is heavy with scorn. "Or is sickness beyond you now?"

Words. They are just words. He takes a breath and takes aim at another tree.

"I have been watching. Listening. From Asia to Europe, the sickness is spreading." A pause, and then: "It's because of the fleas. They're hungry. They cannot be sated, no matter how many times they bite their victims."

Despite himself, he says, "Plague starts with fleas. It swells inside them, blocking their stomachs. When they bite a person, their sickness infects the open wound." *Plague*, he thinks. Not just sickness, but plague. Something stirs in him, an uneasy bubbling in his stomach, and it takes him a moment to recognize it as guilt. Suddenly angry, he releases his arrow. It misses its target. He could blame it on an errant wind, but he knows better.

"I've seen this infection at work. People complain of a headache. Then they have trouble moving, either from feeling too hot or too cold. Some cannot hold down any food or drink." She says this as if she is personally affronted by nausea and vomiting. "Then come the swellings on their necks, under their arms. On their inner thighs. I've watched those lumps grow to the size of oranges."

Of course she would relate to the plague in terms of food. He feels her gaze boring into his back.

"Those boils turn black and split open and leak white liquid and blood." A mirthless laugh, and then: "Black and white and red, intertwined. And it all leads to death."

He growls, "Stop it."

"I can't. It's not my demesne. You fled, and because of that, the plague now runs amok. Only you can rein it in."

He squeezes his eyes closed. His fingers clench around his mortal bow, clench and release, as if they know it is not the proper weapon for him to wield. Beneath his hood, his brow itches.

And he bristles when he feels the weight of her hand on his shoulder.

"King White," she says. "Please."

His mouth twists in a snarl as he whirls to face her. This Famine wears a pointed black cap; beneath it, her plaited auburn hair frames the sides of her pale face. His eyes narrow as he looks at that cap, at those red braids. He thinks of a black beaded wig and of russet skies, and he shouts, "Do not dare! You may be the Black Rider, but you are not *she!*"

"Nor am I trying to be," she says quietly.

He glares at her, takes her in from her ridiculous black gown with its opulent buttons and frills to the lavishly decorated tight black coat trimmed with fur; he sneers at her pointed black shoes. Famine, practically dripping with abundance— it's all but blasphemy. Through gritted teeth he says, "You have no right to use that name with me."

"But I do," she says, imploring. "The spirit of the Black Rider dwells within me, and through it I've seen how she— how *I*—used to be with you."

The words sting him like wasps. "We were never together."

"Not like that. But we were close, once." Shadows play behind her eyes. "How I longed for you to leave your green exile and return. This has all been so . . . overwhelming."

He doesn't want to hear the pain in her voice. "Then tell the Pale Rider that you no longer accept his offer, and be done with the Black!"

"I almost did." She lowers her head as if she cannot meet his gaze. "My predecessor died of heartbreak. I don't know which was worse—trying to control the famine in northern Europe that sprang from her death, or coping with a loss that wasn't mine but that I felt so completely."

Heartbreak.

He thinks of cinnamon and sweet wine, and, deeper than that, of plums.

(Here.)

"Please," says the woman in black. "Please return to us."

Her appeal tears a laugh from his throat. It is a hollow sound, and its emptiness gives voice to his confusion and sorrow and determination. She has not seen what is to come. She doesn't understand that he must stay in the Greenwood, stay there and never return.

(Here he'll stay.)

"If not for the people dying from sickness," she says, "then return for me."

He cannot.

(Here he'll stay, away from the world with its never-ending diseases and hunger and battles at every corner.)

He will not, not even for her, in her borrowed coat of black/

(And Billy suddenly understands.)

||||||

—and in the moment between the White Rider's memories resetting, Billy finally understands what the White was trying to explain. He understands why there are layers of memories and sensations and experiences between him and the Ice Cream Man. And more than that, he knows where the Conqueror is hiding. He's known from the start, but he hasn't realized it until now.

And he knows what he has to do.

White beckons White.

He watches as the memory loops back, skipping past the Greenwood and beginning once more by the docks of Alexandria, where the Conqueror and Famine exchange a heated look. As the two Riders discuss poetry, Billy crouches down and sets himself like a sprinter poised to race. He tells himself he can do this, he's got this. He tells himself he *can*.

Don't be such a girl.

He grits his teeth. *Shut up*, he tells his subconscious, or whatever it is that insists on making him feel like a loser. He has a job to do. Death sent Billy for a reason.

"Whomsoever of men he has once seized he holds fast, and he is hateful even to the deathless gods!"

Billy swallows. Okay, yes, that Death—Death of centuries past—is way more frightening than the modern version that Billy knows. Maybe the Pale Rider has mellowed over the millennia. It doesn't change the fact that Death tapped Billy to bring back the White Rider from the depths of memory—the one place that even Death cannot go.

White beckons White.

A thought nags at Billy, and it burrows into him like a worm through an apple. What if Death *doesn't* think Billy can succeed? What if the only reason Death asked Billy to do this is because the Conqueror tricked Billy into becoming the next White Rider?

What if Billy isn't the best option, but the *only* option?

. . . such a girl . . .

Billy Ballard, constantly picked last for any team. The kid who's always pushed around.

Death's cold voice, echoing from somewhere in the White: *The natural order is one of push and pull.*

Billy feels himself starting to panic—that can't-breathe, suffocating sensation that creeps up his chest and squeezes his throat and makes his head slam into overdrive. Who's he kidding? He's just a kid, a doormat, a punching bag. He's just Billy Ballard, the wimp who can't even fight back because he's such a coward.

Shut up, says Marianne.

And then, deeper than the panic, there's a feeling of warmth, of comfort, centered in his chest, his heart. His soul. He feels it there, pulsing gently, soothing him with every beat of his heart. And in the middle of that feeling is a voice, a thought, a notion that was given to him by someone he misses so completely that he feels that loss in every waking moment.

(*Believe and stand tall.*)

He remembers his grandfather, back when he was a bear of a man. Gramps hoisting Billy high on his shoulders and running with him around the backyard fast enough for Billy to feel like he was flying.

The worm pauses.

Death again, from a memory that isn't his own: *There are times when the ills of the living become too great to bear. And that's when the Horsemen set it right.*

Set it right.

Deep in the White, the Conqueror tells Famine to wait, and he asks her how long the darkened sun will reign. She opens her mouth to answer—

"*She proved her point,*" said Death.

"*What point?*"

"*That you people are worth saving.*"

Yes. *Yes.* For all that Death is upsetting and frightening, he also hasn't lied — not to Mita, all those years ago, and not to Billy. Death told Billy that it's a Horseman's job to save the world. He wouldn't have offered Billy up like some desperate sacrifice to an uncaring god.

(*Believe.*)

Death believes in Billy.

So does Marianne, for reasons Billy still can't fathom. Maybe that's just what friends do: They believe in you, no matter what.

And his mother believes in him — because really, she wouldn't leave Gramps alone with Billy if she didn't completely trust her son to watch over her father.

And Gramps — the Gramps of old, who sometimes winks through the doppelganger wearing his grandfather's skin — Gramps believes in him.

The scene in the White shifts, and now the man pretending to be the human Robert Hode is shooting arrows at trees while the next incarnation of Famine is begging him to listen to her.

Billy nods, determined. Yes, he has people who believe in him. Time for him to make them proud.

Time for him to believe in himself.

And the worm turns.

Billy takes a deep breath and throws himself into the White —

|||||||

— and with a defiant cry, he tackles the man disguised as a human forester —

|||||||

—and the two of them flew in a tangle of limbs, the Conqueror screeching and Billy howling, wrapping himself around the man to keep him from escaping. They landed hard on the leaf-covered ground, rolling until they came to a halt. Billy held fast to the man's arm.

"I'm Billy Ballard," he said over the mad drumming of his heart. "And I've come to take you back."

CHAPTER 17

AS BILLY WATCHED . . .

. . . the human guise bubbled away from the Conqueror's face, leaving behind the twisted visage of the Ice Cream Man. His features were more horrifying than Billy remembered—the sunken, bloodshot eyes fixed on him, searing him with hatred, and both the ruined nose and lipless mouth were nearly lost within lumpy, pockmarked skin—but surprisingly, Billy found that he was no longer frightened by what he saw. Maybe years of nightmares had inoculated him from the melted-wax horror that was the White Rider's face.

"No!" Spittle flew from the Conqueror's mouth, and it sizzled in the air. "No! No no no no NO!" He yanked his arm, but Billy had dug in like a tick. The White Rider's eyes flashed, hot and violent, and he bellowed his denial, his desperation, his utter fury: *"NO!"*

Billy felt sickness hit him dead on, slamming into his body and rolling over him like a tempestuous wave. Not just any sickness but a *calamity* of sicknesses, all pounding him and pushing through his defenses until his immune system was left tattered and wheezing. His muscles constricted and his brain caught fire; his stomach rebelled and his bowels knotted and his heart stuttered. His skin bumped with chill; his flesh cooked with heat. He opened his mouth to scream and vomit erupted. His limbs jerking, he collapsed to the ground. He barely felt the White Rider pull out of his grip.

There on the forest floor, Billy Ballard began to die.

Please, he thought despairingly. Not *no*, not *stop*, not some primeval war cry that voiced his rage, but *please*. After years of just taking it whenever Eddie Glass or any of the other bullies hurt him, Billy didn't know how to fight back.

The answer came to him in a small, still voice: *Focus.*

He closed his eyes and focused. And two things suddenly became clear.

One: He *did* know how to fight back. He had, earlier today, when Eddie had gotten in his face one time too many. And again, when Kurt and Joe had embarrassed him in the cafeteria. He'd done it. He'd gotten pushed and he'd pushed back, hard.

Two: As real as everything seemed right now, he was in a memory.

Perhaps in counterpoint, his stomach twisted and he vomited a second time. Sweat beaded on his forehead and then evaporated as his body tried to regulate its fluctuating temperature.

Memory or not, disease was eating away at him. Destroying him. He even knew what the ingredients were in the cocktail of contagions: influenza and pneumonia and Ebola. Maybe that knowledge was the White Rider in him. A definite plus when taking biology exams, but not so great at practical applications of that knowledge. He would have laughed if he hadn't been struggling for breath.

Again, a gentle nudge, asking him to do one thing: *Focus.*

All right, focusing. He was in a forest, or the memory of a forest, even though he himself had never been in such a place.

He knew other places far better—the pizzeria, where he'd sit with Marianne and watch her oregano her slice to death; the sanctuary of his room, with its posters and music and a door that locked; the booby-trapped hallways of school, filled with people who enjoyed hurting him for no better reason than it was easy to hurt him and with teachers whose eyes were on only their lesson plans . . .

And then, a question from his bio quiz—the one he hadn't needed to study for, because he'd magically known the answers —floated to the front of his mind:

How many leucocytes are in a drop of blood?

Answer: Anywhere from 7,000 to 25,000

Now Billy could hear his biology teacher's nasal whine as he went on and on about *lymphocytes* and *neutrophils*, and how *macrophages phagocytized pathogens.* Or, as he'd loosely translated to Marianne the other week when they'd been do-ing homework together: When a disease invaded the body, the white blood cells attacked.

White blood cells, the soldiers of the human body.

It was an a-ha moment, all "Eureka!" and "Of course!" with the barest hint of "Duh." His mind was telling him what his body already knew: Billy had been fighting back from the mo-ment Pestilence struck.

He could see it now—a swarm of giant white blood cells chasing after the contagions in his body, surrounding them and, one by one, destroying them. As if inspired by Billy's at-tention, the cells redoubled their efforts, annihilating all for-eign entities in his bloodstream. When the overstressed cells began to fall, more rose up to take their place. It was the natural order of things: Disease and infection invaded, and Billy's immune system worked to save him.

In the real world, perhaps it wouldn't have been enough, for the Conqueror's attack had been brutally efficient. In the real world, even when you worked to keep the ball in play, you could still get viciously elbowed and then go down for the count. But here, in the White? And now, since he understood that he wasn't the same walking target he'd been just a few days ago?

"Got it," he croaked.

And he did. Billy went deep inside himself, into his bone marrow, and created more and more cell soldiers to take up arms against the invading diseases. He did this in the way that people breathe—he didn't pause to wonder how he was coaxing his stem cells to produce thousands more white blood cells. He simply did it. He was the White Rider, and his blood was a battleground.

And as with all such battlefields, there came a point when the fighting ceased because there was nothing left for him to fight.

He'd won. The Conqueror had unleashed a horror of illnesses upon him . . . and Billy survived. For the first time that he could remember, he was victorious.

For a while, he just lay on the forest floor, too drained to do anything other than get his breathing under control. Eventually, it sank in that the longer he stayed sprawled on the leafy ground, the more time the Conqueror had to run. With a groan, he climbed to his feet.

"Please," said the woman in black, her eyes wide and imploring. "Please return to us."

That she wasn't looking at Billy when she spoke didn't alter the feeling that she was trying to talk to him, even though she was using previously scripted words. Or maybe he was just a sucker for girls in black.

"Oh, he will," said Billy. "He can't hide anymore."

It was true. Billy had the feeling of the Conqueror now, a nagging, tickling sensation in the base of his skull that felt, for lack of a better word, White. The man who had been King Mita was out there, somewhere in the Greenwood; Billy knew it. *Felt* it. Maybe Billy's presence somehow anchored the Conqueror, forced him to remain in this particular memoryscape; maybe the White Rider had forgotten how to leave. Maybe something else entirely. It didn't matter. The Conqueror was there — on the run, on the lam, hoofing it, had hit the trail, was making serious tracks, was gone, baby, gone. That, too, didn't matter.

No matter how far the Conqueror went, no matter how cleverly he hid, Billy was going to find him.

"Return for me," pleaded Famine, looking where her Conqueror had been.

"Hold that thought," said Billy. And then he took off after the White Rider.

|||||||

Billy tried not to be distracted by the Greenwood as he went hunting for the elusive White Rider, but damn, it was difficult. Even peripherally, the forest was magnificent. Filled with trees that would have given skyscrapers a case of the nerves, the woodland made his senses hum. The earthy, herbal smells of dirt and wood and plant pleasantly stung his nostrils, making him think of the potpourri his mother kept in bowls in the living room. Over the sounds of his feet snapping fallen twigs and dead leaves came the squawking of birds hidden in the trees. But what impressed him the most was the size of the woods. He'd been to Los Angeles years ago, and at the time he'd been stunned by how vast the city was, with block to sprawling block crammed with stores and apartments and people, so many people they were like a disease. But this forest made LA look insignificant.

That being said, he wouldn't have minded a sidewalk.

Time passed as he marched. Well, more like as he moved at a steady plodding sort of pace. His feet had turned to cement some time ago, making it difficult for him not to slip or get his legs tangled in the thorny undergrowth. He'd expected a proper path, even a road, but if there was such a thing, the Conqueror avoided it. Billy pushed on, trying not to grumble. Who knew that rocks and other hard things could be felt so easily under sneakers?

Or that there were streams in the forest, with ice-cold water that soaked right through those very same sneakers?

Squelching as he walked, Billy tried to pretend he wasn't cold. Or wet. Or that he wasn't getting bitten to death. Killing yet another bug, he fervently hoped that his own itching was due to mosquitoes and not fleas. For a memory, this forest had teeth.

At one point, after climbing over yet another fallen tree that was far too large to walk around (and disturbing the writhing mass of beetles clustered on the trunk), he thought he saw a man waving at him. But when Billy turned, he was alone in the woods.

He frowned, and squinted . . . and there, there was the man again, grinning at him and waving him over. Not the Conqueror—the insistent tickle in the back of his head was quite certain of that—and not the dying Robert Hode, come to seek final refuge in the Greenwood. This man was dressed in a dark red that was completely out of place with all the greenery, and he was grinning fit to burst. But as Billy approached, the man blurred until he was nothing more than a smudge of scarlet, and then that, too, was gone.

Huh.

Still frowning, Billy headed back to the fallen tree and continued his hunt for the Conqueror.

The next time he saw someone in the woods, it was at arrowpoint.

He had just decided that trees were highly overrated. Maybe he was just sick of looking at them, to say nothing of all the *green*—green leaves on branches, low enough to slap a face or poke an eye; green bushes filled with thorny plants, sharp enough to sting his legs even through his jeans; green above, forming a canopy that barely let sunlight speckle through; green below, the grass just tall enough to disguise roots that grabbed his feet. Everywhere he looked: green.

Which was why he didn't see the cloaked man in his forest greens until it was too late. The man sprang up from behind a large shrub, a bow in his hands, the arrow nocked and aimed right at Billy's chest.

With a shout, Billy threw his hands up in a universal Don't Shoot gesture.

The archer took a step toward Billy, then misted into nothingness.

Billy stared at the spot where the archer had been. *They're not real,* he told himself. *Maybe they were at one point, but now they're just ghosts haunting a memory.* Still, he had no intention of getting shot with a ghost arrow. The bug bites sure felt real; he absolutely didn't want to learn the hard way whether arrow wounds also felt real.

He kept on going, paying more attention to the nagging itch that was the White Rider's presence and less to the flashes of people scattered in the forest. Some, though, were impossible to ignore—the giant of a man, for example, who held an enormous staff and blocked passage across a log bridge. Billy nearly fell into the river when that staff swung for his legs: He hopped backwards with a squawk, saved from an unintentional dunk by madly pinwheeling his arms (and more than a little luck). The giant laughed and vanished. Good riddance.

And there was a girl. Older than Billy, and dressed like someone going to a Renaissance festival, she suddenly appeared by his side, smiling at him coyly, as if she knew him far, far too well. Looking at her made him feel Marianne's absence so completely that it was like someone had scooped out his heart. He turned his head away and picked up his pace, but the girl stuck by his side. He thought he heard musical laughter before she, too, faded to nothing.

Listening to the White whisper in his brain, Billy kept searching.

He didn't know when he first became aware of the sound; maybe it had been building gradually in the background as he'd stumbled onto a forest trail and he just hadn't noticed it until now, when the birds and squirrels and other woodland creatures paused in their chatter. But he heard it now: the bubbling, rippling sound of rushing water. Soon the rush grew into a roar, and he came upon a waterfall, cresting over three levels of rock and coming to land in a river that flowed across their path. A fallen tree stretched across the width of the water, acting as a bridge.

Billy stared, awestruck. This was nothing like the chiseled fountains he'd seen in parks, with gentle flows of water spouting from tapered marble mouths; this tumble of water surged before him, shouting rapturously as it soared and crashed, soared and crashed. Sunlight danced in the spray, dazzling him with rainbow light.

And then the sunlight dimmed, and the water stopped mid-tumble.

"White Rider," said a cold voice.

He whirled around to see a tall figure standing a few paces behind him. A long robe covered the stranger from neck to toe, and a hood left the face cloaked with shadow. Flanking him were two horses, one pale, one white.

Billy's stomach twisted and a chill worked its way through him, turning his legs weak and sealing his mouth tight. He didn't need to see the man's face to know he had bottomless blue eyes.

The Pale Rider had come calling.

"I come for thee," said Death.

Billy's mouth opened and closed, and his heart skipped

wildly. How could a memory of Death see him? Billy worked up some moisture in his throat and opened his mouth, even though he had no idea what he was going to say.

And from behind him, on the other side of the river, a man's voice called out, "I shall not ride!"

Again, Billy spun around, and this time he saw the forester Robert Hode standing on the end of the log bridge. But the forester image was just a memory; Billy could see, could *feel* the presence of the Conqueror swimming beneath the mortal skin. Here was the White Rider, both present and past.

A burst of lightning tore the sky, and thunder rolled over the treetops. The air was heavy with humidity, but no rain fell.

The Conqueror called out: "I will not help you bring about the end of everything!"

Another lightning flash, and an afterimage burned in Billy's mind: Death, walking around in Billy's living room, telling him about the Four Horsemen of the Apocalypse.

"Is the world going to end?" Billy whispered.

"Of course it will," Death said cheerfully. "But not today. Really, you people get so hung up on the smallest things. Apocalypse is just a word, William. If everything were coming to a crashing halt, you'd know."

"You walked away from your responsibility for more than seventy years," Death said to the White Rider of the past. "You presume the Crown is still yours to wear."

And Billy said to the Conqueror hiding within the memory: "It's not the end of the world."

"I know better." The White Rider stood tall at the end of the bridge, and Billy couldn't tell if it was the memory addressing Death or the Conqueror replying to Billy directly. "The Crown is mine to keep. As long as the White Rider does not ride, the world cannot end."

Behind Billy came a phlegmy snort.

"Your steed disagrees," Death commented.

"You're wrong," said Billy, shaking his head. "Hiding here in a memory, or in the memory of a memory, doesn't save the world."

The Conqueror balled his fists. "I won't listen to you."

"But you know I'm right," said Billy, taking one careful step onto the log bridge. "You thought you were being clever by going into a coma and hiding in a memory. In a coma, you can't ride, but you're still alive, so Death can't take back the Crown. You thought you finally found a way to keep the White Rider from going out into the world." Billy took another step. "But there's still disease. Pestilence still exists." Billy knew that last part all too well.

"If you won't listen to me, or to your steed," said Death, "then listen to the world. It cries beneath the burden you shoved upon it. It screams. You walked away from your Crown, leaving the Great Pestilence in your wake."

"There will always be sickness," said the man pretending to be Robert Hode.

"Not like this." Death's voice held no pity, no mercy. "I have been riding through the world, bearing witness to millions falling ill and dying. *Scores* of millions."

"The Conqueror still has the Crown," said Billy. "But Pestilence has a Bow that shoots poisoned arrows. You haven't stopped anything by hiding here."

The White Rider said nothing. Overhead, the sky raged.

"Don't you get it?" Billy said, taking another step on the

bridge. He was close enough now to see the features of the man's face—the eyes wide and shocked, the mouth pressed into a tight line, the tension on his brow, which seemed to beg for a Crown to cover it. "By staying here, in a memory, you're allowing disease to run free in the real world." He spread his hands helplessly. "Pestilence can't control disease. Only the Conqueror of sickness and health can do that."

Something played in the Conqueror's eyes—recognition, perhaps, or remembered horror.

"I have run out of patience." Thunder punctuated Death's words. "Thou art the White Rider. Either ride once more, or take thy rest."

"Are you the White Rider," said Billy, "who can save the world when disease runs out of control? Or are you just a little king who's dooming the kingdom of the earth?"

Death's voice, commanding and cold: "Choose."

Deep in the memory of stolen time in a shire wood, the White Rider closed his eyes and shuddered. Billy, more than halfway across the bridge, held his breath.

And finally, the Conqueror opened his red-rimmed eyes. "You have reminded me of my duty," he rasped. "I'll not forget this." He strode forward—and walked right through Billy.

The first contact was the bite of winter wind, the splash of water hitting the face, the shock of walking into a punch; the Conqueror stepped through him, and Billy was left squeezed out, empty. He thought he heard a voice, heavy with phlegm, and that voice said: *I'll not forget you, Billy Ballard.*

Shivering, Billy turned to watch the Conqueror climb atop the white steed. With a shout that might have been a sneeze, Rider and horse left the forest to face the world.

Another clap of thunder, one that Billy felt in his teeth. Next to the pale steed, Death paused . . .

. . . and turned his head to look at Billy.

He can't see me, Billy thought wildly. *He can't. He's just a memory!*

"Even memories die."

Whether it was from Death's words or from the absence of the Conqueror or from something else entirely, the forest began to change. The waterfall shimmered once, brightly, and then it folded in on itself, leaving behind a massive wall of gray. Not like rain clouds or turbulent waters, but *gray*, winter-sky gray, the gray of in between. As Billy stared, the gray nibbled at the edges of leaves, at the branches, at the very air itself, eating away everything with any color or spark of life. A sound like a groan, and then it felt soft beneath Billy's sneakers, as if he was standing in mud. He looked down and saw that he'd sunk ankle-deep into what had been a fallen tree. With a yelp, he pulled his feet out, nearly losing his shoes in the process. And he immediately began to sink again, this time up to his shins.

Not like mud at all. More like quicksand.

Panicked, he freed himself from the softening bridge. Standing on the grass, Billy thought the ground felt . . . spongy. Overhead, the gray silently ate the world.

"You should run," said Death.

Billy ran.

||||||

He's running through the forest, not stopping to worry about thorns or rocks or half-hidden springs. He's charging through the woods, a scream building in his throat as all around him the green leaches away into gray. Something brushes against him, cold and familiar, like snowflakes on skin, and Billy hears a word—

Gotcha

—and then something's got him by the hair, is pulling him, reeling him in as around him the world falls away to nothing. Billy releases the scream as he's pulled out of the dying memory—

||||||

—and, still screaming, he sprawled to the floor. He scrambled to his feet and froze, knees bent, arms out, ready to run, to flee, to bolt for his life. Panting, he darted his gaze around, quick flicks as he breathed in and breathed out, one two, breathing, just breathing and looking until two things penetrated the rush of adrenaline and terror: one, he wasn't in the forest anymore; and two, Death—grunger Death, street musician Death— was standing in front of him, grinning hugely and giving him a thumbs-up.

"And that," said the Pale Rider, "is how a Horseman pulls off a rescue."

Billy blinked stupidly. Slowly, he realized he was back in the Greek hospital, clutching the Bow in one hand and sporting a killer headache. Wincing, he raised his free hand and rubbed his forehead. His neck hurt, too, as if he'd slept wrong.

"The Conqueror?" he asked. His voice sounded strange to his ears, off somehow, as if it were coming from some great distance. And there was something wrong with the temperature in the hospital room, because he'd begun to sweat like crazy.

"Out of bed, and riding in the world." Death motioned to the empty hospital bed. "His steed sends its thanks, by the way."

Billy's thoughts felt soupy and slow. He repeated, "Steed?"

"The white horse. It's tough on steeds when their Riders don't ride. And that particular steed gets nervous when its Rider neglects it." Death smiled, shrugged. "Abandonment issues."

Billy thought of the powerful white horse from his nightmares, and then of the rather ordinary horse he'd seen in the Conqueror's memories of Alexandria and the Greenwood, and he couldn't imagine them being the same animal. Riders changed over the years; did their steeds?

"Of course they do," said Death. "Nothing lives forever, not even Apocalyptic horses. But as with their Riders, the essences of those steeds are passed down from horse to horse. Collective memory, some would say. Very convenient, if you're not able to take notes or read."

Billy's head pounded fiercely. He wanted to ask Death why he still had the Bow if the Conqueror had finally gotten out of bed, but his mouth refused to work any longer, and his legs must have decided to go on strike, because he slid to the floor. A tremor worked its way along his shoulders and arms, and his neck was horrible, and his head was threatening to split open.

He whispered, "What's wrong with me?"

Silence, broken only by the sounds of Billy's labored breathing. Finally, Death replied, "At times, the Conqueror can bear a grudge."

Billy closed his eyes and wished his head would stop hurting; it felt like Eddie Glass was using it as a soccer ball. He sensed movement over him, and he tried to open his eyes to see what Death was doing, but his body no longer obeyed his brain.

The Bow, he thought, or tried to think, but it was so hard to focus on anything over the incessant pounding of his head.

"No worries, William," said a still, small voice. "I'll see you soon."

And then something cold touched his forehead—

||||||

—and Billy Ballard woke up.

He was in a hospital bed, with tubes and machines attached to him. His mother and grandfather were there in the room, and his mother cried with relief when Billy opened his eyes. Things slipped in and out of focus for a bit, but when he woke up for real, he learned that he'd gotten sick with bacterial meningitis. He'd been rushed from school, where he'd collapsed, to the hospital, and he'd been dosed with antibiotics and other medicines. Now his fever had broken, and soon he'd be allowed to go home, and look, said his mom, look, everything's going to be just fine.

But she didn't see what was leaning against the corner of the hospital room. In fact, no one saw the thin black limb, polished so that it gleamed in the harsh florescent lighting—an intricately carved limb that looked like a walking stick but wasn't that at all.

Staring at the Bow, Billy understood that no, everything was not going to be fine, not by a long shot.

PART THREE

PESTILENCE AND THE CONQUEROR

CHAPTER 18

BILLY'S IN THE SANDBOX AGAIN . . .

. . . but this time he's solemn as he works on the ultimate castle, where the battle of Good versus Evil is supposed to play out. His heart's not in it, and this shows in the sloppy work by the towers; if it were a real castle, guards would lose their footing on the uneven ground and easily topple over the edge to their deaths. Billy doesn't care about that, and he doesn't care that sand is sifting down the sides of the fortress, making a dune where the moat should be. The problem is he knows that Good and Evil aren't so clear-cut; sometimes, good people do evil things, and, more confusingly, evil people sometimes do good things. Even kings might let people die, all for the greater good.

"Balance," he says aloud. It's a stupid word, and it shouldn't be part of the battle between Good and Evil, and yet there it is. There has to be a balance between the two, because one is defined by the absence of the other.

He knocks down one of the towers, and takes no pleasure in the wanton destruction. He's too old to be playing in a sandbox.

It's a turbulent spring day, the sort that can't decide if it really wants to be jacket weather or not. The wind is a little too strong, and clouds barricade the sun. The trees aren't convinced that winter is truly gone, so they haven't yet budded with new leaves. The playground carries echoes of children laughing and parents calling out warnings to be careful and let your brother play and other such soft reprimands, but the voices are just ghosts in the breeze; the playground itself is deserted.

A cloud passes over Billy, and he feels a tickle in his nose. He fights the sneeze until the feeling passes. Now his nose is leaking and his eyes are watering. He sniffles and blinks until his nose behaves and his eyes know better.

A shadow falls over him.

Billy stares at the ruined sand tower, and he doesn't understand the sense of grief and loss that is bubbling inside him, sour as heartburn.

"It won't last," says a man's voice.

Billy, unsurprised, turns around and sees a tall man dressed in white. The man looks sickly, for he's far too thin: His coat, although clean, is much too big for him, and his pants are baggy. His face is a ruin of melted wax. On his brow, a silver circlet gleams.

"Nothing ever lasts," says the man in white. "Not health. Not peace. Not abundance. Not life. Oh, no, especially not life."

Part of Billy wants to shout for his mom, but that's five-year-old Billy, the part of him who still can build sandcastles and is sure that all the problems of the world can be solved by superheroes. The rest of him, the William Ballard part that's traveled to a distant land and has crossed through time and memory, isn't frightened by the man in white.

"I know you," says Billy. "You're the Conqueror."

"I was, perhaps." The man lowers his head, and his long greasy hair shrouds his face. "But now? Now I am the defeated."

Billy's brow crinkles as he tries to make sense of the man's words. "Defeated? By what?"

"Everything. All my plans are undone. All my fears are real-

ized." His voice drops to a whisper, which rattles in the air as if the wind is coughing. "I am nothing."

Billy considers this. "You're still the Ice Cream Man," he finally replies, although that isn't quite correct; the Ice Cream Man had been a thing of nightmares. This man, this one-time king, looks tired and used up. Not the walking dead, for death is not his demesne, but perhaps the walking ill.

The man in white smiles slowly. It's rather horrible to look at. "I had been many things. Why not an ice cream man as well?"

Billy nods somberly.

"Come with me," says the Ice Cream Man, who turns his back on Billy and starts to walk off the playground, his white boots kicking up a cloud of dust. Billy Ballard follows as if in a dream.

At the edge of the park, Billy sees a white horse. Not a merry-go-round horse, either, but a real live horse, large and so white that it's like staring at the sun. Its eyes are pale green, like springtime peeking through cracks of ice, and those eyes are gazing at him intently, as if the horse is waiting for Billy to do something.

"It's a sad thing when a horse wants for a Rider," says the Ice Cream Man.

Billy frowns. "But you're the White Rider."

"I was."

"You still are."

"You agreed to wear the Crown when the time comes. This Crown," says the Ice Cream Man, motioning to his forehead.

Billy squints at the thin silver band nestled over the man's eyebrows. "But you're still wearing it."

"For now. It won't last. Nothing lasts."

"Why me?" Billy asks. "Why did you trick me into making a deal I didn't understand?"

"Because I remembered you, Billy Ballard. I remembered you, and I came to you with an offer. You agreed to wear the Crown, and to get a ride on my fine white steed." The man in white grins, and Billy sees rotted stumps where there should be teeth. "I saved you from your meager little life."

There's a pit in Billy's stomach, and it's white and filled with bugs. "You didn't save me! You stole my future!"

The Ice Cream Man throws back his head and laughs, laughs like the roar of a waterfall. "What makes you think there's a future for anyone? Don't you understand yet?"

"Understand what?"

Around them, the edge of the park begins to bleed into gray —and beneath the gray, the White beckons.

"Come here, Billy," hisses the Ice Cream Man. "Come here and see the end of the world."

The man in white reaches out to Billy, who sees that the man's gloved hand is twisted into a monster's claw, and Billy opens his mouth to scream—

||||||

—and Billy Ballard shook himself awake. He was in bed, his heart beating too fast, sweat already drying on his face. It was the fourth night he was home from the hospital, the fourth night that he'd had the same dream. And why not? He'd first known the Conqueror as the Ice Cream Man, the Nightmare Man, all those years ago. Why wouldn't he be dreaming about him once more?

As he got his breathing under control, something itched in the back of his mind.

Billy forced himself to think about returning to school—anything to stop thinking about the incessant tickle worming around in his head. His doctor had finally given him an official note that would return him to the hell that was high school, and tomorrow was the big day. Billy sat in bed, thinking about what waited for him in the hallways, or lurked in the cafeteria, or loomed just outside of the bathroom, and even though he had a vague disquiet about Eddie and the Bruisers, it wasn't the all-encompassing terror from before.

The itching grew stronger.

Billy turned to his reliable fantasy of kissing Marianne Bixby. He'd been texting with his favorite girl in black all throughout the week he'd been out of school, so he knew that even though he was the only one from school who'd been admitted to the hospital with meningitis, nearly everyone else in the school had gotten pumped full of antibiotics by their doctors. He also knew that besides his illness, there had been a rash of other sicknesses: Eddie had gotten a nasty stomach flu, and Kurt, Joe, and the lunch monitor had been stricken by salmonella, so now the school was getting sued. Between the freaking out over a possible meningitis outbreak and the food-poisoning lawsuits, the high school had been featured repeatedly on the local news—and that had temporarily turned Billy's classmates into minor celebrities. "You'll see when you're back tomorrow," Marianne had said earlier, laughing over the phone. "Some of them were such camera whores, chasing after anyone with a microphone. I swear, it's like they think there's a reality TV show in their future, all because Eddie puked, a few guys got food poisoning, and you were recovering from the brink of death!" Now as Billy lay in bed, he tried imagining the sound of Marianne's laughter, but it warped into a scratchy whine, like the sound of a mosquito's hum.

It whined, and the itching grew.

Since coming home—since having the new dream about the Conqueror—Billy had felt a nagging sensation near the base of his skull. He'd also felt uncomfortable and irritable, and at first he'd chalked everything up to his regimen of antibiotics. But as the days passed and the nagging itch didn't go away, he'd started daydreaming about wielding the Bow. Hadn't it felt right in his hands? Hadn't it made him strong? All he had to do was summon the Bow, and everything would change. If he held it, he wouldn't have to worry about Eddie Glass or anyone else, because he would be powerful. Confident. All he had to do was draw back the string and let fly its poisoned arrows. Just wield the Bow, and nothing else would matter.

When Billy had realized what he'd been thinking, he understood what the itching in his mind truly was, and he despaired.

It was the sound of the White calling to him.

And now, as he lay in bed in the midnight darkness of his room, neither the fear of Eddie's fists nor the promise of Marianne's smile could distract him from the urge to pick up the Bow.

Thou art the White Rider. Go thee out unto the world.

I'm supposed to be done with this, he thought as he stared at the ceiling and felt the White crawling around in his head. *Get the Conqueror out of bed and back to work, Death said, and I wouldn't have to be Pestilence. That was the deal.*

But if there was one thing Billy Ballard had learned, it was that deals were rarely what they seemed to be—especially when offered by Horsemen.

He rolled on his side and curled into a ball and wished the whispering in his head would go away.

(*Wishes and horses.*)

He could hear Gramps's voice — the voice of years ago, back when Gramps was still Gramps and the doppelganger in the old man's skin was a future yet to come — and Gramps was telling him that if wishes were horses, dreamers would ride. It had been a favorite catchphrase. When Billy was a child, he'd thought that dreams came to people on horseback. Why else would bad dreams be called nightmares? Dreams arrived on horses, and the horses were made of wishes.

The White whispered to him, but now beneath the sound was a thought. *Horses.* Something about horses, or maybe about the white horse . . .

The thought unraveled, leaving Billy uneasy as he lay in his bed, not thinking about school and not thinking about Marianne and absolutely not listening to the maddening whisper of the White in his mind. Until tonight, it had been manageable. But the itch had blossomed into a full-blown rash, and now it was all he could do to not summon the Bow.

He buried his head under his pillow. *Go away!* he shouted at the White.

The only reply was another nagging urge for him to feel the power of the Bow flow through him.

He threw his pillow on the floor. He rolled over. He rolled the other way. He kicked off his blanket. And still the White just wouldn't shut up. He tried to listen to the silence of nighttime, but it was filled with White noise.

Billy got out of bed and stormed into the bathroom. Standing in front of the sink, he splashed water on his face and stared in the mirror. The cheerful nightlight—a must-have ever since Gramps started wandering out of his bedroom in the middle of the night—threw just enough light on his face for him to see that the white patch in his hair had gotten bigger.

(*Marked.*)

He stared at the white strands, remembered the feeling of being forced out of the Conqueror's memory and out of the White.

(*Marked so's you won't get lost.*)

Had Death grabbed him by his hair and pulled him back into the present? Or had he escaped on his own? He leaned in closer to the mirror as a third possibility loomed: Maybe the Conqueror and Death and War and Famine were all in his head. Maybe he'd lost his mind and just hadn't noticed; after all, how many times could someone get punched and kicked and slammed into lockers before all the physical damage took its toll mentally? Maybe his brain was severely messed up, and a lifetime of antipsychotic meds awaited him.

Death's voice, cool and bemused: *It's amazing to see just how far you people go to lie to yourselves.*

Billy slunk back to his room and cocooned himself within his blanket. *Forget about the Horsemen,* he told himself. *Go to sleep, because tomorrow's going to be a long day.* It was true; whether or not he was making up the Riders of the Apocalypse, he had to return to school in the morning after a week's absence.

He closed his eyes and saw the Ice Cream Man at the edge of the world, standing on a sheet of white.

Billy's eyes snapped open. He could still see the afterimage of the Conqueror, burned behind his gaze as if he'd been staring into the sun.

(*Come here, Billy.*)

Heart slamming in his chest, Billy sat up. The incessant, nagging itch that was the White tugged at him, but now there was a frantic quality to that feeling—less temptation, more desperation. The White wasn't trying to lure him into summoning the Bow; it was begging him to feel the Bow's weight in his hands.

(*Come and see the end of the world.*)

Billy was tired, and scared, and horribly uncertain. But deeper than the exhaustion and the fear and the uncertainty was a simmering rage. He was sick of being shoved into responsibilities too great for him to bear, whether at home with his grandfather or in the world with the Conqueror. More than that, he was sick of the constant sense of terror and dread, sick of the never-ending feeling of his nerves being pulled taut because he never knew where the next punch or kick would come from, never knew if his grandfather would be compliant or violent.

And most of all, he was sick to death of not doing anything about that terror, that dread, sick of allowing other people to control his life, to control *him.* Sick of just taking it. Sick of not fighting back. Sick of his life being in a rut that he'd dug for himself without knowing it.

Billy Ballard was sick of being sick. He'd had enough.

As fury worked its way through him, he thought he heard a girl laughing like fire.

Before he could think better of it, he summoned the Bow. It

appeared with a soft pop of displaced air, hovering in front of his hand, waiting for him to claim it for his own.

Billy took a deep breath, and then he wrapped his fingers around the grip.

A surge of power flooded through him, rocking his head back. Part of him wanted to cower, to run, to hide from that skin-crackling energy that threatened to drown him. But that was the part of him that still believed in sandcastles. Billy said goodbye to that five-year-old boy and opened himself up to the White—

||||||

—and he's working his way along a twisted mass of power knotted together to keep it contained but as he moves he sees the strands are fraying and he knows that when the final piece snaps it will bring the end of everything in a sheet of White because the Conqueror is there he's already there he's standing on top of a mountain of ice and his arms are raised high as he calls the diseases of the world to attention and it doesn't matter what she's saying to him because her words are nothing but a memory and he's concentrating on the sounds of sickness the soothing music of coughs and wheezes and groans the sounds of humanity succumbing to pestilence the sounds that will let him conquer all and save the world . . .

||||||

Nauseated, Billy pulled back. The White still coursed through him, but at the quiet flow of a brook instead of the scream of a waterfall. His fingers still gripped the Bow, but they shook from tiny aftershocks, either from the power itself or from the horror of what he'd just witnessed.

"He's insane," he said aloud.

"It's not his fault."

He looked up to see Death standing by his bedroom door, the outline of his blond hair barely visible in the dark room. Maybe Billy would have been surprised by the Pale Rider's sudden appearance if he weren't in shock over what the White had just shown him. "The Conqueror thinks he's saving the world," he said numbly. "He thinks he can claim humanity through sickness, that he can protect everyone from death. From you," he said, staring at Death.

"Yes," Death agreed.

"I felt it," Billy said, shivering. "I felt what he's doing. It's not colds or allergies or anything small. He wants something permanent. He's going to unleash the plague."

"Yes," Death said again.

"He's going to kill everyone."

"Quite possibly." This said in the same tone that a weather forecaster would use when saying there was a chance of rain.

Wide-eyed, Billy shouted, "You have to *do* something!"

"I can't," said Death, lifting one shoulder in a casual shrug. "Pestilence is not my demesne."

The Bow suddenly weighed a thousand pounds.

Voice hoarse, Billy asked, "Why are you here?"

"You already know the answer, William Ballard."

And he did. "That's why I still have the Bow," he said bitterly, tossing the weapon onto his bed. "So I can stop the Conqueror."

"You have it because the White Rider didn't take it back."

A pause, and then Death added, "It's not like he needs it to spread disease. It's a tool, nothing more. It gives him focus. What he's doing now requires no such focus."

Of course not; destruction was easy. Five-year-old Billy knocked down a sandcastle, and sand soldiers fell to their deaths. He shuddered as he felt the White flowing through him, quiet now, patient. Waiting.

Waiting for him.

"I am not charging you to do anything more," Death said gently. "You can simply live your life."

Billy spluttered, "But the world is going to end!"

A soft laugh, like sand blowing in a desert wind. "The world is *always* about to end, William Ballard. The nature of life is to be always on the brink of death."

Knowing that didn't make Billy feel any better. "You stopped him before," he said desperately. "When he was hiding in the Greenwood. You came for him and told him to ride or die."

"He wasn't doing his job then. Now he is. Granted, he's doing it radically, and the results may not be ideal. But it's still his job." Death flicked a smile. "I'm many things, but not a micromanager."

Billy squeezed his eyes shut as another shudder ran through him. If he were brave, he'd tell Death that sure, he'd stop the Conqueror. But he wasn't brave. He was fifteen, and any hint of confidence had long since been pounded out of him. His spine was already broken; he couldn't bear to have the weight of the world on his shoulders.

"I don't have to do anything," he said.

"No," agreed Death.

"But you want me to."

"What I want has little to do with it. Whether you decide to try to stop the Conqueror is up to you and you alone."

Billy could do nothing. He knew this. He could do nothing and live his life, going through the motions until the very end, whenever that would be. He could pretend that everything was fine, pretend that things would eventually get better while the truth sucked away at him like leeches. Or he could try to do something to change the way things were—risk getting hurt more brutally than ever before, risk failing completely.

He thought of his mom, his grandfather, his absentee dad. He thought of Marianne and her heartbreakingly beautiful smile. He thought of Eddie and Kurt and Joe, of beanpole Sean and the PE instructor and his classmates. He thought of Mita touching his daughter's cheek as he told her goodbye for the final time. He thought of all of these things, and many more, all in the space of a handful of heartbeats.

He could do nothing, but then he would never know if he could have done something.

Billy opened his eyes. "How do I get to the Conqueror?"

In the darkness, Death smiled. "You ride."

CHAPTER 19

FOR THE SECOND TIME . . .

. . . Billy followed the Pale Rider out the front door. He wasn't exactly dressed for world saving, not in his ripped T-shirt and baggy sweatpants and bare feet, but once he'd made the decision to stop the Conqueror, he hadn't wanted to stop to change clothing. He might have lost his conviction while rummaging for a hoodie.

After he shut the door softly behind him, he paused on the front stoop and felt his nerve drain away.

There, in the dark, the pale horse waited. It seemed bigger than before—which might have been possible, given that it was really a horse/car. And Billy could have sworn it was smiling at him. Before he could ask Death if there was another option for the whole riding thing, the horse snorted and stepped aside to reveal a second horse.

Billy's mouth gaped open.

Spotlighted by the moon, the white steed stood quietly. It was a tall animal, but its neck was bent in a way that made it appear smaller. The body was sleek with muscle, and it would have made another horse seem powerful, even majestic. A tremor worked its way along the white steed's frame, there and then gone, like a shimmer of heat in the summer. Its nostrils flared and contracted as it blew out a breath. Half hidden beneath its mane, its ears quivered. Its eyes, though, were what made Billy's breath catch in his throat. Those eyes were pale, leeched of color and hinting of sickness and emptiness. If a cough had a color, it would be the color of those eyes. But as Billy looked deeper, he saw the emotion swirling there, hiding behind the glaze of disease. And as he looked within those eyes, he saw fear, and loneliness, and resignation, as if the horse were waiting for the next betrayal that surely was to come.

Billy Ballard looked into the eyes of the White Rider's steed, and he saw himself.

"Pestilence, meet thy steed," said Death. And then he neighed. It wasn't the sound of a human mimicking a horse. It was truly a horse's neigh, coming from a human mouth. The white steed's ears flickered in response.

If Billy hadn't seen Death's horse turn into a car, he probably would have been more weirded out by the whole thing. "Um," he said. "Hi."

"It's a little skittish," Death said, not quite apologetically. *It's a sad thing when a horse wants for a Rider.*

"Abandonment issues," Billy said softly.

"Yes."

He took a step forward, then stopped. "Um. I'm not sure what to do."

"It's not sure what you're going to do, either," said Death, grinning. "You two are meant for each other."

Billy took a deep breath, then moved forward again, taking one slow, exaggerated step. He placed his hand out in front of him, palm up, the way he'd approach a dog or a cat. "Hey," he said, "I'm Billy." He paused. "And I just introduced myself to a horse."

The white horse nickered softly.

"It said hello," Death translated. "Actually, it said, 'Please don't hurt me.' But you get the idea. It's trying to be polite."

The pale steed snorted, loudly.

"What?" Death said. "It is. Saying 'Don't hurt me' is considered good manners for many species. Just, apparently, not for transmogrifiers."

The pale horse snorted again.

"Now that," said Death, "isn't polite in *any* language."

Billy took another slow step toward the white horse, keeping his hands out and his voice steady. "I'm completely terrified right now," he said to the steed. "Horses scare me."

The white horse blinked its rheumy eyes.

"I had a bad dream when I was a kid," said Billy, moving slowly to the horse's left. "You were in it. Well. A white horse was in it. Maybe it wasn't you exactly. But it was the Conqueror's horse." He was close enough now to reach out and touch the horse's neck, just slightly, brushing his fingertips along the coat. He felt the steed shiver beneath his hand, and he knew that it was about three seconds away from bolting. So he stopped where he was and kept his hand resting gently on the horse's neck. "I wanted to ride that horse so badly," said Billy, "so I made a really stupid deal."

The horse still trembled, but the sense of panic slowly diminished.

"I agreed to wear the Conqueror's Crown, just so I could get a ride on the white horse. And then everything changed. The Conqueror scared me, and I ran." Billy sighed. "I never rode the horse. I ran away and didn't get what I'd bargained for. I was a kid, but I guess that doesn't matter. And I thought it was all just a dream. But I guess that doesn't matter, either. Since then, horses have scared me."

Beneath his fingers, the trembling slowed.

"Maybe you're scared too," he said. "You've been doing everything you're supposed to do, but your Rider keeps leaving you. Maybe you think you're doing something wrong. That it's you. Maybe you think you're getting what you deserve. That you're not worth having a Rider who returns to you and trusts you and depends on you. But it's not you," said Billy, stroking the steed's neck. "It's not your fault that your Rider lost his mind. You're a good steed."

There was one last shiver, and then the white horse stood still as Billy continued to move his hand over its broad neck.

"Do you have a name?" Billy asked.

"Horses don't use names the way that humans do," said Death. "It's the white steed. That's its definition and its purpose."

"The good white steed," Billy murmured. "A very good horse. One that's worthy of a good Rider."

The white horse's ears quivered, perhaps by way of thanks.

"I'm still scared," Billy admitted, patting the horse's neck. And maybe you are too. Let's be scared together."

The steed blew out a breath through its nostrils and knelt down. Billy hoisted himself up until he was seated on the horse's back, and as the steed rose to its full height, he threaded his fingers through the white mane and trusted that he wouldn't fall—and, more important, he trusted that the steed wouldn't let him fall.

"We can do this," he whispered.

"Return to the White Rider," said Death, punctuating the words with a whinny.

The white horse snorted, or maybe coughed, and then it leapt into the sky and rocketed away, with Billy clinging to it like a tick.

|||||

Billy held on, white-knuckled, his mouth clamped firmly shut so there wouldn't be any chance of him freaking out—or, loosely translated, screaming in terror. He wasn't one for roller coasters on his best day. Riding atop a flying horse that left jet planes in its wake? Gah. He was about three minutes away from leaning over and vomiting into the nighttime sky. How's that for an excuse to stay home from school? *Billy couldn't make it today because he puked his guts out over the Appalachians.* He swallowed thickly and tried not to look down as the white steed soared over the mountains.

Breathe in, breathe out. Just like that. Breathe in, breathe out.

At least the air quality was nice. A bit cold, but he wasn't about to complain. The last thing he wanted to do was upset the horse. Actually, the last thing he wanted to do was plummet to his death, but at the moment, that went hand in hand with him not upsetting the horse. And that meant he had to be calm. He had a feeling—or maybe it was a nudge from the White—that the horse could pick up on his emotions; if he panicked, the horse would too. And that wouldn't be good for him or the horse—but especially not for him, here above the clouds. So he breathed in and breathed out, and he pressed his legs against the horse's sides and forced himself to slightly

—*slightly*—loosen his death grip on the steed's mane.

They flew on. Or, more accurately, the horse flew, and Billy hung on.

He closed his eyes and hummed Green Day songs, his voice lost in the wind. At one point, he thought the horse was harmonizing, but that would have been crazy. And then he remembered that he was on a flying horse, on the way to stop the Horseman of all disease from destroying the world, and he decided that crazy was relative.

They cruised in the wind, buffered by songs and slowly learning to trust each other, until they hit a bump. Specifically, Billy suddenly jerked, and the horse floundered. For a heart-stopping moment, the two plummeted in free fall until the white steed shook its head and began to gallop in the air once more, and they quickly steadied. Billy, sweating and breathless, patted the horse's neck. "Good horse," he croaked. "Good horse."

The thing that had tugged at Billy's consciousness hooked him again, but this time, he was ready for it and didn't flinch. Despite his fear of heights, he looked down at the world below and saw a massive area of greenish yellow—a sickly color, like infected mucus. The landscape stretched out, leading in one direction to a palette of sandy browns and in the other to a mountain range. They were too high up for him to make out any living things on the surface. That didn't include a glimpse of red whisking past the mountaintops—fire dancing with the wind, flaring brilliantly then winking down to nothing.

And he knew, without knowing how he knew, that he'd just witnessed the path of War.

In his head, he felt the White . . . shift. Billy understood that it was a reaction to the Red Rider, but he had no idea what it meant. And he also didn't have time to puzzle over it. Maybe, once he stopped the Conqueror from infecting the entire world with plague, he'd go into therapy and figure out the relationship between disease and destruction.

Okay, maybe not.

He leaned into the steed and pressed his legs a little tighter, but not so tight as to spook the animal. The horse obliged by pouring on the speed. In a blink, the landmass and the Red Rider were behind them, nothing but memories.

We are the Riders of the Apocalypse, and we herald the end of everything!

Billy gritted his teeth. No, that War, the War from Mita's past, wanted to see the end of the world, eagerly awaited the final battle that would annihilate every living thing. That War reveled in the thought of the Apocalypse. But the girl in the alleyway, the one who'd helped Billy up after Eddie Glass had jumped him, that girl in red was not the same War. Riders changed over time. He thought briefly of the Black Rider, first of the exotic woman by the docks of Alexandria and then of the pale, proper woman in the depths of the Greenwood, and he remembered how she'd called him King White.

"You have no right to use that name with me," snarled the man who would be Robert Hode.

"But I do," said Famine. *"The spirit of the Black Rider dwells within me, and through it I've seen how she—how I—used to be with you."*

The people who were Horsemen changed over the years, but the thing that made them Horsemen—the spirit, according to Famine—remained the same. So was the girl in red who'd helped him just a different version of the brutal woman in armor who enjoyed causing pain?

Billy felt the White crawling in his head, and he forced himself not to shiver. It didn't matter, he told himself. He was going to stop the Conqueror and make him take back the Bow, and then he'd be done with all of this. White and red and black would go back to being only colors.

Under him, the horse flew on, and Billy felt a stab of guilt. Maybe the White Rider would return to his senses and take care of the horse. Yes, maybe.

Wishes and horses, said Gramps.

The white steed will be all right, he wished, he hoped—no, he insisted. The horse would be all right. They would save the world, and the white horse would have a Rider it could depend on.

Wishes and horses.

All too soon, Billy felt his stomach drop, signaling that they had begun their descent. To keep himself from worrying over what would happen once they landed, he risked looking down.

Floating on the wide-open ocean was a vast expanse of green-tinged white, filled with cracks of dark blue that threaded the surface like veins. As they circled down, he saw that the ground was littered with ridges and bumps, and he thought of the White Rider's melting face. Closer now, Billy was able to make out ponds of turquoise and aquamarine, the colors a brilliant contrast to the surrounding bed of white. There was a splash of ink against the snow-capped ice, and as the white steed glided down, the darkness pulled into the shape of a horse.

A black horse.

They touched down, and the steed of Famine met them as they landed. The horse twined its neck around the white's in an equine hug, and the two animals exchanged blows of breath that sounded almost intimate.

Over the horses' greetings, Billy heard a woman's voice rising and falling, imploring. Begging.

As if in response, the White scratched at Billy's mind, urging him to hurry.

Right, he thought. *I'm hurrying. And not at all panicking.*

He pulled himself off the white horse's back, and his bare feet landed in snow that he couldn't feel. He was breathing too fast, and he was fairly certain he was a candidate for cardiac arrest based on how his heart was pounding, but at least he was standing on his own two feet. Around him was a land of white on white, a place of eternal winter. Snow drifts piled on top of a sheet of ice, stretching as far as he could see. His breath frosted, and he wondered why he wasn't cold.

As if Death would let him come all this way just to die from hypothermia. That would be completely lame.

He peered up a slope that was splotched with hoof prints. Clearly, the black horse had made its way down the incline the traditional equestrian way. Maybe it had been too tired to fly. There was a question his math teacher would love: How many calories does an Apocalyptic steed burn when it flies across the Western Hemisphere in ten minutes? Answer: lots.

The woman's voice rose once more, and now Billy could make out a word: *Please.* And then he heard nothing at all.

No time for fear.

He set off at a run, crunching through the snow fast enough that his PE instructor would have been impressed. Yet another thing for him to consider, should he survive the upcoming encounter: try out for the varsity track team. He grinned madly as he worked his way up the slope. *Save the world in under two minutes—go!*

His mouth set in a rictus, he loped over a swell of ice and snow at the top of the hill . . . and came to a stumbling halt.

There, on a flat expanse of snow framed by icy knolls, stood the Ice Cream Man, caught in profile. An arctic gust snatched his long hair and the ends of his coat, slapping at him furiously. His head was thrown back as if in ecstasy, and his arms stretched high above as if he were orchestrating the movement of the wind. A nimbus of filth surrounded him in an aura of frozen dust, and he stood in the center of a cesspool of disease, disease that was invisible to Billy's eyes but strong enough to make his skin crawl.

The White pulled at him, demanded that he move forward, but the sight of the shadow at the Conqueror's feet rooted him to the spot. A woman in black sprawled on the ground, unconscious or worse. Billy stared at her, transfixed by the spill of black-clad limbs against the snow, and he thought of Marianne, his Marianne, telling him that he was a hero, and imagined her crushed by the madness of the White Rider.

A surge of fury, white hot and blinding, burned away any vestiges of panic. "Stop!" he shouted, his voice echoing across the frozen wasteland.

The White Rider paused, then pivoted to face him. Beneath strands of greasy black hair, the silver Crown gleamed on his pockmarked brow. The Conqueror grinned, a thing of stillborn dreams and bloody nightmares. "Come here," he said with a bubbling laugh. "Come here and see the end of the world."

And then, still grinning madly, he unleashed the White upon Billy Ballard.

CHAPTER 20

BILLY SAW THE FLARE OF WHITE . . .

. . . around the Conqueror's hands, saw those hands come together and aim right at him, and for a moment he was tempted to take it, to roll with the punches because that's what he always did—just tense up for the punch in the gut, the kick when you're down; let the worst happen because soon enough, it will pass.

(*It won't last*, a man's voice insisted.)

And then Billy's survival instinct kicked into overdrive. With a yelp, he threw himself to the snowy ground just before something careened over him. He sensed it as it zoomed by, understood with still-unfamiliar senses that it was a bolt of pure White, a thing of disease given form as it soared past. His arm had gone up automatically to shield his head, and now, down on the ground with his face in the snow, he felt something settle over the bare skin of his arm, brushing against him like ashes.

Five-year-old Billy sang, *Ashes, ashes, we all fall down!*

Fifteen-year-old Billy ignored the playful singsong and scrambled to his feet—just in time to see the White Rider take aim. He dove to the right, barely avoiding another blast.

"The end of the world," said the Conqueror, his voice thick with laughter and menace. "The end of *everything*."

His arm stinging, his heart pounding, Billy desperately

wished he were anywhere but there. *Wishes and horses,* Gramps would have said. *Wishes and horses.*

|||||||

The white steed danced in place, eager to move. Even the closeness of Famine's horse couldn't soothe it; the black steed nickered softly and tried to nuzzle against it, but the white horse moved out of reach. It didn't want to be soothed. It sensed its Rider—both of its Riders, the man and the boy—somewhere above, somewhere amid all the White.

Two Riders.

The notion made the horse giddy. Two! Two Riders to carry; two Riders to belong to. It wanted to canter in a circle and give voice to its joy. Two Riders meant the steed would not be left alone anymore, would not be overlooked or ignored—would not be left waiting as the seasons came and went and the world grew ever older, waiting for a Rider to pat its neck and climb atop its back, ready to be borne across the sky in a wave of White. Two Riders meant that the horse was still needed.

Yes. Two Riders meant that the white steed still *mattered.*

The horse snorted with happiness and impatience. It wanted to prance up the snow-covered hill and present itself to its Riders, show them that it was a good steed and would do whatever either one of them, the man or the boy, asked of it. Fly to the highest mountain? Cross the ocean faster than thought? Go deep beneath the earth where the blind things crawled? Whatever its Rider—its *Riders*—wanted, it would do.

The good steed, the boy had called it. *The good white horse.*

The horse jumped in the air and flipped head over hooves.

It would prove itself to the boy, to the man, and it would never be alone again!

As it landed on the icy ground, a pale hand patted its neck fondly.

"You *are* a good steed," Death said, speaking perfect Horse. "He was absolutely right about that."

If horses could blush, the white steed would have been pink.

"Go on, then," said Death. "Present yourself. I bet they'll both be genuinely happy to see you."

The white steed snorted its thanks and charged up the hill.

||||||

Billy, still on the snow-covered ground, looked up to see the White Rider looming over him. Cracked lips twisted into a manic grin, revealing rotted teeth; black eyes shone brightly with either sickness or madness. Billy stared into those darkly gleaming eyes, felt the heat of the Conqueror's insanity, and realized that he was utterly, completely terrified.

"Come watch the end of the world," the Ice Cream Man said with a giggle. His white-gloved hands began to glow, giving them an aura of dusty moonlight. "It arrives on a sheet of white."

Billy felt his bladder threaten to let go. He opened his mouth to speak sense, to beg for mercy, to say something, even if it was just noise, but then a whinny pealed across the ice and snow.

The White Rider's head jerked to the side, and Billy watched as something caught between delight and regret played across the man's ruined face. "Hello," he said, his voice brimming with apology. "Did I forget you again?"

A snort, or maybe a sneeze, and then the white horse trotted into view. It looked bigger than Billy remembered, which was crazy because he'd just ridden with it halfway across the world, but he couldn't deny that the white steed seemed bigger somehow. Taller. Or maybe Billy's perception was skewed by relief, because damned if the White Rider hadn't just forgotten all about him. The Conqueror reached out to the horse, murmuring things that Billy couldn't hear, and the horse bowed its snowy head as its Rider ran white-gloved fingers through its mane. There was a contented sigh, and Billy had no idea if it came from the man or the horse.

Right. He knew a cue when he got one.

Heart careening in his chest, he pulled himself up as silently as he could, paused to make sure that the Conqueror wasn't looking, then he lunged for the nearest hillock. Once behind the icy hill, he squatted there, limbs shaking with adrenaline as he strained to hear if the Ice Cream Man was coming after him. He caught snatches of the Conqueror's phlegmy voice, of the white steed's blows of air, and Billy decided that for the moment, he was safe.

Well. As safe as he could be with the Conqueror about to summon enough plague to blanket the world. Billy let out an exhausted sigh. The White Rider really was going to kill everyone.

He thought he heard Death's bemused voice: *The nature of life is to be always on the brink of death.*

No, that was just philosophical bullshit. The nature of life was to *live*, period. He was only fifteen, but even he knew that. Maybe Death didn't care if the entire world went up in a sneeze of White, but Billy sure did.

"You walk like a man," Mita said, "but beneath the skin, you're inhuman."

And Death replied, "I never claimed to be human."

The Riders are human, Billy thought as he hid behind the icy knoll, *with the Horseman spirit or soul or whatever inside of them. But Death . . . Death isn't human.*

I don't think he ever was.

With that uneasy thought, Billy decided to stop pondering the nature of Death—if thinking about the nature of life was just philosophical bullshit, thinking about the nature of death was just grim. His left arm itched madly; when he glanced down at it, he wasn't surprised to see a score of hives clustered along the length of his forearm, staining the flesh sunburned red. And now that he was focusing on his arm, he realized that his armpit was horrifically sore. As was his neck. He remembered the feeling of something like ashes or maybe snowflakes landing on his exposed skin after the White Rider had tried to blast him. Whatever disease the Conqueror was throwing around, Billy clearly was allergic to it.

Yeah, I'd say I'm allergic to plague. His stomach roiled unhappily, and he fought down the urge to be sick. *Oh my God—do I have the plague?*

His breath started to come in shallow bursts, and he desperately tried to get it under control before it bloomed into hyperventilation. But the White whispered to him, told him that yes, the plague was festering inside of him, that he'd skipped the incubation period and gone straight to bubonic symptoms, and that at this rate he'd hit septicemic plague and then pneumonic plague in a matter of minutes. And then he'd get to see Death again, and maybe he could ask him directly about his nature.

He wanted to throw back his head and howl that it wasn't fair, but that wasn't going to change anything. He had the plague, a preview of what was coming for everyone, and if he didn't do anything about it, he was going to die.

Don't panic, he told himself, clenching his teeth. *Can't think if you panic. Now. Calm. Down.*

It took him more than a minute to wrestle his breathing into something close to normal, and by that point his head had started throbbing and he was pretty sure he'd spiked a fever. He leaned his head against the icy knoll and tried to think.

The Conqueror hit me with disease before, and I fought back. I healed myself.

But that had been in the White, floating above a pool of memories. This was the real world. Real disease. When Death had pulled him out of the White, he'd been slammed with bacterial meningitis and was in the hospital for a small slice of eternity.

Yeah, well, that option's off the table. Sweat popped on his brow, and his teeth chattered with sudden chill. If he didn't fight off the infection, he would die. Period.

His eyes slipped closed, and he felt the White slithering in his mind. Desperate, he opened himself up to it . . .

||||||

. . . and he feels the yersinia pestis *inside of him, evading and attacking his white blood cells, feels the bacteria spreading through his bloodstream and infecting his liver and kidneys, decimating his lymph nodes, but now the White is working in him, working with him and creating an antibiotic, one that inhibits bacterial growth,*

giving his white blood cells the chance to reform and swarm and now the yersinia pestis *is floundering as the white blood cells soldier up and destroy every invading bacterium and his ravaged organs begin to regenerate . . .*

||||||

In the arctic wasteland, behind a hill of ice and snow, the White saved Billy Ballard's life.

||||||

The red horse kept its distance from the others. Even though its Rider was no longer at odds with her companions, old habits died hard.

On the flat expanse of pancake ice, War stood by the Pale Rider's side. Though their forms did not touch, their shadows intertwined, black on black, in a smoky caress.

"Knew you'd come," Death said cheerfully.

She smiled, and that slow motion of her lips hinted at many things. "The White Rider divided, and the world on the brink of destruction. How could I stay away?"

"I could set my watch by you."

"You don't have a watch." Her smile broadened into a grin. "An hourglass, maybe . . ."

"Please, not another joke about a scythe . . ."

She mimed zipping her mouth shut.

A pause, as they listened to the sounds of the boy healing and the man summoning doom.

"I like him," War said.

Even though she hadn't specified whether she meant the boy
or the man, Death smiled and nodded. "Me too."

"You like everyone."

"Well, yes."

The two shared a quiet laugh, their voices mingling in perfect harmony.

A longer pause, and then War asked, "What of Famine?"

"What of her? She's not mine. Not yet, anyway. She will be
soon enough."

The Red Rider slid him a look. "That's cold, even for you."

"Eh, just practical." A shrug. "Everyone comes to me eventually. It's the journey that makes it interesting."

"Such a people person!"

He flashed her a grin. "My best quality."

"Oh," said War, sliding her gloved hand into his pale one, "I
can think of others that are better."

||||||

Shaking with exhaustion and the aftereffects of adrenaline,
Billy opened his eyes. He was still leaning against the hillock,
and part of him wanted to just curl up and sleep for a month.
But he didn't have time.

Time. How much time did he lose?

Where was the White Rider?

He cocked his head and listened, but he didn't hear anything over the sound of his own heavy breathing. Had the
white steed's appearance knocked some sense into the Conqueror? Maybe the two had flown off for some Rider/steed
bonding. Maybe Billy didn't have to save the world after all—

which would be fine with him, thank you very much, because what he really wanted was to sleep. And eat. Maybe eat while he was sleeping.

Up, he told himself. *Sleep when you're dead. Which will be soon, if the Conqueror gets his way.*

Suppressing a groan, he forced himself to his feet. God, he felt like he'd been pureed in a blender. He swayed for a moment, teetered on the point of collapse, then forced himself to stand tall. Okay, good start. *A* for effort. Trying not to think about how wrecked he was, he peered around the side of the knoll —and then he quickly ducked his head back. One glance had been enough to show him that the White Rider was once again standing on the icy ground, his arms up and his head thrown back, a sickly aura surrounding him in filthy white, purity gone corrupt. By his booted feet, the Black Rider hadn't moved. The white steed was nearby, waiting as its Rider worked.

For the Conqueror was, indeed, working. Now that Billy wasn't distracted by his exhaustion, he sensed the slow, steady building of pressure, as if the world were preparing for a massive storm. But this would be a storm of disease, a tempest from which there would be no shelter.

In Billy's head, the White churned violently.

He needed to do something—but what? He could fight back disease within his own body, but on a global scale? Death had told him that it was the Crown that made the White Rider the Conqueror of health and disease; all Billy had was the Bow.

His eyes widened. *The Bow!*

Fight fire with fire, the saying went. Well, he could fight White with White.

He held out his hand and commanded the Bow to appear.

It did, with a soft pop of displaced air, hovering for a moment before his fingers closed around it. The White surged in his mind; power danced along his skin. The warmth of confidence flooded him, spiced his blood and made him stand taller. He was Pestilence, the White Rider, and he wielded his Bow.

More than that, he was Billy Ballard, and it was time for him to make his stand.

He stepped away from the safety of the hillock. Raising the Bow before him like a staff, he called out, "Mita! Stop!"

The Conqueror's head jerked, and then he turned toward the sound. His gaze fixed on Billy. This time, there was no sign of either madness or acceptance in his eyes. Billy watched recognition dawn, quickly followed by rage. Maybe the Ice Cream Man hadn't understood who Billy was before, when he hadn't been wielding the Bow, but now there was no question that the Conqueror recognized Pestilence. And he clearly didn't like what he saw.

Cracked lips peeled back in a sneer. *"You."*

"Me," Billy agreed.

The White Rider bellowed, the sound of his wrath thundering over the ice and snow, filling the white-streaked air. And then he attacked.

CHAPTER 21

THIS . . .

. . . is Billy Ballard, fifteen years old, standing on an icy peak as
the Conqueror bears down on him—

. . . and this is Billy Ballard, five years old, two weeks before
he meets the White Rider for the first time; he's in pre-K and
he's sitting next to a girl with black hair, and she's crying because her crayon broke and so he gives her his crayon, and it's
not a big deal because he's done coloring anyway and besides,
he doesn't want her to cry anymore and so he gives her a crayon
and in return she gives him a radiant smile that he'll treasure in
his deepest heart for years to come—

. . . and this is Billy Ballard, six and lousy at baseball; he's so
bad, in fact, that his father stops coming to the games, and not
even six months later his father will go away and never come
back—

. . . and this is Billy Ballard, age seven, packing away his
beloved Cookie Monster plush doll because he knows how the
world works now, that it's a place where dads are happier without their children and so Billy is too old for toys and never
mind how he's crying as he seals the box—

. . . and this is eight-year-old Billy Ballard, shrieking for joy
as he pedals his new bicycle and his grandfather waves him on
as he tears down the road—

. . . and this, too, is Billy Ballard, nine and on the ground, crying because the biggest kid in third grade, Eddie Glass, shoved him so hard that Billy banged his knee when he landed; in three minutes, Billy will discover that the Law of the Playground is much stronger than the promise of justice, that teachers don't see everything and even if they do, they may not do anything about it —

. . . this is Billy Ballard, learning what it's like to be the one who nobody wants on the team —

. . . and this is Billy Ballard, getting yelled at by his grandfather for no reason, no reason at all, and he's afraid to tell his mom that Gramps has been acting weird and forgetful and violent, afraid to say that Gramps is scaring him —

. . . and this is Billy Ballard, bringing home another hundred on his test and getting a huge hug from his mother, who tells him that if he keeps working hard, he can do anything he puts his mind to; in four years, he'll still be working hard so that there will be a chance at a full scholarship to a college far, far away from home, far enough for him to leave his life behind —

. . . and this is Billy Ballard in seventh grade, picking up his books and papers from the hallway floor and ignoring the way his face burns as Eddie laughs at him, and when he's done gathering his things he Keeps His Head Down and shuffles off to class, pretending he doesn't hear the mocking jeers of the other students —

. . . and this is Billy Ballard, pleading a stomachache so he can stay home from school, because Gramps has been acting almost normal and Eddie has teamed up with Kurt and Joe to make Billy's school life unbearable — . . .

. . . and this is Billy Ballard, eating pizza with Marianne and noticing, for the first time, the way the sunlight hits her black hair and gives her the most amazing blue highlights, and she's laughing at something and the sound of her laughter is like music—

. . . and this is Billy Ballard sitting on his bed as his mom explains that Gramps has Alzheimer's, and Billy says the word to himself again and again as he feels the world slowly crash down around him; in six months' time, his mom will have a second job to help pay for the medical bills and Billy will start playing babysitter because his grandfather can't be left alone—

. . . and this is Billy Ballard getting the snot pounded out of him, again, and Billy is just taking it because he knows it will be over soon, real soon, and if he just protects his head and stays curled into a ball, Eddie will get bored and stomp away and then Billy can go on with his life—

. . . and now Billy Ballard is standing on an ice peak as the Conqueror bears down on him, and Billy clenches his fist and stands his ground, because this is Billy Ballard who has had enough of taking it, enough of getting hurt and Keeping His Head Down, enough of being a walking target.

This is Billy Ballard, fifteen and finally fighting back.

|||||||

He saw the blast coming, but he didn't move to avoid it. Empowered by the White, Billy positioned the Bow in front of him like a shield and planted his feet. The blow slammed into the polished wood, and Billy's entire body vibrated from the impact, but he himself was unhurt. In his hands, the black unstrung bow gleamed.

Billy had a moment to think, *That worked!* But then another bolt of disease was already headed toward him. His arm shook as the Bow absorbed the second assault, and his teeth clicked together hard enough that his tongue would have been severed. The wood now glowed slightly, as if the White were illuminating it from within.

The Conqueror roared. Spittle flying as he swore blistering curses, he leveled another attack.

Billy grunted as the blast hit the Bow. Once again, it absorbed the impact; the weapon was warm in his hand now, and smoke wafted from either end. Probably not a good sign; it might not be able to withstand another onslaught.

His turn.

Chin high, Billy nocked an arrow of disease and drew back the bowstring. This time, he could actually see the arrow and the string outlined in white fire as he took aim—an aftereffect from absorbing all of the White, perhaps, or maybe Billy was finally looking at the Bow properly. It was a majestic weapon, worthy of fiery arrows and a string that rivaled an aurora borealis; the Bow belonged in the hands of a warrior or a hero. Or a king.

Thinking of Famine calling the Conqueror *King White* —Famine, who was now nothing more than a broken doll discarded on the ground—Billy Ballard let fly his poisoned arrow.

His aim was true. The shaft slammed into the Conqueror's stomach and faded upon contact. Even as the White Rider snarled with fury, Billy shot a second arrow, and then a third, a fourth, one-two-three-four, all with the smooth precision of a master archer. The Bow's power had awoken Billy's confidence, and he welcomed it without reservation. They worked together, the White and Pestilence, as he unleashed disease.

Like Billy, the Conqueror didn't try to get out of the way. Each arrow struck home, boring into his torso and chest, but instead of infecting the man, the attacks merely enraged him.

"Your fault," he roared, throwing his arm back as if to pitch a fastball. "All your fault!"

The White rocketed at Billy, who barely got the Bow braced in time for impact. The bolt slammed into the black wood hard enough to knock him backwards.

"All of this, because of you!" the Conqueror screeched, hurling another blast, one that sent Billy to his knees. "You tricked me into leaving the Greenwood!"

Billy, off-balance and furious, shouted, "*You* don't get to be mad at *me! You're* the one who tricked me!" The words flew out of his mouth, desperate for freedom after simmering in venomous hatred for ten years, and he couldn't control his tongue even if he tried. "You tricked me when I was a kid, got me to agree to something I didn't understand! Grownups are supposed to protect kids, *but you betrayed me!*"

And the White Rider paused in his fury.

Billy clambered to his feet and nocked an arrow. "You betrayed me," he said again, "and I didn't even know you." He let fly.

The Conqueror didn't move as the arrow tore into him. He stared owlishly at Billy, peering at his face. "Yes," he said slowly in his phlegm-filled voice. "I remember you, Billy Ballard."

"You stole my future," Billy spat, aiming another arrow.

"And you sealed my fate." The Conqueror let out a bitter laugh. "You should have left me in the Greenwood."

"And you should have left me alone to play in the sandbox."

"Should, could, would." Another laugh, this one tinged with madness. "Do you like the Bow, little boy Pestilence? Do you think you'll grow into it?"

"I don't want it," Billy said tightly, still aiming at the Conqueror's chest. "I never wanted any of this."

"And I don't want the world to end," said the White Rider. "And yet here we are."

"We're here because of *you*," shouted Billy. "Don't you see that? What you're doing now is going to kill everyone!"

And it was; Billy still felt the pressure of the White all around him, felt the bacteria and viruses and germs and carcinogens tainting the air, waiting impatiently to be released upon the world. The Conqueror might not have delivered his plague-o-gram yet, but he'd stuffed and sealed the envelope.

"Little boy Pestilence," laughed the Conqueror. "You still don't understand. I've seen the end of the world, and it arrives on a sheet of white. This sheet," he said, stomping his foot on the snow-covered ground.

"Because of you," Billy said. His fingers ached from keeping the tension in the bowstring, but he didn't want to fire, not if he could keep the Conqueror talking, maybe get him to see that what he was trying to do couldn't possibly work.

"Because of *him*," said the Conqueror, his voice dropping to a hiss. "The world echoes his mood. When it warms, he is content with his lot. But when it grows colder, then despair, little boy Pestilence! Despair!"

So this is what it's like to talk to a crazy person. "You're not making sense," Billy said.

"The world is nothing more than a reflection of his soul. And his soul is black and twisted and cold, so very cold. A sheet of ice." The White Rider stomped his foot once more. "He gives everything life, and life begets all evils in the world."

Billy was completely lost. "What are you talking about?"

"All of this," the Conqueror said, motioning to the land and beyond, "is because of Death."

Billy stared at the White Rider, and he couldn't think of a single thing to say. How did he convince an insane Horseman that he was, in fact, insane?

"Death is here, right now," said the Conqueror.

If only, Billy thought. His arms had begun to shake from the pressure of the bowstring, so he finally removed the arrow. It vanished as soon as it stopped touching the string. Maybe it popped into Pestilence's quiver, wherever that was. Billy didn't know, and he didn't care; he was still working to keep the Bow itself raised in front of him. He didn't dare lower it, in case the Conqueror decided to attack him again, but it was getting harder to keep his arms raised.

"Death is in all things," the Conqueror continued, babbling now, his words like wasps in Billy's ears. "He is the alpha and the omega, and we exist only on his whim. And he is done with whimsy! I've seen the end of the world," shouted the White Rider, pointing to the icy ground, "and it begins with a sheet of white!"

"It begins with *you*," Billy said through gritted teeth. "But you can stop it, Mita. Call back the White."

A pause, and for a moment, Billy thought that his plea had actually worked. But then the Conqueror said, "No."

"Call it back!"

"No."

Brandishing the Bow, Billy demanded once more, "Mita! Call back the White!"

The Conqueror grinned hugely; on his brow, the Crown gleamed. "No!"

The word echoed over the frozen wasteland, slowly fading to the whine of arctic wind. The silence stretched taut; around them, disease pressed against the air, eager to fly free.

In Billy's unsteady hands, the Bow waivered. *What do I do now?*

He was at a loss. He couldn't stop the Conqueror; Billy knew that now, as surely as he knew his own name. The arrows were useless — after all, how could sickness affect the one person who controlled all health? Horror clutched at his heart, squeezing it in panic, and dread filled his stomach like acid. He'd failed. He'd come all this way, had pushed himself further than he'd ever gone, and it was all for nothing.

A small, still voice whispered: *Focus.*

Alone and afraid, Billy focused. He gripped the Bow tightly, felt the weight in his hands, how evenly balanced it was, how solid . . . and in that moment, he had an idea, born of equal parts revelation and desperation.

He lowered his weapon and closed the distance between himself and the mad king. His voice pitched low, he said, "Your daughter would be so disappointed."

Rage warped the Conqueror's pox-riddled face, twisting it into a grotesque lump of wax. "This is *for* my daughter," he shrieked to the white-tinged sky, "for *all* daughters and sons! This is so that no one need ever die again! Sickness will take

them all, and then I'll save them, each and every one of them!"
He raised his arms high, urging the plague to go forth. "The
world will be bathed in White!"

Billy brought the Bow over his shoulder and lunged forward, swinging the Bow, going for the home run that would
win the game. It connected solidly against the Conqueror's
head, denting his skull and knocking the Crown askew. With a
shout that would have done War proud, Billy swung the Bow
back again, smashing it against the White Rider's misshapen
head. The Bow splintered and cracked—and the Crown flew
free. The silver circlet landed in the snow with an unceremonious thump.

The Ice Cream Man blinked, then raised his shaking his
hands to touch the doughy mass of his bare forehead.

"Oh," he breathed, a radiant smile softening the features of
his ravaged face. "Plums."

And then Mita, king of Phrygia, crumbled to ash.

CHAPTER 22

THE WHITE RIDER IS DEAD . . .

. . . Billy thought wildly, staring at the pile of ashes that had
been a man. *The Bow is broken and the White Rider is dead and
I killed him, I killed him, oh God I killed him and I want to go
home now. Please, can I go home now?*

Around him, the White howled.

The shattered Bow slipped from his numb fingers and
landed in the snow with a soft *pfft*. Billy barely noticed; he was
still staring wide-eyed where Mita had died, staring at all that
remained of him.

Ashes, ashes, sang five-year-old Billy, *We all! Fall! Down!*

Fifteen-year-old Billy sank to his knees. He'd stopped the
Conqueror—*Not stopped, no, I killed him, killed him dead*—
but it wasn't enough. Or maybe it would have been enough,
but he had run out of time. Even though the Conqueror was
dead, Billy still felt the press of sickness upon the air, sensed
each bacterium, each virus, felt the rising wave of disease swell
higher and higher, a crescendo of pestilence that would drown
the world.

His stomach lurched, and Billy vomited noisily on the snow.
You can simply live your life.

Could he walk away now, knowing what would happen if
he did? Could he go home and pretend that the world wasn't
about to be blanketed with a plague of Biblical proportion?

The world is always about to end, William Ballard.

Maybe. But if he didn't do anything about it, he wouldn't be able to live with himself.

He let out a croaking laugh as he wiped his mouth. Granted, he wouldn't have to live with himself for very long, what with the world ending. Cold comfort, that. He stared at the silver circlet, which lay upon a bed of ice and snow. It looked tarnished, as if its contact with the Conqueror had stained it.

"Will you wear the Crown, Billy Ballard?"

Billy said, *"A crown. Like a king?"*

"This Crown," said the Ice Cream Man, motioning to his forehead.

A spasm wracked him, and he shuddered violently. He didn't want to do this.

"I don't want to be Pestilence!"

"It matters little what you want. The Conqueror tricked you into agreeing to wear the Crown when the time came. That time is now."

No, he didn't want this at all. But it was his penance and his promise. He'd already made his choice—first when he was five and he let the Ice Cream Man tempt him with visions of white horses; and again the other week when he followed Death out of his house because the Pale Rider had asked for Billy's help; and a third time, just a little while ago, when Death had once again come calling.

In the snow, the silver band winked.

"I can't give you the White Rider's Crown," Death said, *"because he wears it still. It would have made you the conqueror of health and sickness alike."*

No, Death couldn't give him the Crown. But Billy could take it.

He pulled himself to his feet and stumbled over to the circlet that would change him forever. He wasn't thinking of his mom or his absentee dad, wasn't thinking of his grandfather —not the Gramps of the past, not the old man of the present. He wasn't thinking of Marianne. No, Billy was thinking of a blue plush doll, worn with age and love, long packed away in a crate in his attic.

Saying goodbye to his childhood for the last time, he took a deep breath and reached for the Crown. It was a plain silver band, thin and unassuming, and it was surprisingly light in his hands.

Diseased air pressed down on him, squeezing him, making him dizzy. The plague raged within and all around, fighting against its cage, ready to tear its way free.

Billy Ballard placed the Crown upon his brow—

—and the power sears him scorches him burns him alive it's alive in him in all things it's everything it's light it's light it's the White and it hurts oh God it hurts him so much and he can't think past the pain he can't control it can't wield it can't use it and all he wants is to make the pain stop stop stop—

—and light erupted from his skin, fountaining from his pores, his eyes, his mouth. He couldn't take it, couldn't stop it, couldn't hold it back, though he tried frantically; it was like trying to build sandcastles out of smoke as fire cooked his flesh. His body clenched and he threw his head back, giving voice to his agony as the White consumed him from within. He screamed until his throat was raw, and then he screamed anew. Only when his voice failed and his screams were nothing but excruciating silence did he hear Death whisper to him.

You wear the Crown, William. Don't let the Crown wear you.

It hurts! he cried out. *It hurts so much!*

You're fighting it, said Death. *Stand tall, William.*

I don't know how!

Of course you do, Death replied, his cool voice like balm. *Stand tall, and wear the Crown.*

Billy struggled against the pain a moment longer, and then he stopped fighting and gave himself to the White. It wasn't surrender as much as a leap of faith, the desperation of an atheist in front of a firing squad.

Billy Ballard stood tall.

The White still burned, but now it was a cleansing fire, a purifying flame that revealed his soul and the soul of all living things. He felt the light rush through him and he opened his eyes and saw the light of the world and saw disease starting to worm its way into the light, tainting what it touched, dimming the White and threatening to leech it pale. Billy reached for that infection, grasped it and held tight, but as he tried to destroy it the sickness squirmed out of his grip. He reached for it once more, but this time it eluded him, maneuvered around him as he flailed.

Focus.

Billy felt the White connecting him to all life, blood to blood, and he felt his own blood responding to the disease around him, felt white blood cells swarm and strike. He urged them on and led them to battle, and as they fought he reached deep within himself and summoned more cell soldiers, threw them at the infection that tried to eat the world.

And slowly, the disease weakened.

Strengthened by his success, Billy created more and more cellular warriors and fueled them for their surge. They rushed forward, surrounding the plague and attacking it, fighting until the infection trembled and began to die. If disease had a voice, it would have begged for mercy — and it would have discovered that Billy Ballard was no longer a boy with a silver circlet sloping on his brow; he was the Conqueror, wearing the Crown that gave him control over sickness and health.

Dying, the infection launched itself at its enemy.

Billy absorbed the blow and broke it down until there was nothing but White. It flared brilliantly, blinding the sky, and then the White settled into Billy, wrapped itself around him and clothed him, covered him with a shirt and coat and pants and boots, girding him to face the world.

He was the White Rider, and today the Apocalypse was just a word.

||||||

He'd done it. He'd stood tall and saved the world.

Drained, Billy sank to his knees. So much for the "standing tall" part. A manic laugh bubbled out of him, and the sound filled the air, taking up the space that just a moment ago had been filled with plague. Billy laughed with relief, with joy, with the pride of a job well done.

And then he saw the black horse nudging the still form of Famine.

His elation faded as he watched the steed nose its way into her coat pocket. It rooted there for a moment, then pulled back, revealing a sugar cube between its teeth. It gently placed the cube on Famine's mouth, then stepped back and waited. The white confection sparkled like snowflakes in winter starlight, and there it stayed on the Black Rider's lips, uneaten. The black horse chuffed, then it lowered its sleek head, its mane tangling in the arctic wind. Near it, the white horse nickered softly, but the other steed didn't respond.

Billy tried to get up, but he couldn't summon the energy. "Please," he said, his voice cracking. "Please bring her to me."

The black horse flattened its ears.

The white steed approached the other horse and blew out a quick burst of air, then nuzzled against the black's neck. Famine's steed swiveled to look at Billy, who saw such pain and loss in those glowing white eyes that it stole his breath.

"Let me try," he pleaded.

The black horse sighed, in the way that horses do, and then it took one of the Black Rider's sleeves in its mouth, and the white horse took the other, and together the steeds dragged Famine to where the Conqueror knelt in the snow.

He murmured a thank you as he gazed upon the Black Rider's face. It was woefully gaunt and pale, and purple splotches stained her mouth and jaw. He whispered, "Plums," and he didn't know if that was his voice or Mita's. He reached for the White, coaxed it to spark enough for him to sense the plague contaminating Famine's body. She must have been dying even before he'd put on the Crown. Now there was almost nothing left to her but disease. He'd saved the world, but he'd been too late to help the Black Rider.

Mita's daughter took one last strangled breath, and then she breathed no more.

Billy's eyes narrowed, and his hands ball into fists. No. He refused to watch her die. He was exhausted, spent, too tired to even stand, but this was Famine, Lady Black, the one who had fascinated the White Rider for eons—the one who reminded Billy of a girl in black who waited for him at home.

He placed his hands upon her head and closed his eyes. And then he stoked the White into a blazing fire, and with it he burned away the disease that had eaten her body from within. It left her desiccated, wasted, and Billy told himself that was wrong, she was supposed to be healthy, and he heard Mita whisper to him, telling him how to turn a battle into a breath, how to stop fighting sickness and start nurturing the body left behind. Billy listened, and with the last of his strength, he dove into the Black Rider's soul—

—and he's hovering over the floe, looking down at himself working to save the woman in black, and he turns to face the Black Rider floating above him. Do you want me to heal you? *he asks in a voice of smoke and spirit, and she gazes at him with black, black eyes and she says,* Yes, *and so he opens his arms wide and she moves into his embrace, and they merge, Black and White, swirling together until the world is filled with shades of gray—*

The Black Rider took a shuddering breath, and then she opened her eyes.

"Hey." Billy offered her a tired smile. "Welcome back."

"Thank you," she said, her voice gruff. She propped herself onto her elbow and faced him, gazing deeply into his eyes, then at the silver circlet on his brow. "You stopped him."

He nodded.

She sighed and bowed her head.

In that wordless sigh, Billy heard her sorrow, her bitterness, felt the pain of her loss. "He wasn't always mad," she said quietly. "When he'd forget that he'd been anything other than the White Rider, he did his job well."

Billy knew this; he'd seen it in the White, and he felt it now, stirring in the back of his mind as Mita whispered to him. "I'm so sorry," he said softly. "I just wanted to stop him. I didn't mean—" His voice broke, and no more words would come.

She looked up at him, her face unreadable. "King White is dead, but the Conqueror lives on."

He hissed out a breath, half denial, half apology.

Famine slowly pulled herself to her feet. Her steed appeared by her side, and she leaned heavily against it, stroking its neck and murmuring something Billy couldn't hear. The horse snorted softly, and it knelt so that the Black Rider could climb atop its back. Now seated upon her steed, she looked down at Billy, who was sitting in the snow because he was too tired to stand. Her voice clipped, she said, "I look forward to working with you, White."

And then the black horse leapt into the sky and the Black Rider was gone.

From behind him came the sound of a girl's laughter. "Don't mind her. She believes in an economy of words. Actually, for her, that was practically a soliloquy."

Billy turned and looked up to see a girl in red, standing over him and grinning fit to burst.

"Hello, Pestilence," she said, offering him a hand. "I'm War."

CHAPTER 23

BILLY HAD A MOMENT OF DEJÀ VU . . .

. . . as he stared at the offered hand, not surprised that the leather glove was a dull brown instead of red. *It should be red,* he thought as he took her hand; everything about the girl should be red.

"The red belongs to the office," said the girl, pulling him to his feet. "The gloves are mine."

He blinked at the casual display of mind reading. When Death had done it, that had been . . . well, not acceptable, exactly, but understandable. Having War flit about in his head was just obnoxious.

She squeezed his hand once, playfully, then let go. "I've been called worse."

His mouth pulled into a humorless smile. "Me too."

War was older than he was, maybe by a year or two, but he was taller. Except for her head and her hands, she was covered in red — not the lush red of cherries or the cheerful red of strawberries but volcanic red, hot red, the red of fast cars and dangerous intentions. He looked down at his own clothing, at the startlingly white leather coat and pants, the boots that nearly blended with the snowy ground — Mita's uniform, but cleaner. Purer. And, happily, a bit more modern. Maybe before he'd accepted the White, Billy would have felt ridiculous wearing it. But not now. Now the outfit seemed—no, felt—exactly right, as if it were meant for him.

"You wear it well," said War, smiling wickedly.

He felt his cheeks flush. "Um. Thanks." Belatedly remembering that she'd introduced herself, he said, "I'm Billy Ballard."

She looked at him, this girl who was carved from fire, and she asked, "So, Billy Ballard, do you know yourself yet?"

After a pause, he replied, "I'm learning."

War grinned. "Good answer." She walked over to a red horse waiting near the far side of the floe, its coat like spilled blood against the backdrop of snow and ice. It looked at Billy—no, it *glared* at him, glared so fiercely that Billy took an involuntary step backward—and then the horse snorted as War petted its side. She murmured something to it, and then she climbed up in a fluid motion.

Billy blinked again as she settled into the saddle that absolutely hadn't been there a moment ago. One of her brown-gloved hands now held a pair of reins, and ditto on the not-being-there-before thing.

Okay. That was a neat trick.

"There's more where that came from," War called out. "Pleasure to meet you, Billy Ballard!" And then the horse launched itself across the sky in a streak of red, taking the Red Rider far away.

He watched War's fiery path cut across the horizon, and only after it faded to an afterthought did he say, "How long have you been here?"

A quiet laugh, the sound like snowfall, and then a cold voice replied, "Since before the first living thing took its first gasping breath."

There was a sense of movement behind him, and then Death was standing by his side, slouching comfortably, his hands resting in the front pockets of his faded jeans. The Pale Rider smiled warmly at Billy, belying the chill of his voice. "Good job saving the world. That's the sort of thing that wows them on résumés."

"Thanks." Billy stared at the pile of ashes that had been the Conqueror, and a lump formed in his throat, one that had nothing to do with sickness. "I killed him."

"Only technically."

Death the lawyer. So Billy was only technically a murderer. Yeah, that made him feel worlds better.

"The man who had been King Mita died long and long ago," Death said. "And the man who became the Conqueror was insane, more often than not, and his bite was poisonous. Would you call it murder to put down a rabid dog?"

The Crown felt heavy on Billy's head. "If I were the dog, yeah."

"You did what needed to be done. You saved the world and healed the Black Rider. Be content with that, William Ballard."

He looked into Death's bottomless eyes, those empty eyes, and he asked, "Is he happy now? Can you tell me that much?"

Death smiled whimsically. "Do *you* think he's happy now?"

He thought of the father who'd mourned his daughter, of the king who'd sacrificed everything for his kingdom. He thought of the man who learned that because he'd run away to save the world, the woman he loved died of heartbreak. Billy didn't know if there were such things as happy endings, but Mita of

Phrygia deserved one. "Yes," he decided. "Yes, he's happy now."

"And so you have your answer."

No, he didn't. But he understood that was all he was going to get. Death kept his secrets well.

"Death is in all things," the Conqueror said. "He is the alpha and the omega, and we exist only on his whim. And he is done with whimsy! I've seen the end of the world, and it begins with a sheet of white!"

"That was the Atlantic pack ice, about eight hundred years ago," said Death. "He'd seen the first pieces forming in the ocean and moving south."

Billy frowned. "So that's the end of the world? Icebergs?"

"It is for certain passenger ships."

"The world echoes his mood," the Conqueror hissed. "When it warms, he is content with his lot. But when it grows colder, then despair, little boy Pestilence! Despair!"

"He thought that when the world grew colder, that was because of you," Billy said. "He thought that the world is here only because of you."

"Did he now?" Death smiled ruefully as he walked over to the pile of ashes. Squatting, he scooped them into his hand and cupped them gently, almost reverently.

There was a pause in which the world held its breath, and words filled the wind in a whisper of frost: *Fare thee well, Mita, White Rider, colleague, king.*

The ashes glinted in Death's palm and then shot out of his hand and spirited off into the arctic sky. In Death's hand, two pennies winked.

Awed, Billy whispered, "Was he right?"

Still squatting, Death closed his fist over the pennies and

turned his head to face Billy. The human guise slipped, only for a breath, and Billy glimpsed something beyond his comprehension; then he blinked and the Pale Rider was once again a thin blond man with hands meant for strumming a guitar and a voice meant for song. He smiled a smile filled with the mysteries of the universe, and he said, "What do *you* think?"

Billy had no idea. And that was all right, he decided. If Death really was the start and end of everything, he really didn't want to know.

"So," said Death as he rose to his full height and put the pennies into his jeans pocket, "we come now to a crossroads. When you were five, you agreed to wear the Conqueror's Crown at the right time. The one with whom you made your compact is dead. All previous agreements are forgiven. And," he added, eyes sparkling with mischief, "some might argue that you fulfilled the terms of that agreement. Either way, you've done your job."

"Um," said Billy, suddenly sheepish. "I sort of broke the Bow. It was an accident. But, um. Yeah. I broke it."

"That Bow?" Death pointed to Billy's left—and there it was, lying on the snow in one complete piece: the unstrung bow, its black wood gleaming, inviting. "It takes more than that to break it permanently. But it wants you to know that it doesn't appreciate being treated like a baseball bat."

Billy's mouth opened and closed, and then it opened again and he said, "Um. Thanks. And, ah, I'm sorry. About the baseball bat thing."

Death winked. "No worries. The Bow has been through worse. And now, William Ballard, you have a choice."

Billy held his breath.

"You may choose to remain Pestilence, Conqueror of Health, Bringer of Disease, White Rider of the Apocalypse. Or you may reject the Crown and simply be William Ballard and live your life."

Billy's head spun, showing him images too fast for him to follow, leaving him with impressions of people and memories — Marianne and Gramps and his mom and his dad, his Cookie Monster doll and Eddie Glass, Kurt and Joe and the others from school. And now he saw Famine, or Famines — the exotic woman in black who'd held the Conqueror's heart, and the prim woman in black who'd reminded him of his duty, and the painfully thin woman in black who'd nearly died and had a horse that tried to feed her sugar cubes. And he saw War, both the female knight with her terrifying laughter and the girl in red with her wicked grin.

Do you know yourself yet?

Did he?

"Tell me," said Death. "Are you William Ballard? Or are you Pestilence?"

No matter what he chose, he wasn't the same Billy Ballard as before. He'd felt the light of the world flowing through him, connecting him to all living things. He'd seen the impossible and had traveled through time. He'd stood tall and fought back the plague. He'd saved the world.

Marianne's voice, full of wonder: *Billy Ballard, you were a hero today. You hear me? You were a hero.*

He felt the weight of the Crown upon his head, felt the mad beating of his heart as he thought of his favorite girl in black.

And then, locking his gaze on to Death's empty blue eyes, Billy Ballard made his choice.

CHAPTER 24

AND THEN . . .

. . . it was the next morning and Billy was getting ready for school. He'd been away for a week and now had fully recuperated, bounced back, turned the corner, got better, healed up, and, all in all, was feeling pretty good. A hot shower to scrub away the last dregs of sleep, a quick tooth brushing to kill off bad breath, a comb through the hair in an attempt to tame it—these were the tools of the mundane, the everyday, the ordinary.

Billy Ballard couldn't be happier.

He smiled as he looked at his reflection in the bathroom mirror. The white patch in his hair, noticeably bigger, looked brighter today. Whiter. Maybe with a glint of silver beneath it. He decided that he liked it.

Dressed for the day, and never mind whether he had PE or not—he'd change in the locker room, like the other guys. He grabbed his phone and wallet, threw them into his backpack, and then shut and locked his bedroom door. Keys in his pocket, he walked down the hallway, waving to the ghosts of photographs on the walls. As he went by, the impressions of the past echoed; it wasn't an unpleasant sensation, but a restless one. Over there had been a portrait of his grandparents on their wedding day, and here used to hang a framed shot

of Billy and his dad, the Ballard boys, grinning like scoun-
drels ready to make mischief. He touched his fingers over the
spot where his dad's face used to be, and he felt a pang in his
chest—a small sadness, a tiny piece of loss. Billy acknowledged
the feeling and then let it go. It was time, he decided, to put
those ghosts to rest. After school, he'd talk to his mom about
painting the walls, either a new coat of what was there already
or, better, something new, lively. Paint was cheap, and he could
do it himself—and maybe even Gramps could help. He didn't
have to be a wild conversationalist to hold a roller, and Billy
thought the old man would enjoy the activity.

In the kitchen, he gave his mom a quick kiss on the cheek
and smiled a hello to his grandfather. Gramps looked more
there today, like there was someone home behind his eyes.

"Sleep well?" Billy asked, and shock of shocks, his grandfather smiled and nodded and smacked his toast with his tooth-
less gums, one part mastication and two parts saliva.

"It's the new meds," chirped his mother as she offered Billy
a bowl of cereal. "They're not underperforming."

"Yeah," Billy agreed, grinning as he poured milk. The meds
absolutely were not underperforming, not any more. He had
a good feeling that this time, his grandfather's lucid period
would hang around for a while.

Billy had a good feeling about a lot of things.

|||||||

Before PE, Billy would have to experience the joys of trigonometry, biology, and American history, all of which redefined

tedium. If Billy weren't feeling so awake, he'd have had plenty of time to catch up on his sleep.

Walking to his locker to get his books for his morning classes, he noticed that some of the other students in the hallway were casting him odd looks, like they didn't know how to react. Maybe it was because he was in a great mood, and so he was walking taller, prouder, as if there were an invisible crown on his head. Or maybe it was just because he'd been stricken with potentially deadly bacterial meningitis and therefore had helped launch the school into its brief televised career. Celebrity by proxy. He grinned at everyone, just because, and — second shock of shocks — some of them even smiled back. Sure, they were all from the misfits' table in the cafeteria. But for the first time in a long time, Billy didn't feel like a pariah.

A shove from behind, making him stumble.

"Watch it, loser," said Kurt.

Well. It was sort of comforting to know some things hadn't changed.

Billy regained his footing and turned to face Kurt, who had Joe by his side. Kurt looked particularly stupid this morning; maybe he'd had an extra helping of dumb for breakfast. Joe just looked mean, but Billy had to admit, Joe rocked that look.

"What're you looking at, Birdy?" Kurt sneered.

This was the part where Billy was supposed to cringe and try to turn invisible as the verbal abuse hit home. The other students were supposed to point and laugh and get in on the taunting, maybe spice it up with a fly-by noogie. And a part of Billy was ready to jump back into character and play the victim role the way he'd been playing it for years. That part of Billy still had nightmares about the Ice Cream Man, was still desperate to Keep His Head Down and hope that soon, real soon, the monsters would move on to other prey.

But the rest of Billy remembered that he had saved the world.

I even saved you, he thought, looking at Kurt and Joe and not flinching. *It's like the Apocalypse—their words are just words.*

And the thing about words? He didn't have to listen to them.

Billy smiled, because really, he was having a terrific day and not even Kurt and Joe could ruin that, and he kept walking toward his locker.

This time, a hand on his shoulder stopped him and spun him around. He looked up into the piggy eyes of Eddie Glass.

"You just walk away like that?" Eddie said. "My boy Kurt talks to you, and you just ignore him?" The large boy leaned in close, and Billy smelled something foul on his breath. "Bad manners, Birdy."

Part of him wanted to cower.

Part of him wanted to run.

And part of him wished he could draw the Bow and riddle Eddie with disease after disease, slam his hatred and fury into him arrow by arrow until there was nothing left of Eddie Glass but a smear on the ground.

He thought he heard a small, still voice telling him to focus.

Billy looked at the bully who had plagued him for years, really looked at him, and he didn't see a raging giant but just a large boy with anger in his eyes and something to prove to the world, something that had nothing to do with Billy. In that crystalline moment, he understood that Eddie had his own Ice Cream Man haunting him.

"I get it," Billy said, and he did. He'd spent so many years being afraid of Eddie Glass, and then, after he'd used the Bow in anger, he'd been afraid of becoming Eddie Glass. But now he knew that he'd surpassed Eddie Glass, had left him far behind. Billy had confronted his demon, while Eddie was still pretending that he wasn't scared.

Billy had never thought he'd see the day when he pitied Eddie.

Maybe that showed on his face, because something lit behind Eddie's eyes, something ugly and small. "You're *going* to get it," he breathed, getting in Billy's face.

Billy met his gaze and didn't look away.

The two faced off, the bully and the bullied, until someone called Eddie's name. The bigger boy's eyes narrowed, and he growled, "This isn't done." He shoved past Billy to join his friends, walking big and talking bigger.

No, it wasn't done for good. But it was done for now.

Smiling to himself, Billy finally got to his locker. His favorite girl in black was waiting for him, waving as he arrived.

"So glad you're back," Marianne said, grinning. "You wouldn't *believe* the stupid assignment we've got for history. Get this, we have to compare the Vietnam War to spaghetti, to *spaghetti*, can you believe that? I'm thinking of saying, Yeah, it's like pasta because it's pointless carbs . . ." Her voice trailed off as she searched his face, and an odd smile played on her lips.

"You're brilliant," he said, enamored. Because she was — brilliant and gorgeous and amazing and the best friend he could ever ask for.

"And you're looking at me in a goofy way." A faint blush

touched her cheeks, and her smile bloomed into something magical.

"I'm feeling goofy," he said, grinning at her as he dropped his backpack to the floor and wrapped his arms around her. "I've been thinking about you."

And then Billy Ballard finally kissed the girl.

Authors should never fall in love with ideas. Therein lies madness. Or, at least, many sleepless nights.

I had two ideas for *Loss* that I absolutely, positively loved. I was passionate about these ideas. And by God, I was going to make them work!

Neither of them made it to the final draft. At least, not in the form that I had originally envisioned.

The first idea was that the main issue of *Loss* would be coping with Alzheimer's. This would have tackled the disease mostly from a caregiver's point of view, but also from the actual patient's. I've seen firsthand how Alzheimer's and dementia rob people of their dignity. It's frightening to behold. It's even more frightening to think that one day, that could be my parents. That could be *me*. One day, I might not recognize my children. Excuse me while I quietly freak out.

Coping with Alzheimer's was the top spot on my list. The second? Robin Hood. That's right: Originally, the entire second section of *Loss* was going to be about Robin Hood and Will Scarlet—or, in this case, Will Scarlock. No, I'm not an Errol Flynn junkie. And I haven't seen the Russell Crowe version of the movie. Pestilence has a Bow, so I thought of Robin Hood. Simple, really.

So I had these ideas, and I loved these ideas. And I was going to make *Loss* all about them.

Twenty-two drafts later, that didn't happen.

The Robin Hood thing didn't work because frankly, this wasn't the right story for it. I tried; oh yes, I tried. One thing I've discovered: If you force a story to go a certain way, the story will fight you. (Thus: twenty-two drafts.) I wound up keeping a little bit of the idea — Robert Hode is Robin Hood, and the ghosts that Billy sees when he's in the Greenwood are all that remain of Little John, Will Scarlet, and Maid Marian.

As for the Alzheimer's, that was reduced to a subplot. Billy Ballard became much more than just his grandfather's caregiver as I started writing the book. I realized fairly quickly that he was horribly bullied. That idea resonated, and so that became the major focus of *Loss:* bullying.

Billy had a lot to say about the subject. As it turns out, so do I.

||||||

In eighth grade, I got mean.

I was lucky growing up. I wasn't bullied, not more so than anyone else. Sure, there were lunchbox wars in second grade, and the girls tended to play mercy a lot, but I didn't mind those things; I usually got my metal lunchbox up in time to block a swing, and I actually rocked at mercy. I was active in school: I was the fourth grade class president and the sixth grade co-president, and I participated in the annual storytelling contest. I had friends. I invited kids to my birthday parties, and they always came. It didn't matter to me that I was always one of the last kids picked for any sport; I wasn't good at sports. That was all right. Elementary school, overall, was all right.

But then came junior high.

I was an art geek. My school had talents, or majors, and mine was studio art. So I hung out with some of the art kids and some of the kids in my homeroom. Seventh grade was okay. Mostly, I watched things happen from a distance.

But by eighth grade, the insults started coming my way. One guy—Vinny? Victor? Something like that—started calling me Jerky Horse, which rhymed with Jackie Morse. Someone else called me Thunder Thighs. And from there came the rank-outs, everything from "Your momma" to cursing. So I learned how to curse. I remember walking down the hall with my friend Carol, and some guy named Dennis shouted something at me. I don't remember the words, but I remember that it was an insult. I shouted back, "Shut up, Dennis, you prick!" I didn't even know what a prick was—but he shut up. And Carol cracked up.

That's when I learned how to be mean.

I wasn't a total jerk; I didn't walk around insulting people just because I could. But there were two distinct times when I did something horrible. The first was to this girl who was on my bus. I changed the lyrics to a commercial jingle and made it about the girl's weight. I sang it to some of the other kids on the bus. It was funny, you see. Hee-lar-i-ous. Boy, was I a riot. I have no idea if she knew about it. Thinking back, I'm pretty sure she did.

That was shitty of me. I'm sorry, Kelly.

The other time was to a girl I'd known for years, because our grandparents were friends. Eighth grade can be an awkward period; for me, my face had exploded with acne (a condition that wouldn't get under control until I was in my twenties), and I was short and chubby with no fashion sense (conditions that have yet to get under control). For this girl, Lisa (no—not from *Hunger;* that's just one of those strange coincidences), it was her teeth. She had buckteeth. And one day, this guy called her Beaver to her face. And I laughed. Because, you know, it was hee-ster-i-cal.

Sorry, Lisa. That was shitty of me too.

By the time I was in high school, a lot of that shitty attitude was gone. I wasn't mean anymore. Maybe that's because I was mostly invisible. I had my core group of friends—we were the rocker crowd—and I didn't venture out of my social circle. I didn't dare. Sharks swam in those waters. I didn't have the right clothes, or the right accessories. I didn't listen to the right music. I didn't get the right grades. I didn't get involved in high school politics or popularity contests. High school, for me, was a series of *I Didn'ts*. It was my version of Keeping My Head Down. I did do some things, like play varsity soccer (man, was I bad) and be art director for Sing (think *High School Musical*, but with a much smaller budget). But for the most part, people had no idea who I was. I wasn't bullied. And I didn't bully. I was inconsequential.

Soon I had an eating disorder, but that's another story.

|||||||

Soapbox time. You've been warned.

Here's the thing: Bullies tell you all about themselves when they bully you.

That nasty song I wrote about poor Kelly? That was a weight issue. And God knows, I had—and have—major weight issues. Laughing at someone's appearance? That's a self-esteem issue. I'm still working on that one.

When Victor (or Vinny) called me Jerky Horse, well, I guess he was worried that he was a jerk. Either that, or he just had a penchant for rhyming. And I know for certain that the guy who called me Thunder Thighs was—and is—extremely image-focused. If you looked up the word *superficial,* you'd probably see his face there in the dictionary.

So if someone calls you a name, keep in mind that it's less about you, and more about the person who's calling you the name. That doesn't make it right, but it might make it easier to get through.

And you will get through it. You will. You know why? Eighth grade isn't forever. And while high school may feel like an eternity, it's not.

You must have heard of the It Gets Better Project. It's there for a reason. It does get better. It does. Here's the main link: **www.itgetsbetter.org.**

If you're getting bullied, talk to someone. A parent. A teacher. The school counselor. A friend. If the first person you talk to can't help, try someone else. And someone else. Keep on talking. You'll find someone who listens. I promise you, you're not alone.

Maybe you're not the one being bullied. Maybe you're the one who laughs when someone says something mean. Maybe you even get inspired to say, or do, something mean yourself. If you are . . . just think about what you're doing, okay? Think about how your words matter. Think about how they can hurt.

Think about how easy it would be instead to make your words help.

Be stronger than the bullies.

Speak out.

||||||

Everyone has their thing, you know. For some, it may be cancer. For others, high blood pressure. For me, it's Alzheimer's. I watched one of my grandmothers slowly succumb to the disease. Witnessing this strong, determined, proud, clever, marvelous woman erode into a shell of her former self was devastating.

Millions of people are affected by Alzheimer's. It's a progressive disease, and as of today, there is no cure. Research is under way, however, and current Alzheimer's treatments are able to temporarily slow the symptoms.

That's why a portion of *Loss* proceeds will be donated to the Alzheimer's Association. Even if the disease won't be eradicated in my lifetime, I hope that by the time my kids have kids, Alzheimer's will be a thing of the past. For more about the Alzheimer's Association — including the terrific section called Living with Alzheimer's, which helps support those who have Alzheimer's as well as their caregivers — please visit www.alz.org.

If you bought a copy of *Loss,* thank you for helping to make a difference.

USA 7

Jackie Morse Kessler grew up in Brooklyn, New York, with a cranky cat and shelves overflowing with dolls and books. Now she's in upstate New York with another cranky cat, a loving husband, two sons, and shelves overflowing with dragons and books (except when her sons steal her dragons). Her previous books in the Riders of the Apocalypse series told the stories of Famine (*Hunger*) and War (*Rage*). For more about Jackie, visit her website: **www.jackiemorsekessler.com.**